— *Praise for*

"This book was exactly what I needed. A heartfelt love story about learning to overcome being hurt in love before, taking a leap on something that is outside of your norm, and taking a leap of faith on love again."

— *Short and Sassy Book Blurbs*

"A great story of finding someone when you least expect it and not letting misunderstandings stop you from being together. A fun sweet romance to curl in a chair with and get lost in."

— *Books Are Love*

"*Mending Heartstrings* is a splendid romance read. It's a great choice for someone that wants more character-driven plot as opposed to hot and steamy. With fun characters, a few twists in the plot, and plenty of emotion, I recommend checking it out."

— *Jennifer Streck, Psychocat Reads*

ALSO BY
ARIA GLAZKI

Mortal Musings

Mending Heartstrings

ARIA GLAZKI

ANIKA PRESS

Cover design by Paper & Sage
Cover photo by Jillian Rubman

ISBN: 978-1-943572-04-5

Second Edition

To Dr. Moisey Kagan,
who knew love needs no words

One

Kane walked out of the private back room of Nashville's Fiddle and Steel and headed straight for the bar. Every so often, he'd still try out his new material at their open mic nights. But tonight, the initially warm reception of the regulars had fizzled out as he played. They hadn't really responded to any of his three songs. He needed a beer.

A couple of the regulars greeted him, and Kane paused to exchange pleasantries. The laid-back atmosphere of the bar put everyone at ease, which was the great thing about playing there. The locals who knew him weren't intimidated by his relative fame, and he wasn't a big enough deal yet for the occasional tourist to recognize him. He relied on the reactions of this comfortable community. And they sure didn't mind telling him he had more work to do before his next tour.

When he finally reached the bar, he flagged down Cody, tearing the younger man away from a pretty brunette who was probably underage. He greeted Kane with a subtle lift of his chin.

"How's it going, man?" Kane asked.

"Just got better," Cody answered, looking over Kane's shoulder.

Kane followed his gaze to a group of women who'd just walked in but turned back after barely a moment. He definitely wouldn't mind a distraction. First, though, he really did want that beer. "Get your mind back on your work, boy," Kane scolded with a smile.

Cody's mama hadn't raised an idiot. "You just want them for yourself."

Kane grinned. "It's no competition."

"Only 'cause those three didn't hear you flame out tonight."

"Yeah, well. Some of us can rely on our good looks." Kane kept an easy smile on his face. The ribbing shouldn't have bothered him, but he was having an off night. The songs he'd played could have passed muster most anywhere else, but Nashville knew its country music. "Get me a beer, would ya?" he asked.

"Yeah, yeah." Cody slapped a coaster onto the bar in front of Kane then headed to the fridge to grab Kane's favorite.

Kane rested his forearms on the bar and bent his head down, exhaling. As always, he'd scanned the audience a few times while he played, trying to read the room's reactions. Tonight, too many people had been absorbed in their own conversations around the bar's simple wooden tables. Only one pair of eyes had met his. A striking, unwavering pair of eyes.

She'd been standing toward the back, alone. He'd felt her watching him even when he'd closed his eyes.

But she hadn't been standing there when he'd come back out. Probably just as well.

Cody set down a chilled beer in front of Kane. He tipped it toward the bartender as thanks. A couple drinks, a little bit of flirting, and there'd be no more need to think about his songs tonight.

Turning back toward the room, Kane bumped a girl he hadn't noticed seated next to him at the bar. "Ah! Sorry 'bout that," he said with a half-smile, ramping up the charm.

She twisted toward him. "I'll survive." The corners of her mouth pulled up, but Kane couldn't look away from her eyes. *Hazel*, he realized. Unlike when he'd been on stage, her gaze fell, and she started to turn back to the bar.

"Kane," he offered, shifting his beer to his left hand and offering up his right. *A handshake. Smooth.* This really was an off night.

Her eyes flicked down to his hand then laughingly back to his face. Her eyebrows drew up in a small challenge as she placed her hand in his. "Like the sugar, or the stick?"

"With a K…" He leaned back against the bar, resting on one elbow.

"So, not Abel's brother. Good to know."

Normally he'd have walked away at a line like that, but it wasn't like he'd been offering conversational gold. Maybe this would help him shake it off before he made his move on the trio Cody'd pointed out. And then there were those eyes… "Go ahead and joke. I've probably heard them all."

"Don't tempt me." Her lips curved softly. Mischief glinted in her eyes.

"And how could I do that?" Kane let himself relax, sliding back into the easy feel of the bar. Unlike his performance, this conversation didn't really matter.

"I'm sure you have a few tricks up your sleeves." She picked up the glass of white wine she'd been nursing and took a sip, without dropping her smile or taking her eyes off him.

A local girl would've been drinking beer. But then, a local girl would've known exactly who he was, which could lead to nothing more than a mildly satisfying romp in the sack. He remembered his own beer and took a swig.

"Worried?" he asked, after she set her glass back down.

That got him a bigger smile. "Please, I can take anything you throw at me."

"Maybe we should test that theory." He took another sip of beer. This was getting more and more interesting.

"By all means," she replied, not missing a beat.

He was used to women flattering him, fawning over him. His Southern charm had rarely failed him, and as a singer, he wasn't hurting for female attention, especially since country music wannabes thought he'd be a perfect springboard for their careers. But he hadn't met someone who actually intrigued him in a while. Too long.

He turned to face her, leaving his elbow resting on the bar, and set down his beer. "I didn't catch your name."

"Call me Elle," she answered, tilting her head slightly, a silent question on the change in direction. Her eyelashes didn't flutter with calculated coyness, and her direct gaze didn't falter.

Kane straightened, suddenly inspired. "Pleased to meet you, Elle. Excuse me a sec?" He grabbed the bottle he'd just set down and turned away from her. Another swig and he returned to the back room. This was nothing short of crazy, but he picked up his guitar anyway and walked back to the small stage.

Sabella had barely returned to her wine when she heard the slight strumming of a guitar as someone settled in front of the microphone. She wasn't certain what had prompted Kane to leave so abruptly, but she was definitely disappointed. Not that she was star-struck or anything. The fact that she had dressed up to venture outside her hotel room, to the Fiddle and Steel Guitar Bar, simply because she had heard that Kane Hartridge would possibly be trying out new material at their open mic night, did *not* mean she was star-struck. If anything, she was underwhelmed by his song choices tonight, and even more so by her awkward attempt at flirting. Men like Kane didn't waste their attentions on women like her.

She took another sip of the perfectly nice Riesling and silently deliberated whether she would stay past draining her glass. This bar did have a certain, inexplicably innate, country charm that she wouldn't mind exploring and observing further. After all, she had come to Nashville to learn what she could about the culture of country music.

As far as she could tell, the room around her was furnished with exactly the same style of unadorned, wooden furniture and boasted a similar smattering of booths around the perimeter as any other bar. Nothing about the décor particularly screamed "country." No posters of country stars lined the walls, and if it weren't for the distinct twang emanating from the patrons' conversations and through the speakers, she could have been back home. If she could figure out what exactly made this bar so popular among the locals, the night wouldn't have to be a complete waste. Plus, her flight the next day wasn't until the afternoon, so she could afford to stay out awhile.

"Hey, guys." Kane's voice carried through the speaker system, quieting the room. Someone shut off the recorded music that had been playing ever since he had left the small stage, his performance intended as the finale of their open mic night. Sabella twisted on her barstool to face the stage. Kane and his guitar once again occupied the unadorned chair set behind the single microphone. His beer bottle rested just behind his leg. "Don't mean to pull y'all away, but I have a friend in from out of town who is dyin', she's absolutely dyin', to sing for you. Please join me in welcomin' Elle—over by the bar, there, in the purple, that's Elle—welcomin' her to the Fiddle an' Steel stage."

Most of the patrons shifted their attention toward the bar, trying to find Kane's "friend." Sabella froze, schooling her expression. *I can take anything you throw at me*, she had said. He was clearly testing her claim. What in the world had she been thinking?

"C'mon, Elle," Kane called through the microphone. "Here's your chance." His mouth pulled into a half smile, intended to portray solicitous charm, no doubt, not the baiting nature of his challenge.

She took a deep breath, reminding herself she would likely never see any of these people again, and slid off the barstool. Apparently, her customarily rigid practicality had been dislodged the second he'd bumped into her. Not that he was giving her much choice.

The stage was closer than she would have preferred, but the walk over from the bar still gave Sabella plenty of time to admire Kane's comfortable posture. He wore jeans and a faded, black, button-down shirt, with a few buttons left unfastened and rolled-up sleeves. With his brown hair cut raggedly to slightly above his ears in front, somewhat longer in back, and his stunning green eyes, he really was more handsome than any man had a right to be. Especially one who was trying to embarrass her in front of a bar full of people.

"What exactly do you have in mind?" she murmured as she took the short step onto the stage.

He covered the microphone. "Name a country duet."

At least he wasn't going to force her to sing alone. Still, she wasn't exactly a country music savant. "The only one that comes to mind is 'Picture.'" That wasn't strictly speaking true, but she was betting he would be even less thrilled with her choice if she had named one with Kelly Clarkson.

All Kane said was, "All right." He shifted his chair so it wasn't squarely facing the microphone then started to play an intro. "Not the newest song in the book, but a guilty pleasure for some of y'all, I'm sure," he drawled, smiling at the crowd.

His voice captured her as he sang, its purity reminding her why his was the only country music to which she really listened. As she watched him, Sabella almost forgot he had manipulated her into joining him on stage—for a *duet*. She looked out over their somewhat captive audience, filled with men in worn-out jeans and flannel shirts—even a cowboy hat or two—and some amazingly beautiful women. Maybe this was actually a bizarre dream, and in reality she was sleeping in her hotel room, or even back home in her bed. If only.

When Kane finished the first chorus, he looked up at her in anticipation. Little crinkles appeared around his eyes. He didn't think she would do it.

To be fair, normally she wouldn't have. *This is simply a more active form of research,* she assured herself. Sticky sweat still gathered between her fingers and coated her palms. Sabella surreptitiously wiped her hands on her thighs and stepped marginally closer to the microphone.

She scrambled to remember the lyrics, staring at the floor as she sang. When no one booed by the end of the stanza, she risked a glance out at the room. About half of the tables had reverted to quiet conversation, but others appeared to be listening. At the end of her chorus, she looked over at Kane.

He was watching her, eyebrows drawn slightly together, as if he wasn't altogether sure what he was seeing. Maybe he was shocked she was still singing, despite the blatant difference in their abilities. She had never been one for public displays of foolery, and the remaining shreds of her rationality were appalled by the ridiculousness of her behavior. Running off the stage would be worse, though, or at the very least more memorable.

She finished their interchanging lines with her eyes on him. The last chord he strummed hung in the air until the murmuring of patrons' conversations wiped it away. Sabella backed away from Kane and the microphone, then turned to step off the stage, and wove her way toward the hallway that led to the bar's restrooms and a door with an "Employees Only" sign. She pressed her back to the wall for support and resolutely steadied her breathing. This night wasn't turning out anything like she could have expected.

Kane stayed on stage through the applause that started just as Elle left. It was more applause than he'd gotten alone tonight, not that he was surprised. She sang purely, without flourish. She sure wouldn't be making a career of this, but something about her singing had captivated their audience, and him. It was so…earnest. Unassuming. Maybe that's what he had glimpsed in her eyes.

Falling back on his ingrained charm, Kane offered a smile and a "good night" to the audience. He followed Elle's route to the bar's back rooms, taking his guitar with him. Cody might whine later that he'd left the beer for the boy to pick up, but Kane didn't care.

He found her leaning against the wall that faced the ladies' room. "Waiting for a friend?"

Her head jerked toward him. She straightened from the wall and turned to face him. "Did you enjoy the show?" She wasn't smiling now.

A Southern girl would've chewed his hide for that stunt. And if she really hadn't wanted to sing, she would've found a way to bow out, or plain old told him to go to hell.

"You surprised me," he answered honestly. "You have a nice voice." *And gumption.*

"That's somewhat patronizing coming from you, don't you think?"

He smiled. "A fan, are you?" he teased, though she obviously wasn't. But that suited him just fine.

She raised her eyebrows. A second later her shoulders shrugged, and she looked down. He was pretty sure he saw a hint of a smile.

"C'mon," he said then turned toward the private room to put away his guitar. Maybe this night had potential yet.

"Shouldn't you be getting back out to your adoring fans?" Sabella asked as she followed Kane through the "Employees Only" door. Probably not her wisest move, reminding him of the significantly more enchanting company he could be keeping. She couldn't compete with the leggy, sleekly styled beauties she had overheard him and the bartender discussing earlier. Apparently, though, her tenacity in staying through the whole song despite her lack of talent meant she held his attention for at least a bit longer.

Kane ignored her question, focusing instead on placing his guitar in a solid, somewhat beat-up case. A knotted, Native-American-style bracelet on his right wrist drew her attention to his hands and his long, skilled fingers. "Elegant" sprang to her mind—not that she would ever describe them that way to him.

With his guitar safely put away, Kane sat down on a comfortable-looking leather couch and gestured for her to join him. Sabella remained standing, absorbing her surroundings: cozy chic furniture that had undoubtedly found its way here naturally, not from the pages of some magazine; flyers from past Fiddle and Steel Guitar events on the walls overlapped with autographed posters of country stars; and boxes of extra bar supplies that were stacked as out of the way as possible. Her eyes stalled on a poster of Kane, hanging slightly slanted toward the corner on the wall behind him. She was in the private, back room of a country bar with Kane Hartridge.

The reminder prompted her to return her attention to where it belonged. He looked back at her with good-humored eyes, set under slightly arched eyebrows. His bowed upper lip rested in a sharp line over a barely rounded lower lip, as if his mouth was the result of the swift swipe of a knife, though she had already seen those lips soften as they curved into a smile, simultaneously rounding the otherwise sleek lines of his cheeks. Painfully handsome.

She had to stop watching him, or he might think she was an obsessed fangirl. "So how did you know I was from out of town?" She hadn't thought she stood out quite so blatantly, and there were plenty of people in Nashville without Southern accents, so that couldn't have given her away.

"You don't act like a local girl," he answered, relaxing back into the couch. His hands rested gently on his thighs, and he sat with his ankles crossed. He looked so perfectly comfortable that she felt even more self-conscious, standing in the middle of the room, thumbs tucked into the pockets of her jeans.

"And how do local girls act?" she asked curiously, shifting her weight to one hip to appear more relaxed.

"Confident. Assertive. They know exactly what they bring to the table, and exactly what they want to take away." He paused. She felt herself swallow but continued to watch him. "But they rarely take any real risks," he finished.

Kane stood and stepped forward, which brought him a touch closer to her than would have been casual. Sabella could see the stubble beginning to grow over his angled jaw and slightly rounded chin, his hair brushing over the tops of his ears and down to the back of his shirt collar, the thin scar that angled from right above his lip toward his left cheek, and the slightly flattened line of his nose that told her it had been broken at least once. He smelled faintly of wood with an overlay of beer, a combination she never would have imagined to be alluring.

She shifted moderately closer to him. If his assessment of these women was accurate, she definitely had little in common with them. Maybe it was her natural curiosity, but she almost never knew well enough to avoid taking risks, though she relentlessly attempted to impose sensible limitations on herself. Clearly that wasn't working so well tonight.

Over a foot remained between them, yet their stance felt oddly intimate. Until the door was opened by an older woman in a jean skirt, black halter top, and well-worn leather boots.

Sabella took a hasty step back, but the woman was looking at Kane. He hadn't reacted as sharply as she had, but rather did a slow half turn toward the door.

"Amber Lynn," he said by way of greeting and smiled somewhat crookedly.

"Kane," she responded, with a voice so husky she must have spent years shouting to be heard. "Not your best night," she said casually then turned toward Sabella. "Now you must be why the boys keep on askin' me for a karaoke night." Her eyes took in Sabella's silky purple top, manicured hands, casual sandals, and loosely waved hair, which didn't accurately reflect the fact that it had taken almost an hour to style. She took her time, as if her eyes moved through the same honey that dripped from her voice—though that's how Sabella thought of most country accents she had heard in her brief time in Nashville.

"Amber Lynn here's the owner of the Fiddle an' Steel," Kane explained. His drawl was actually not thick, with only a hint of flattened vowels and that light softening to some of his consonants.

"Pleasure to meet you," Sabella offered politely.

"Welcome to Nashville," Amber Lynn replied. "What're you hidin' in here for? A lotta them boys would sure love to get to know ya better after that little show y'all put on." The last few words were directed at Kane. Amber Lynn narrowed her eyes a bit and pursed her lips, as if trying to discern Kane's motives.

"Give 'er a chance to recover, Amber Lynn." Kane's innocent smile never wavered.

Amber Lynn considered him for a moment, glanced again

at Sabella, and turned back toward the door. "Behave yourself, boy," she threw over her shoulder as she walked out.

"You know me!" he called after her, grinning. "So." He turned back to Sabella, and his mouth settled into a half smile. "Can I buy you a drink?"

One drink quickly turned into a few. In a corner booth that was somewhat secluded from the majority of the bar's patrons, Kane regaled her with stories from his childhood in eastern Oklahoma and of his road to relative fame. He was charmingly down-to-earth, understating how far he had already come in his career. She in turn described to him how she had recently experienced a turnaround in perspective on the country music scene, which inspired her idea for a series of articles on the various cultures of different genres—the reason behind her research trip to Nashville.

All too soon, the bar had nearly emptied. Kane, the paragon of Southern charm, offered to escort her back to her hotel, and Sabella found herself accepting. By then, the city that had been throbbing with music mere hours ago had fallen mostly silent.

The DoubleTree hotel where she was staying was less than a couple blocks from the Fiddle and Steel Guitar, but Kane led her on something of a detour. Sabella stifled the rational voice that insisted wandering around an unfamiliar city at night with a virtual stranger was a horrible idea. *What better way to see a new city than with a local?*

Kane took her first past Nashville's City Hall. It hadn't been particularly interesting when she had explored the city during the day, but at night, with both the building and the fountains in front of it alight, not to mention Kane's company and a few drinks in her, it was transformed.

From there, he led her by the edge of the Cumberland River, doubling back past the bar, until they reached the iconic Shelby Street Bridge. As she looked out over the city, Kane stood protectively behind her, hands braced around her on the railing, sheltering her from the wind.

They hadn't talked much since leaving the bar, but the silence felt comfortable in the night's darkness.

"Beautiful," she whispered, looking out over the lights of Nashville's skyline.

"Absolutely." His voice was low, coming from right beside her ear. He placed his hand on her arm, gently. His touch was warm through the bell sleeves of her top, and she turned to face him. All the lights of Nashville twinkled at her back, but they weren't nearly as mesmerizing as Kane's eyes.

She would always remember the swell of his biceps under her hands, the heat of his palms when they came to rest slightly below her waist. She looked from his eyes to his mouth a heartbeat before he kissed her.

The kiss was soft, starting with a brush of their lips and growing into a slow taste of each other. In writing it, she would have claimed time stilled, but in reality, wind whipped her hair around them, and she shivered under its onslaught.

Kane broke their kiss and wrapped his arm around her shoulders. Occasionally commenting on their surroundings, he led them off the bridge, meandering through downtown, past the Country Music Hall of Fame and the Convention Center, until they reached the abstractly decorated, and intensely red, DoubleTree lobby. He kept his arm draped over her shoulders until they came to the bank of elevators.

Sabella knew they should part ways, but she didn't want this fantasy night to end quite yet. An elderly couple joined them in the elevator, and they all remained silent. When the doors opened, she walked ahead of him to her room, acutely aware of him behind her. At her door, she turned to face him, and to say goodbye.

The fingers of his right hand grazed hers as his left came up to cup her jaw.

"We should say good night," she whispered.

"All right," Kane breathed against her mouth before kissing her again. This time the kiss was harder, lips crushing together and tongues intertwining as if that touch would be enough to keep the two of them together. He pressed her against the door, stepping closer so virtually no space remained between them. Her hands came up, brushing through his silky hair before drifting to his shoulders. When the kiss broke, the rapid expansion of her lungs mirrored the rise and fall of his shoulders against her palms.

"Don't leave tomorrow," she barely heard him whisper. "Stay with me."

"I wish I could…" she murmured sincerely. But fairy tales too often turned into nightmares in the morning.

Kane nodded, exhaled, and said, "G'night."

"Bye," she breathed in return. She watched him walk down the hallway, admiring his naturally fluid movement. He glanced back, and she nearly called out. Instead, she reminded herself to be sensible, certain later she'd be grateful for her strict guidelines, even though right then, she despised them.

When he turned the corner, Sabella let her head fall back against the door and shut her eyes. This was one risk she knew better than to take.

Two

eeks later, Sabella still couldn't believe she had spent her last night in Nashville with Kane Hartridge, and she couldn't stop thinking about it either. Physically, she had returned to her Portland apartment, but her mind kept drifting back to that night of its own volition.

She pulled a mug from her kitchen cabinet and poured herself some freshly brewed coffee. She needed to get back to work, but her ability to focus had gotten lost somewhere in Nashville. Her last few attempts had felt forced, and she didn't want to pitch poorly written articles. Mostly, she wanted to return to that night, to feel Kane's arms braced protectively around her and his lips on hers.

She couldn't regret sticking to her self-imposed rules—they existed for a reason—but that didn't keep her from picturing what would have happened had she invited him in.

Stay with me. The plea replayed in her mind at least a dozen times a day. Too often, she wished she had agreed, but it wasn't like she could have simply disappeared from her life back home, putting everything on hold for however long, or short, of a time he wanted her there. For all she knew, he would have come to his senses in the sober light of day, and she would have been crushed by her poor decision-making. At this point, he probably didn't even remember her.

Not for the first time, Sabella considered finding a way to contact him. Instead, she made her way to her couch, set her mug on the coffee table, and picked up her laptop. Her living room was the only room in her corner apartment that didn't have a window, but it was home to most of her literary collection. A waist-high shelf placed perpendicular to the couch created separation between her entryway and the living room, and tall bookcases covered the entire wall opposite it. Another bookshelf leveled off the protrusion created by her bedroom closet. She had set a pair of cozy armchairs in that corner, across from the open space that led into both her kitchen and her dining room and allowed for natural light from those rooms' windows.

No matter where she sat in this room, books surrounded her. Leather-bound collections of works by Shakespeare, Poe, Austen and their like mingled with the writings of Voltaire, Salinger, Molière, and more. Usually, this beautiful literature inspired her as she tried to write; it welcomed her, beckoning. Now, her beloved books seemed to chastise her for reliving one night rather than working on a potential chef d'oeuvre.

Still the memories played on a ceaseless loop.

"Focus, Sabella," she muttered. She wasn't about to lose her apartment or anything quite so drastic, but it might come to that if she couldn't write and sell a few articles or short stories relatively soon, which was the downside of working freelance.

A couple of hours and a not altogether terrible article on how to choose a career path later, Sabella was interrupted by the doorbell. She shut and set down her laptop and made her way over to the door, stretching as she walked around the shelf. Remembering her disheveled appearance, she pulled out her hairband and ran her fingers through her hair. No matter who was waiting on the other side, she didn't want to come off as a completely crazy shut-in.

She twisted the deadbolt and pulled open the door, then froze. Either she had progressed to full-blown hallucinations, or… "Kane?"

"Hey," he said, flashing her an uncertain smile.

"What are you doing here?" she managed to ask, still not quite believing this was happening.

"Ninety percent of life is showin' up," he answered with a small shrug. He was wearing a blue tee shirt layered over a white, long-sleeved shirt and jeans, and he was really, it seemed, standing in her doorway.

Sabella stepped back and gestured for him to come in. He took a couple steps inside, filling the space between her kitchen wall and the barrier-shelf. She pushed the door shut and stood there, unmoving.

They stared at each other silently. What was there to say? She probably should have asked how he had found her, but in that moment, it mattered less than the fact that he had.

Kane moved toward her, stepping so close that she could feel the heat from his body and smell the faint, pleasant scent of what was presumably cologne. Absolutely willing in that moment to slip off into this dream or fairy tale that had apparently followed her home, she tilted her chin up. Kane took it as the invitation it was, leaning in to kiss her. For a moment, only their lips touched, but then his hands came to her waist, finding skin and reminding Sabella she wasn't exactly dressed for company.

She did a small jump backward, almost knocking into the wooden shelf. "Be right back," she said, rushing past him and into her bedroom. With the door firmly shut, she blew her breath out, trying to ignore the flurry of questions racing through her mind. First things first: she had to get dressed.

Kane waited for a moment then followed the direction she'd gone. To his left stood a small dining set and a few barstools by an island counter. The door she'd gone through was closed on his right. He pulled out a stool and sat, leaning his elbows onto the island. His eyes closed to savor the image of her running away in only soft, and very short, shorts and a tank top. Her tousled honeyed-brown hair had whipped around when she'd turned sharply into the doorway.

It hadn't taken him long after that night to get her address, but he'd waited to come out and see her. He'd tried to distract himself with the bounty of local girls, but more often than not, he found himself thinking of her, especially when he tried to write. Somehow, that one night provided many snippets of material: their soft kiss on the bridge, her self-conscious smile, the challenge in her eyes during their first conversation, his last glimpse of her as he walked away... So many inspiring moments. Eventually he realized he couldn't put that night behind him without seeing her again, so he'd hopped on a plane.

Somewhere between the flight and parking his rental car, Kane had wondered if she'd welcome his visit. He'd decided it didn't matter. Either way, it was unlikely they'd have a repeat of that night's chemistry. He'd finally be able to put it firmly in the past—something to pull from for his music maybe, but nothing more. He'd even brought his guitar, so he could work on some of his songs if he had time to kill after seeing her.

The way she'd welcomed his kiss made him question how much spare time he'd really have. But then, she might always throw him out on his ear when she came out of that room. Kane ran his fingers through his hair, combing it into place. What would they do when she reappeared? He could probably charm her into spending the day, and even night, together, but at thirty-two, he was starting to find nights like that hollow.

❖ ❖ ❖

When Sabella came out of her bedroom, she found Kane sitting at the island that separated her kitchen from the dining room, his eyes closed and brows angled together, with a scowl starting to form. He looked chiseled, formidable, and ready to take on the world. Incredibly attractive.

She had replaced her flimsy terrycloth shorts with cargostyle pants and swapped the lace-trimmed tank for a palegreen, cold-shoulder top with a deep surplice neckline that her best friend, Gina, had convinced her to buy. Thankfully, she always did her makeup at the mirrored armoire in her bedroom, so she hadn't had to choose between changing and running to the bathroom for eyeliner and mascara. She had foregone lip gloss, in case it was too apparent a change, and resigned herself to looking not as well put-together as he had last seen her—far from it, actually, but there was nothing she could do about that without making him wait for much too long.

"So, can I get you something?" she offered, breaking the silence. His eyes snapped open, and he turned his head toward her. She walked into the kitchen for the relative barrier the dark, granite island provided. "Coffee? Beer?"

"No, thank you."

She had missed his voice. Since she had returned home, she hadn't allowed herself to listen to his music in a fruitless attempt to move past the memories of Nashville.

She leaned against the corner counter across from the island, leaving about as much space as was possible between them. He kept watching her intently, making her worry she had somehow smeared lipstick that she hadn't even used all over her face. Resisting the urge to wipe at the imagined smudge, Sabella asked, "So, how did you find me?"

He had the grace to look a bit sheepish. "I, uh, I asked somebody at the hotel."

"And they just offered up my address? You must be quite convincing."

"Well, I've known the concierge for a few years," he said, as if that explained everything.

"Still, though. They could have gotten in trouble for giving you confidential information." She could easily see him charming a female concierge, an ex-lover perhaps, but it wasn't likely a woman would be thrilled to give him another woman's contact information.

"It didn't hurt that he's a fan," Kane admitted. "I told him you'd forgotten somethin' at the bar. Just wanted to get it back to you."

"Did I?"

"Not at the bar." His cheeks rounded with the suggestive glint in his eyes.

"And what did I forget?" she inquired in return, following the bait.

"To give me your number. Or tell me your real name…"

"I told you my real name," she half asked, half insisted. His left eyebrow lifted in challenge. "Well, the name I go by in general," she clarified.

"Sabella is a pretty name."

"It doesn't suit me."

"Sure it does. Has the word 'beautiful' right in it. It's perfect for you." He said it so matter-of-factly that Sabella didn't know how to respond—a rare occurrence.

"Why did you come here?" she finally asked, intentionally changing the topic.

He turned and tilted his head slightly, asking, "Would you like me to leave?"

"No, that isn't what I meant," she answered without hesitation. She licked her lips—a bad habit, which was another reason she hadn't worn lip gloss, and rarely did. "I'm just trying to understand."

"I wanted to see you," he answered simply. He rose from the barstool then walked around the island so he stood blocking the opening to her kitchen. Her heartbeat quickened.

"So, you've seen me," she said deliberately. "What now?"

"You tell me," he answered, forcing her to take the lead.

"How long are you here?"

"Flight back's tomorrow." He leaned against the wall side of the opening. He had an uncanny ability to appear comfortable anywhere, she decided.

She wasn't sure she wanted to know where he planned to stay, so she didn't ask. Either he expected she would fall into his arms and let him fall into her bed, or he had made alternate arrangements. Both options were strangely unsettling. She didn't want to be merely a temporary escape from his routine any more than she wanted to be a cross-country booty call. Although, technically, he had come to her.

"Is there anywhere you have to be?" she ventured.

"I'm all yours, Bella." He smiled, seeing right through her question, then melted into the wall supporting him, truly relaxing, as if his previous stance had been calculated, imitating calm.

Sabella didn't comment on his shortening of her name to the Italian word for beautiful; far be it from her to point out the many flaws in her figure. Instead, she glanced around the kitchen, trying to come up with an idea of something they could do. "It looks like a beautiful day outside. We could have a picnic or something," she suggested, shrugging faintly so he would know she wasn't committed to the idea.

"That sounds great," he answered, pushing off the wall to stand straight. He really did have an impressive stance when he chose to take control. "I'll drive. Is there a deli or somethin' 'round here?"

Well done, Sabella, she chastised silently. The last thing she should have proposed was the two of them being alone, and there wasn't much likelihood of any of the local parks being particularly populated on a weekday afternoon so early in May. *What have you gotten yourself into?*

Three

Kane shrugged the growing tension from his shoulders. Sabella'd grabbed a sleeping bag from her bedroom and plucked her purse from a hook by her door before they left. Now they stood in line at a café. He couldn't wait to get to whatever park she had in mind. A picnic, his guitar, hopefully somewhere secluded—it was perfect.

Mostly he just wanted to tug her into his arms. Even though she'd changed from the skimpy outfit he'd found her in, she still looked unbelievably sexy. There was just something about her curves… And he didn't mind the fact that she was short enough to nestle comfortably under his arm.

He was ready to be disappointed by a cold dose of reality, but he had to get the fantasy out of his mind. For weeks, all he'd had were memories of her. That had been torment enough but nothing like actually having her near.

"What are you in the mood for?" Sabella asked, twisting back to him.

Kane cleared his throat. "Whatever you're having," he heard himself answering.

"Two vegan salads it is," she said, though he caught a twinkle in her eyes.

"Definitely not." He glanced up at the menu board. "How about a roast beef sandwich?" He hadn't had anything other than a croissant and coffee on the plane. He wanted something a bit more filling, even if food wasn't his top priority right now.

"Okay, then," she said and turned back toward the cashier. Finally the last person in front of them was done, and Sabella placed their order: two roast beef sandwiches, a couple iced teas, and she added a side of potato salad. *Not bad.*

Kane pulled out his credit card, handing it to the cashier before Sabella had a chance to take out her wallet. She started to protest, but he cut her off. "Where I come from, the man pays." A part of him expected her to protest anyway.

Instead, she cocked an eyebrow, smiled, and remained silent. The cashier shifted her gaze between the two of them, unsure if she should run the card. Kane looked back at her, about to turn on the charm, when Sabella nodded at the girl. "Go ahead, Daisy."

After he'd gotten his card back, the two of them stepped out of the way to wait for their order. "You come here often?" Kane asked, though it wasn't really a question.

"Sometimes, when I'm tired of writing at home." They stood in silence for a minute. "They have pretty great sandwiches, actually," Sabella added.

Kane nodded in response. The ease of their night in Nashville was clearly gone. It was exactly what he'd expected, but he still found himself disappointed.

Sabella puffed her breath out as the two of them walked to Kane's rental car. He was being perfectly polite, the epitome of a good old Southern boy, even going as far as to insist on carrying their food, but somehow it all reminded her that, ultimately, they were strangers. Maybe their chemistry had been a perfectly normal side effect of alcohol consumption. *How depressing.*

The car chirped, and Kane opened the passenger door for her, ever the gentleman. Sabella kept her eyes down, desperately looking for something to say. Her eyes fell on the back seat, but all she saw there was a jacket, the sleeping bag Kane had tossed in, and a guitar case she hadn't noticed earlier. Her head jerked up. "You brought your guitar?" she asked, looking up at him. Other than the metal door between them, they were standing closer than she had previously realized.

The question seemed to catch him off-guard. "I, uh, yeah. I take it everywhere," he answered after a moment.

Sabella smiled, slipped the bag of food from his left hand, and slid into the seat. Kane hesitated for a second, then shut the door and rounded the car.

Once they'd made their way out of the parking lot, Sabella directed him to the Waterfront Park. Portland had no shortage of parks, both in downtown and outside of the city center, but she loved sitting on the waterfront, alternately looking over the river and facing the city, depending on her mood. Maybe sitting by the river would somehow help revive the chemistry they had had in Nashville.

In the park, she chose a solid-looking tree with full branches—one of her personal favorites. People passed by on the bike path that snaked near the water. They were few and far between, and the path itself was still a ways away, but the two of them wouldn't be completely alone.

"What do you think?" she asked, turning back to Kane.

"Looks good." He set down his guitar and laid out the sleeping bag between them.

Sabella knelt on the edge and pulled out the sandwiches, salad, forks, napkins, and iced teas, placing everything between her spot and the tree. Kane still stood near the other edge of the sleeping bag, by his guitar case, as if uncertain whether he should sit down.

"Are you going to join me?" she asked tentatively. Suddenly, the reality of the situation pressed around her. What was she doing on a *picnic* with Kane Hartridge? It wasn't as though she was particularly fascinating or pretty, or anything resembling his type, which probably tended more toward leggy, gorgeous, and effortlessly flirty women. She would have been only mildly surprised if he had chosen to turn around and drive off right then.

❖ ❖ ❖

Sabella stiffened then licked her lips. She looked unsure, expectant. Kane lowered himself to the corner of the sleeping bag on the other side of the tree from where she sat, letting his legs go off the edge and into the grass. He kept one knee bent and leaned onto his right hand. Sabella shifted onto one hip, leaving her legs folded to her side. Both of them were left awkwardly just a bit too far from the food she'd laid out. She'd gotten nervous, but he wasn't sure why. He did know how to put a girl at ease, though.

He flashed her a smile. "You're right, this does look good."

Sabella exhaled and said, "Hopefully, it tastes even better." She cocked her head and added, "You must be pretty hungry if you just flew in."

"That I am." He waited for her to make a move toward the food.

She looked at him, the hint of a smile back in her eyes. "It's not poisoned. Well." She paused. "Not as far as I know."

Kane pushed up from his position and resettled closer to the tree. He reached for an iced tea, twisted it open, and offered it to her.

"Thanks." She accepted it with a smile. Then she tucked her hair behind her ear and leaned forward to open the box of potato salad. Kane's mama had raised him better, but that didn't stop him from taking in the sight of Sabella's cleavage. It did make him pretend he hadn't when she sat up and held out the opened container to him along with a plastic fork.

They ate seated like that. Occasionally, Kane passed her the potato salad. She would take a couple bites then give it back, so he ended up eating most of it. They chatted a bit, but it was mostly frustrating, idle small talk. When they finished their sandwiches, she gathered the trash and walked it over to a nearby bin. Her hips swayed with every step. He took a sip of iced tea as he watched her walk back toward him. A soft wind tousled her hair, tempting Kane to tangle his fingers in it.

Sabella stopped when she reached the edge of the sleeping bag. "So, are you going to leave your guitar just lying there? Abandoned?"

Kane smiled at the feigned concern on her face. Her expressive eyes showed every emotion. He placed his hand on the guitar case. "What do I get if I take it out?"

"Nothing," she said with a smile. "But," she continued a second later, sitting back down, "you might get something for a song."

That made him chuckle. "What'd that be?"

"It would be a surprise," she answered, barely hesitating.

"Who picks?" Kane asked softly, without humor. His gaze slipped to her lips just as she licked them. He forced himself to focus on her eyes again.

"Depends on how well you sing, I guess." Challenge joined the mischief in her eyes, but her voice sounded a bit breathier.

Kane turned away to get his guitar. There was a chance he'd judged the day too quickly.

Sabella settled comfortably and waited as Kane tuned his guitar. With his focus diverted, she could watch him without any pretense of admiring the nature surrounding them. He sat with both knees bent, one leg laid flat against the sleeping bag while the other supported the guitar. His upper body curved slightly over the instrument while he tuned, which made his hair drift forward on the right side, falling over his eyebrow. His left wrist was adorned with the same woven bracelet he had worn in Nashville. She made a mental note to ask him about it the next time there was a lull in their conversation.

Finished tuning, Kane straightened and brushed his hair back. His voice was incredible: so pure, yet touched with a husky raggedness that heightened the sincerity of the emotions and experiences behind his words. This was why she had made a point of going to the Fiddle and Steel Guitar specifically for their open mic night. She might never come to appreciate the country music genre as a whole, but she definitely didn't mind the country feel to his songs; he was so good, she had no difficulty looking past the genre, or even the occasional syntactical errors in his lyrics, to enjoy his music wholeheartedly.

Like when he had been on stage, Kane alternated between closing his eyes and taking in his surroundings, though this time, there was no question he was looking at her. At the conclusion of the song, a soft smile curled his lips just enough to round his cheeks and narrow his eyes almost imperceptibly.

"Your voice is amazing," Sabella murmured, not wanting to disturb the air, which still felt suffused with his last notes.

For a moment, Kane said nothing; he simply sat, hugging the guitar effortlessly, as if it was an ingrained part of him. "Thanks," he whispered finally, so quietly she realized he had spoken more because his lips moved than anything else.

"I always wish I had learned to play an instrument," Sabella confided. "Music is not really my forte, though," she added, dismissing the idea.

Kane lifted the guitar from his knee. "I could show you."

"You wouldn't mind? I wouldn't want to take advantage of your expertise, or to bore you."

"We got time." He shifted so that he sat with both legs out in front of him, bent at the knees. "Come 'ere," he added.

Sabella lifted onto her knees and scooted closer to him, in what probably looked like an unbecoming half-crawl. She stopped when she was beside his foot and sat back onto her heels.

"What're you, scared of me now?" Kane taunted with a smile and a lift of an eyebrow.

She held her hands out, palms up. "Where do you want me?"

Kane's smile dropped, and suggestion replaced the humor in his eyes.

Sabella opened her mouth to clarify then shut it with an exhale, smiling despite herself. "You know what I meant."

Kane leaned away from the tree trunk and held out his left hand toward her, still holding onto the guitar with his right. She lifted onto her knees again and placed her hand in his, enjoying its warmth and the sensation of his calluses against the softer skin of her palm. He pulled her gently forward and to the side, so she twisted, landing right in front of him with her back to his chest. A new tension vibrated through both of them as Kane straightened his right leg and brought the guitar in front of her so that the head rested against the front of his left knee.

"Watch," he said, drawing her attention first to his face, so close to hers, then down to the neck of the guitar. He placed three fingers deliberately on the strings in sequence, ensuring she had a chance to note the position of each one. When he dropped his hand, Sabella brought hers to the guitar to replicate the position he had demonstrated. He shifted her ring finger so it rested exactly below her middle finger then strummed the chord. "A minor," he told her.

"Okay," she acknowledged.

Kane picked her right arm up from her lap and brought it over the guitar. His muscles shifted against her back with each of his movements. He placed his hand on the body of the guitar, and Sabella took that as an invitation to strum the chord herself. She drew her fingers slowly against the strings, and the guitar sounded each note in succession.

"A little faster," Kane corrected. "Good," he praised when she produced a smooth-sounding chord.

Sabella struck the chord again rather than speaking.

"Now," she felt him say by her ear, "move each finger one string up."

For a second, Sabella debated what he meant by "up," but then she shifted her fingers closer to the sky and strummed the new chord.

"E major," Kane said.

"Easier than I thought it would be." She strummed the chord again then switched back to the first one. "I don't know why I was so impressed." She looked up at him to ensure he had caught her sarcasm.

He was smiling back at her. "Yeah? So you can play me a song now."

"Nah," she backtracked, "I think I'll leave the playing to you, in case you have a superiority complex." She smiled up at him then licked her lips. His vibrantly green eyes melded perfectly with their surroundings, and there was something oddly appealing about the hint of stubble covering his jaw.

"You want to hear somethin' else?" Kane asked without breaking eye contact.

"Yes, please," she said earnestly and returned her attention to the guitar. Maybe it was wishful thinking, but it seemed they had made it past the earlier disconnected unease. *Don't get your hopes up, Sabella.*

"Scootch back a bit," he directed.

She placed her hands on the ground, pushing off so she could lift up and land a touch closer to him. He leaned back against the tree trunk, but she stayed sitting straight until his hand on her shoulder prompted her to settle against him. Kane switched his legs, straightening his left knee so that leg lay straight alongside hers and bringing up his right knee to support the guitar again. Sabella kept both her hands resting on her thighs, but that barely lessened the intimacy of their position. Like it or not, she was nestled against him, surrounded by his body. If she were to be honest with herself, she would have admitted it felt wonderful, but she resolutely avoided thinking about that.

Kane started playing a ballad about a lost high school love. Sabella let the music wash over her, relaxing against his chest. Eventually, she leaned her head back on his shoulder so she could watch him sing. From this angle, she observed the movement of his jaw, saw a slight breeze puff his hair away from his ear for a moment, and noticed the thick, lush branches above them that provided a natural backdrop to his laidback posture. He gazed into the distance, as if seeing the story of the song unfold among the trees before him.

At the song's bridge, Kane turned his head to look at her. He kept playing but didn't continue to sing. After a few bars of them watching each other, he leaned down to kiss her.

Four

Tiny pauses punctuated their kiss, turning it into a gentle series of their lips coming together. At first, Kane kept his fingers idly playing the same chord, but soon he laid the guitar aside. He lifted his hands to her: one cupping her cheek, the other slowly tangling in her hair. Sabella shifted so her back rested against his knee. Kane bent his other knee to give her more space. One of her hands glided through his hair, landing on his shoulder as the other came to rest above his ribs on his left side.

Kane angled her head to deepen their kiss, but he kept it soft. She matched his timing seamlessly. He wouldn't have minded spending the rest of the afternoon kissing her.

Voices drifted to them from the bike path, and she pulled away. Her lips were redder, and her cheeks were flushed, enhancing the color of her eyes. He slid his hands to her shoulders, enjoying the feel of her skin. She started to lean in for another kiss but twisted away at the sound of laughter. Kane followed her gaze to a group of women strolling by the river. Sabella turned back to him but leaned against his knee, keeping as much distance between them as she could without moving away. She lowered her hand from his shoulder. He ran his hands down her arms.

They sat there like that until Kane asked, "Should we get out of here?"

"Did you have something in mind?"

Hell yes. "I'm open to suggestions."

Sabella started to get up, but Kane pulled her in for another kiss. She laughed against his mouth then pulled back. "I thought you wanted to leave?" she teased.

He smiled back at her. "I'm good here."

Sabella reluctantly pulled away from another languid kiss. More and more people were trickling into the park, and she didn't particularly want an audience. Maybe she should have selected a more secluded park after all. She placed her hands on Kane's chest and pushed gently to keep some distance between them. "So, have you ever been to Portland before?" she asked. "We have some peculiarly interesting things to see."

"More interesting than this?" Kane started to lean in for another kiss, but Sabella ducked his attempt, feigning innocence.

"There's the Chinese Garden," she suggested. Kane lifted an eyebrow. "Or, 'Brew and View' movie theaters?"

"Movies and alcohol, huh?" His eyes trailed lasciviously over her upper body.

"Don't get any ideas." She swatted imperceptibly at his chest despite his nearly irresistibly suggestive smile. "Okay, what else…" She looked around them, as if the trees would inspire an idea. "There's old China Town."

Kane ignored her and began nuzzling her neck.

"Or…" She couldn't gather her thoughts with his mouth playing down her neck, then over her collarbone. "There's the Pioneer Courthouse Square," she managed to say, punctuating her words with deep breaths to maintain some control over her voice. Kane's tongue began tracing patterns over her skin, and her fingers curled over his chest. For a brief moment, she gave in to the sensation of being in his arms, of him tasting her neck, of his stubble grazing her skin.

"Oh!" she gasped seconds later when an idea struck her. "There's also Powell's!"

Kane lifted his head, and she practically felt the heat emanating from his eyes. Whatever she had meant to say evaporated from her mind, and Sabella leaned in for another kiss, less gentle than its predecessors. A shout from a passing biker drew both of them back to their surroundings and up for air. Kane brushed his lips over hers once more, then pulled back and sighed. "What's Powell's?" he asked.

Sabella smiled regretfully. "It's a city of books. A bookstore so enormous it covers an entire city block."

"You spend a lot of time there?" he asked with genuine interest, though she was fairly certain his thoughts were elsewhere.

"I try not to—I'm running out of shelf space. But it is considered one of Portland's must-see attractions," she said with an intentionally cheesy, convincing smile.

"Well, then. Let's go see Powell's," he consented, smiling back wryly.

They spent the rest of the afternoon wandering around downtown. Sabella led him through China Town, to Powell's, where he predominately saw her light up with her love for literature, and then down to the courthouse square. He bought them coffee, and they found a spot on the square's steps. They spoke comfortably, sliding back into the easy interaction they had shared in Nashville.

It turned out Kane always wore the bracelet she had noticed as a link to his Native American grandfather, who had wisely gifted a teenage Kane with his first guitar. That heritage was also part of the reason he kept his hair longer. The other part was the effect longer hair had on his image as a musician—and he knew women loved it. At times Sabella felt herself slipping into an interviewer's role, a common complaint from those who spoke to her caused by her bound-less curiosity for the details of people's lives, but Kane redirected the conversation, smoothly balancing out her unfortunate habit. She regaled him with stories of the crazy adventures with which Gina had imbued her life since they had met in their sophomore year of university.

Gina came from a big Italian family, complete with a cheerful yet well-connected father, whom Sabella had no problems imagining as part of the mafia, a bustling, homey mother, and a protective older brother, not to exclude the cheeky youngest boy. The Sabatino family had unreservedly accepted Sabella into their home and their lives.

"What about your family?" Kane asked as the sun began to set.

"What do you mean?" she asked, sipping her coffee.

"I told you 'bout my folks, that I'm part Cherokee, an only child. You've told me a fair bit about Gina's folks. But you haven't said anythin' about your own family."

"You are too perceptive for my own good," she joked.

His brow furrowed, though he didn't press her. Sabella gazed across the square as she answered him. "There really isn't all that much to tell you. My parents live in California, though they're traveling around Europe at the moment. They're extremely intellectual and successful, but they were so encouraging while raising their children that they ended up with an artist and a writer." She turned back to Kane and finished with a fond smile, "My sister, Trisha, is over in New York."

He brushed a strand of hair back from her cheek. Sabella thought he might kiss her again, but instead he asked, "You didn't want to work in New York?"

She shrugged. "I don't really enjoy big cities like New York. Portland has a more laidback and natural atmosphere that suits me better."

"And it has Powell's," he teased.

"And Powell's," she agreed, laughing outright. "So. What would you like to do with your one night in Portland?"

"I get to choose?" he asked shrewdly, accepting the non sequitur.

The suggestiveness in his eyes warmed her cheeks. "Within reasonable limits," Sabella clarified, her lips pressing into a small smile.

"Shame." He smiled back at her, clearly relishing her modest timidity. "Let's grab some dinner?" He stood and offered her his hand.

She took it and stood as well. "What kinds of food do you like?" she asked as they made their way across the square and back to the car.

"Delicious kinds." The answer earned him a reproving glance. "I'm pretty adventurous, so long as it's food, if the food's not vegan or anythin' like that," he elaborated.

"Well, we could go to Nostrano's—fabulous, Italian-inspired cuisine. But, wait." She stopped mid-step and turned toward him. "Where are you staying? I wouldn't want to make you drive around in too many circles."

"Haven't figured that out yet."

"Oh." Sabella considered the man before her then decided to dive in; she had already tried staying practical, ever since Nashville, and that hadn't turned out particularly well. Plus, he had travelled all this way. "You're welcome to stay at my place. I mean, the couch folds out, and it's fairly comfortable."

To his credit, Kane barely reacted to being relegated to the couch. "Thanks, Bella" he said, then placed his arm around her, and continued walking.

Kane parked his rental car back by Sabella's apartment and turned off the engine. Dinner had been fantastic, and the rest of the day had actually turned out much better than he'd expected.

Sabella'd seemed a bit shy at first, quiet. But when they touched on topics she liked, she grew animated, enthralling him. Sometimes, she would catch herself speaking enthusiastically, and she'd pause. Her cheeks would flush slightly, and she'd bite her lip, embarrassed. It was endearing.

Kane rounded the car and opened the door so she could slide out. He blocked her path with his body. She looked up at him, surprised. He took advantage of her gently parted lips to steal a kiss.

She hummed quietly once he'd pulled away. Like for most of the day, a soft smile touched her lips, lighting up her eyes. Her guileless, uncalculated responses enchanted him. She seemed unlike any of the women he'd tangled with.

"I take it you found dinner palatable?" she teased.

"It was great," he answered sincerely. "So, have I earned your number?"

"Well, I suppose that depends." Kane braced himself when she paused. "Am I going to get yours? Since you do have my address already."

He let out the breath he'd been holding. "I think we could work something out," he answered wryly.

"So, right here? Right now?" she asked suggestively when he didn't move. She slipped her phone out of her pocket and held it up between their bodies.

Kane chuckled, relaxing. "If you insist." He took her phone and entered his number, then called his own phone so he'd have hers.

When they walked into her apartment, Sabella gestured over the wooden panel that separated her doorway from the living room. "Make yourself comfortable."

She went to put away the sleeping bag, and Kane rounded the barrier. "You weren't kidding," he called out, when he saw the "panel" was actually a shelf. Packed bookshelves also covered the far wall and evened out a protrusion from the neighboring room. Kane set down his guitar and backpack by the colorful easy chairs in front of the outcropping.

The shelves looked a bit overstuffed. In many spots, little knickknacks stood in front of the books—a painting on glass from Rome, some souvenir glasses, and random figurines. But the books actually seemed well organized, separated into time periods or topics. He was examining her collection when he heard Sabella's voice behind him.

"I really wasn't."

Kane turned to face her.

"Some have called my collection excessive," she continued with a self-deprecating smile, crossing the living room. "I put out a towel and a new toothbrush for you in the bathroom. It's the door in the corner of the dining room." She set the sheets and a pillow she had brought out on the arm of the couch.

Kane joined her silently.

"I should move the coffee table so I can make up the couch," she stated, voicing the excuse as if he'd suggested something.

"I got it." He picked up the basic black table. "Where would you like it?"

"It's actually small enough to fit right by the chairs. Thank you."

She flashed him a simple smile then turned to pull up the couch cushions. He moved the table the few steps away and walked back to the couch. She placed the cushions next to the short shelf then jumped slightly when she saw him back next to her. He stayed facing her as he pulled out the couch, forcing her to move across the room with him. He tried not to smile at her subtle discomfort but wasn't wholly successful.

She exhaled, licked her lips, then walked around the couch to pick up the sheets. Kane offered to help, but she declined, so instead he enjoyed the sight of her bending over the couch as she made it up for him.

"I'm sorry, this definitely isn't the most luxurious bed in the world," she warned, tossing the pillow down.

"I'll survive."

She smiled at the first words she'd said to him. Kane definitely wouldn't have minded replacing the smile with the more serious look of passion. But he'd learned he liked making her smile.

"Care for a nightcap?" Sabella offered.

"Sure." Kane followed her out to the kitchen.

"Coffee? Beer? Something stronger?"

"Do you by chance have any whiskey?"

"Strangely, yes." She turned to the cabinet between her sink and the gray island. "Whiskey it is." She pulled down a bottle and a couple tumblers. "How would you like it?" she asked, glancing over her shoulder.

"Straight up, thanks."

She filled the glasses and handed one to him. "Cheers," she said and raised her glass, smiling shyly this time. Awareness leapt between them.

Kane tilted his head in acknowledgement and clinked his tumbler against hers.

Kane should have looked out of place in her combination library-living room, but somehow, as with everywhere else

Sabella had seen him, he didn't. He had chosen the blue chair, and Sabella sat in the yellow one, with the whiskey bottle on the floor beside her. She had nudged the matching lilac footstool aside in case he wanted to stretch out his legs. For a while, they sat in silence, both sipping the whiskey.

Finally, he asked, "Why didn't you contact me?"

"I…" she started to answer, then paused and sighed. "I didn't think you would want to hear from me." When he didn't say anything, she added tentatively, "I'm really happy you came."

She was about to find some unidentified method of back-tracking when he softly said, "Me too."

As if by tacit agreement, the conversation then returned to less intense topics. On their second round of whiskey, they began discussing music. Surprisingly, the subject hadn't been completely exhausted earlier in the day.

"Well, lots of classical music, some French music, Broadway soundtracks, Matchbox 20, Pink, Secret Garden. Jack Savoretti's pretty good," Sabella listed, self-consciously trying to filter out any of her potentially embarrassing preferences.

"No country artists?" he prompted.

"Well, you know, I don't really like country music, or rather, most country music."

"What do you mean you don't like country music?" Kane asked, aghast.

"I told you when we met. I had recently discovered, to my infinite surprise, a country artist whose music I like," she reminded.

"In Nashville?" He took another swallow.

"No, actually. When I heard his music, I realized there must be something about the country genre I hadn't experienced before, which inspired my foray into that culture."

"Oh yeah? Whose music?" Kane asked, passively curious.

Sabella took a bracing sip of whiskey. "Yours," she admitted.

Kane stiffened. "Mine?"

"Yes. Although, I think part of the reason I liked it was the touch of rock in your sound. Then again, even without that, you have an unbelievably beautiful voice."

Kane gulped down his remaining whiskey and stood. "So you came to Nashville."

Sabella sensed the shift in his mood, but she wasn't certain what had bothered him. "Yes, to do some research, for my article idea," she elaborated, though he hadn't really asked. "I told you that," she added when he didn't say anything.

He ran his hand through his hair, which, coupled with his stony expression, showed unequivocally that he was aggravated. "Research on what exactly?" he probed.

His volatile mood had to have been caused by a simple misunderstanding, but Sabella stood regardless. "On the world of country music. What's wrong?" she asked bluntly.

"Nothing," he answered, all traces of amiability erased from his demeanor.

"Kane." His name came out partially as a plea, but Sabella didn't know what else to say.

"Never mind," he said and stalked to the kitchen.

His tumbler clinked against the counter. She had a sinking feeling his last words referred not solely to the past few minutes but to the entire day. She followed him, intending to fix whatever had shattered, but stopped in the entrance to the kitchen, keeping distance between herself and Kane's turned back. "I knew who you were when we met, but you knew that," she pointed out.

"I thought you'd heard 'em announce me," he snapped without turning around, "not that you were a fan! Why'd you even go to the Fiddle an' Steel?"

"Besides the fact that it was near my hotel and was touted as an ideal example of a country bar?" Kane turned, fixing her with a rather intimidating glare, but Sabella wouldn't be cowed. "I had heard or read somewhere that you occasionally perform at their open mic nights," she acknowledged, crossing her arms in front of her chest.

"What is it you want from me?" Kane asked in a menacingly soft tone.

The implication that she had been manipulating him sparked Sabella's own temper. "Right now? I would mostly like for you to leave," she retorted, setting her glass sharply on the island. "But since you're here for another twelve hours or so, I think the best option is if we both just get some sleep."

Some idealistic part of her hoped Kane would recognize how unfairly he was acting—he was the one who found *her*!—but he remained unyielding. "That's not what I meant," he stated stonily.

Sabella inhaled deeply in an attempt to match his emotionless approach. "What would you like me to say? Would you like to hear that I'm a stalker, and you've fallen prey to my ingeniously malicious plan?" She paused. "Or maybe you'd rather I tell you that it was a magical meet-cute, orchestrated by an unseen power beyond our control? Which fictional story would you like me to tell you?" When he didn't respond, Sabella sighed. "Good night."

She strode into her bedroom, leaving him alone in the kitchen, and pressed her back against the closed door. The evening had switched from charmingly agreeable to abysmal in an instant, and she had been an idiot not to have anticipated it, regardless of how idyllic their day together had been.

Five

Kane couldn't sleep. Instead he sat on the edge of Sabella's unfolded couch, wearing just his jeans, and drank her whiskey. Light still shone from under the door of her bedroom.

He'd acted like an idiot, finding her and coming to Portland, believing she was unlike all the women who'd gone after his image and industry connections instead of him, who'd used him to get ahead. Turned out, different as she was in mannerisms, she was really just like them, only wanting him for a story. He didn't know how she'd pulled it off without him noticing sooner, but she was clearly a master manipulator.

Kane downed the whiskey then found his way to the bathroom, not bothering to turn on any lights until he got there. He ran the water and splashed it over his face. It dripped onto his chest, but Kane paid no attention, leaning over the sink. He'd thought he'd seen every trick in the women's playbook after Felicia Mae, but it turned out, he'd been wrong. He still couldn't figure out how Sabella'd managed to play him.

She hadn't actually forgotten anything in Nashville, like he'd told the hotel clerk. She hadn't invited him into her room, so she couldn't have found him later with a fake, or worse real, pregnancy. She'd looked truly surprised when he'd shown up. Today, once things had clicked, had been unbelievable.

Kane sighed and looked up at the mirror. He wiped off the remaining drops of water with the towel she'd left for him, staring at his brooding reflection. Some part of him had wanted to believe he'd met a girl without ulterior motives, but she'd freely admitted that she'd gone to the Fiddle and Steel to see him. She hadn't even tried to come up with a cover story.

None of which changed that he couldn't get the mixture of hurt and anger in her expression out of his mind. Had it been anger and fear, he'd have been sure she'd tried to use him. As things stood, some last bit of optimism in him clung to her pain. Maybe he'd been wrong to jump down her throat.

Once upon a time, he'd naturally given people the benefit of the doubt. He hadn't been that trusting in years.

Kane turned out the light and stalked out of the bathroom. He intended to pass right by her room but stopped at the sliver of light on the floor. He knocked softly on her bedroom door, then waited a moment but didn't hear anything. He was about to turn the corner and return to the living room when she called out, "Come in."

Kane opened the door slowly to find Sabella sitting on her bed with her laptop. She was dressed again in shorts and a tank top. She looked up at him expectantly. Her expression could have been mistaken for neutral, but to him it looked cold. "I'm sorry," he said stiffly from the doorway. She just continued to watch him. "I shouldn't, I uh. I shouldn't have snapped at you," he forced out. He didn't mind apologizing when he was wrong, but what if this was all somehow part of her plan?

She nodded, pensive. "What is it you want from me?" she quoted back at him.

Kane didn't know the answer. "Good night," he whispered and shut the door.

Sabella woke in a foul mood. Water was running in the bathroom, but under no circumstances would she picture Kane in the shower. At least that meant she could go make coffee before having to face him.

She dragged herself out of bed, pulled on some jeans, added a bra under her tank top, touched up the smudged leftovers of her eyeliner, and tied her hair back in a messy bun before deeming herself sufficiently presentable for a morning goodbye. It wasn't like she'd ever see him again.

She had a pot of coffee brewing and was taking down two of her vibrant, oversized, round coffee mugs when the shower shut off. Even the mugs' perky colors didn't improve her mood, though.

When the bathroom door began to open, Sabella turned back to her coffee maker. Despite herself, she couldn't wholly expunge the picture of him standing shirtless in her bedroom doorway the night before, and her imagination didn't need any more fodder, especially considering how poorly he apparently thought of her. She busied herself with putting away the beans while the coffee finished percolating.

"Good morning," Kane said a few minutes later from behind her.

"Morning," she replied, pouring him some coffee before turning around. He was fully dressed and had leaned his guitar case against the island.

"Thank you," he said politely when she handed him the mug.

Sabella couldn't bring herself to be equally polite by inquiring how he had slept. Besides, if she had, he would likely use it as further twisted evidence that she had manipulated him for some nefarious purpose. *I shouldn't have snapped at you*, he had stated the night before. Sabella paid scrupulous attention to people's words—one of the hazards of being a writer—and she hadn't missed that he hadn't apologized for his mistaken conclusion, only for his tone.

She poured herself a cup of coffee and took a restorative sip. When she turned back around, Kane had set down his cup, still partially filled, and picked up his guitar. He clenched his jaw, as if preventing himself from speaking. They watched each other long enough that she dropped her gaze first.

"I'll see ya," Kane said shortly afterward.

Once she had heard him leave and shut the door, Sabella took her coffee back to her bedroom. She honestly considered climbing back under the covers but refused to wallow. On the plus side, she and Gina had their habitual mid-week lunch later that day.

Six

$\mathcal{Y}$ ou will not *believe* the week I'm having!" Gina exclaimed, plopping down across from Sabella at Tasty and Sons.

The familiar restaurant offered a changing, eclectic menu in a laid-back, earthy atmosphere with just the right touches of class. As usual, Gina's vibrantly patterned outfit was the most colorful thing in the entire restaurant, though that would be true almost anywhere. As the fashion editor of a monthly Portland magazine for women, Gina was a staunch proponent of vivacious and energetic styles that flattered the wearer and drew all eyes. She unyieldingly believed every woman should dress to stand out. Given her stunningly svelte physique, Gina's boundless confidence wasn't surprising. Sabella had long ago accepted the staggering difference between their appearances. Gina's enthusiastic affection eventually won over virtually everyone, and Sabella treasured their unlikely friendship.

"Roger giving you trouble again?" she asked, lips stretching into a smile. Gina's flair for the dramatic was irresistibly entertaining. Roger, Gina's associate editor, somehow lived up to nearly every stereotype of a fashion-obsessed gay man. Since Sabella occasionally wrote for the magazine, he was also one of their close friends.

As Gina filled her in on the latest office drama—Roger had approved photos filled with fashion faux-pas for their summer styles spread then tried to convince her they were *daring* selections—Sabella seized the reprieve from her own unrelenting frustration with yesterday's events. This was exactly what she needed: a return to her real world.

"So anyway, I told him to take responsibility for the mistake and order a reshoot, which is obviously not in the budget. But I just can't allow us to use any of these horrendous photos!" Gina explained.

"None of them?" Sabella probed, effortlessly slipping into her customary role as the voice of reason. "Not even if you cropped them for a 'Summer Separates' spread and postponed the other one?"

Gina pushed her hair behind one ear, revealing a bright-blue, thick hoop earring, and plopped her chin on her hand with a sigh. "Maybe if I look at them again, there'll be something salvageable," she agreed begrudgingly. "Or!" She jerked excitedly to a straight position. "What if we pulled it altogether, and you whipped up an article?"

Sabella busied herself with twirling her fork in her lunch but all too soon looked up to face Gina's hopeful expression.

"Article on what?" she relented with a sigh.

"I don't know. 'Life Hacks for Summer Styles?'" Gina suggested, taking a sip of her strawberry lemonade. She had transitioned into complete business mode. "Or something inspirational for women who haven't met their summer fitness goals? Or—and this would be perfect—a summer guide to fashion 'don'ts'! We could use the photos from that shoot, and you could add tips for quick fixes."

"Sure, if it would help you out, but you know you would be the one actually coming up with 'quick fixes,'" Sabella pointed out.

"Well, obviously," Gina joked. "Hey, you ok?" she asked when Sabella didn't react. "You've been somewhat lackluster since we got here."

Sabella set down her silverware. Gina knew her better than anyone, so if anyone could straighten her out about Kane, it was her best friend. "Okay, well. You remember I told you about my last night in Nashville?"

"Yeah...? You went out to a bar, alone, and the world didn't end," Gina recounted sarcastically.

Sabella narrowed her eyes and smiled wryly in acknowledgement. "I might have skipped over part of the story," she admitted.

"Oh my gosh—are you pregnant?" Gina asked with a mixture of concern and disbelief.

"Gina!" Sabella glanced around self-consciously. Leave it to her best friend to exclaim her unfounded conclusion with no regard for their utter lack of privacy.

"Well, sorry, Sab, but you look so serious."

"It's only been a few weeks!" Sabella pointed out. "And, anyway, nothing like that happened," she quickly tacked on when Gina's eyes grew round.

"But something happened? Why didn't you tell me?" Gina asked. "And why are you telling me now?" she added before Sabella could answer.

"Well, because he showed up yesterday," Sabella answered hesitantly.

"Sabella! I don't know if I should be shocked, proud, or creeped out on your behalf." Her beaming smile indicated she had chosen to be proud.

"It's not like that! Well," she waffled, "it's kind of like that. Or it was." She sighed and picked up her iced tea. "It's complicated," she concluded.

"And you let me go on and on about Roger," Gina accused. "So are you avoiding him?"

"No, he left."

"Okay, Sab. Start at the beginning," Gina commanded.

"Well, we met at that bar. We spent a couple hours there, drinking and chatting, and then he offered to walk me back to the hotel."

Gina's eyebrow crooked.

"Shush," Sabella chided, "just listen. We mostly meandered

around downtown. He kissed me when we were on this beautiful bridge, overlooking the water. Eventually, he did walk me back to my hotel room, and we, well, said goodbye."

"You didn't invite him in," Gina stated.

"We had just met, and my flight was the next day," Sabella explained defensively.

"I know, I know," Gina reassured. "Did you get a picture?"

"I'm sure there are plenty online; he's a somewhat popular singer," Sabella replied bitterly.

"Ouch. What did he do to you?" Gina slipped out her smart phone so Sabella would pull up pictures. Reluctantly, Sabella typed Kane's name into the browser window. "Wow, not bad, Sab!" Gina exclaimed after Sabella handed back the phone.

"I noticed," she said drily.

"A hot musician, you're finally branching out! Okay, wait. So, what, you gave him your address?" Gina prompted.

"No, he actually, well, found it himself." Another eyebrow raise. "And then yesterday, he showed up," Sabella continued.

"Well, that's either really romantic, or actually creepy," Gina remarked. "Must be pretty well known back in Nashville to swing that."

Sabella responded with a noncommittal hum. "I was leaning toward romantic, Gi. And after an admittedly awkward start, yesterday was incredible. Idyllic. Think: cheesy romantic comedy," she said pointedly.

"You always were a sucker for romance," Gina said sympathetically. "So what happened?"

"We went back to my apartment, and everything was wonderful…"

"Ooh la la," Gina joked, but Sabella ignored her.

"Until he basically accused me of manipulating him; using him for, I don't know, something," she finished miserably.

"Oh, Sab," Gina murmured and placed her hand comfortingly over Sabella's. "Sounds like he's a world-class jerk." She stared down at the picture on her phone. "Oh my gosh, this is perfect. I know exactly what you need!" she exclaimed suddenly.

"Uh oh." Gina's ideas were always wild. Even though they usually effectively distracted Sabella from whatever was going on, caution prompted her to ask pointedly, "Don't you have to get back to work?"

"I'm in an impromptu meeting with one of our writers for the rest of the afternoon," Gina answered with a wink. "Speaking of, don't worry about lunch. I'll expense it." When Sabella tried to protest, Gina cut her off. "You, Elle Savvy, are officially on assignment," she declared, using Sabella's pen name.

"Everything all right today, ladies?" their frequent server, Marcy, asked as she laid down their bill.

"It will be," Gina said mischievously and slipped the waitress her credit card. "Thanks, Marce."

When the bill was settled, Gina linked her arm through Sabella's and led her out of the restaurant. "Are you going to tell me where we're going?" Sabella asked. "And are you sure you can take the afternoon off?"

"I'm not taking it off, technically. You said yourself, you need me to walk you through the fashion tips. I'll have Roger email me the photos, and we'll go over them later. Now, come *on*," she insisted, ignoring Sabella's first question.

Gina's impromptu surprise was to drive them over to her favorite hair salon and spa. "This," she said, pulling out her phone to show Sabella a picture she'd chosen of Kane, "would make a killer haircut."

"You think the best way for me to get over Kane is to cut my hair like his?" Sabella asked skeptically.

"Not yours, mine! And not quite like his, but a feminine version. You," Gina clarified, "should get bright highlights. Pink or something."

"Yeah, right." No matter how Gina prodded, Sabella's aversion to pink hadn't wavered over their many years of friendship.

"Oh, come on! I can ask Michel to use a temporary dye if you want. It'll wash out in like a week. And it'll be good for you!"

"I can't believe you want to cut your hair," Sabella said, shifting the subject. "You've been growing it out on purpose, and it looks fantastic." Gina's chestnut hair gleamed and fell in perfect waves around her shoulders, yet another asset to her natural beauty.

Gina shrugged. "I'm up for a change. And you should be, too."

They were interrupted by Michel, Gina's hair stylist, who informed them with dismay that he didn't have an opening for another hour. Gina assured him that they would wait and steered Sabella, who gave herself over to the unstoppable force that was Gina on a roll, to the nail stations for mani-pedis.

A couple of hours later, with bright-blue nails and leaf-green toenails, Sabella watched Michel blow-drying Gina's sheared hair.

"Wow, Gi, I had my doubts, but you look incredible," Sabella said sincerely. The side-swept, unevenly textured bob framed her striking features to perfection.

"One of us is definitely a genius, right, Michel?" Gina teased.

"Magic happens when we're together, *chèrie*," he agreed. Michel, who was as French as his name suggested, sported closely cropped, yet carefully styled, dark hair, a soul patch, and a striped scarf wrapped around his neck, which, as far as Sabella knew, was never bare. He had been Gina's hairdresser of choice for a couple years now—a testament to his skill, given that, until meeting him, Gina had changed stylists and salons with practically every haircut she received since the girls had both moved to Portland.

"You're going to share in this brilliance, right Sab?" Gina asked. "I was kidding about pink, but maybe green highlights?"

"Chlorine chic," Sabella joked. "I'm fine, really. I'm feeling better already." She wagged her painted nails for emphasis.

"Purple," Michel weighed in. "With your honey hair? Purple."

Gina's eyes lit up. "Perfect! And it's *temporary*, Sab," she coaxed.

When the girls left the salon, it was with expertly styled—and in Sabella's case, daringly dyed—coiffures. "I'll meet you back at your place," Gina said, pulling up beside Sabella's car.

"Thanks, Gi." Sabella smiled and reached out for a quick hug. "You were right, as always. I needed this."

Gina shrugged off the gratitude with a cheeky smile. "It's why I'm here."

Sabella switched to her own car and headed home. Occasionally she glimpsed the purple highlights that now adorned her hair in her rear-view mirror, but there was nothing she could do about them now. Theoretically, the color would rinse out in ten to fourteen days. As always, in her own bizarrely effectual way, Gina had reminded Sabella of her unfettered independence, and that she shouldn't be defined by the assumptions of a virtual stranger, no matter how attractive and otherwise charming he may be.

She parked in her designated spot then waited, leaning against her car, for Gina to drive up. She shut her eyes and tilted her face up, enjoying the sunlight. A wolf whistle snapped her out of her carefree moment to see Gina striding across the parking lot. Sabella grinned back at her and walked to meet her partway. As they fell into step with each other, Gina pulled out her phone to verify that Roger had sent the photos they needed. Laughing, she handed Sabella the device so she could read Roger's hilariously passive-aggressive email, bemoaning Gina's lack of trust, visionary gumption, and appreciation for the work of her colleagues.

Fully engrossed in the message, Sabella didn't notice that Gina had stopped in the hallway outside her door until Gina warned, "Sab…"

Sabella shifted her attention from the phone to Gina's face then followed her friend's gaze to the floor. It took a moment for her to process what Gina had seen: a gift box and a bouquet of pink-tipped, peach roses with a few Calla lilies. She handed Gina the phone and crouched to pick up the items. "Heavy," she remarked, shifting the box to her side, so it was wedged between her hip and the arm in which she now also held the flowers. She fished out her keys and opened the door without further comment.

"There's a card," Gina pointed out, trailing after her into the apartment.

Something sloshed inside the gift box when Sabella set it and the flowers on the island. She reached up into the cabinet beside the protrusion to bring down a vase, then went to the sink to fill it up. Gina came up beside her and held out the envelope. "Bella" was scripted across the front.

"Are you going to open it, or should I?" Gina asked bluntly.

Sabella set the vase down and plucked the envelope from Gina's grasp. She stared at the card-sized rectangle for a few heartbeats, distantly registering that the calligraphy was unlikely to have been penned by Kane, then resolutely flipped it over and tore it open. She pulled out the card, covered in a print of more lilies, and flicked it open to see similar script.

"'Thank you for your hospitality. K,'" she read aloud, then tossed the card down on the counter, and retrieved the flowers.

As Sabella removed the cellophane trappings, Gina picked up the card and pulled one of the backless barstools out from under this side of the island to perch on it. She tapped her fingers rhythmically on the gift box.

"Go ahead and open it," Sabella said, occupying herself with arranging the flowers in the vase. She inhaled their fresh fragrance, adamantly silencing the flurry of hopeful thoughts that had begun battering the walls of her mind since she had seen the gift.

"In your place," Gina said, unabashedly tearing at the packaging, "I would throw those out, possibly after chopping them up into little pieces."

Sabella laughed. "I have no doubt you would. But the flowers are beautiful, and their provenance is not their fault."

Gina whistled in appreciation for the contents of the box she had opened. She pulled out a tapered bottle. "Single-barrel Jack Daniel's. Are you *sure* nothing else happened between you yesterday? That's some 'hospitality'…"

Slightly perplexed, Sabella strode over to the living room she hadn't yet reconstructed. She picked up the bottle Kane had left on her displaced coffee table. It hadn't been unopened when they started, but it was now only about one-third full. How much whiskey had he needed to tolerate staying in her apartment? "He was just replacing this," she explained, carrying the bottle back to the kitchen.

Gina watched her with narrowed, discerning eyes but didn't say anything more. Sabella put both whiskey bottles away then carried the crystal vase to her dining room table. Gina twisted to watch her over the island.

"Maybe we should take a look at those photos," Sabella said, decisively changing the topic. "Otherwise you'll be stuck with two blank pages and an inappropriately expensed lunch."

Two hours and fifteen fashion "don'ts" later, Sabella tossed down her notebook and pen between them on the plush, backless bench in front of her latticed dining room windows. "Dinner?" she asked, unfolding from the bench and stretching.

Gina froze, then exhaled, and shut the computer on her lap. "Don't kill me," she started, "but I may have had another motive for our makeover afternoon."

"What are you talking about?" Sabella asked curiously.

"I may have a date tonight. But I can cancel if you want me to!" Gina added quickly.

"Oh, of course not! Why didn't you tell me?"

Gina shot her a pointed look.

"I'm fine," Sabella insisted. "Tell me about your date!"

"Well,"—Gina shifted the computer onto the bench and settled against the armrest—"he's one of those straight-laced, business types. I met him in the lobby of our building, so I asked around, and it turns out he owns one of the financial companies—the one on the top floor."

Sabella plopped back down on the other end of the bench. "Sounds like he's exactly your type," she said sardonically.

Gina tossed the pen at her. "No, but I think I'm exactly what he needs. He seems like he's in dire need of some excitement."

"Well, no one's more exciting than you, Gi." Sabella tossed the pen back with a grin. "Won't you be bored, though?"

"Who knows? Guys like him sometimes have the craziest, hidden wild side. He's well dressed, cute, charming…" She broke off and shrugged.

"Well you look gorgeous. In fact, he might not be able to stop staring long enough to say anything all night."

"Why thank you," Gina answered with a sassy grin. "Actually, while I'm here, would you mind if I borrowed one of your tops? Might need to ease him in to the craziness." She shook her head, sending her daring new style flying demonstrably.

"You know you never have to ask, if you can find something that fits." Sabella's curvy figure didn't match Gina's slinkier body, but Gina could work miracles with clothing. "I will expect a full report, though!" she called as Gina went to scour her wardrobe, no doubt for one of the daring tops she herself had convinced Sabella to buy.

Meanwhile, Sabella headed to the living room to set everything back in order. She stripped the sheets off, dumping them on the floor, and reassembled the couch, then nudged the coffee table back into place. "How are you doing?" she called out, picking up the sheets and spare pillow so she could put them away: sheets to the hamper in the bathroom, pillow back in one of the drawers in the dining room bench. She had filled the small apartment with a variety of such multi-purpose furniture, generally for additional, discrete storage space.

Gina came to the bedroom doorway holding up two tops. "What do you think?"

"The forest-green one," Sabella suggested from across the dining room. "The surplice neckline will look modest on you, and the solid color won't pull focus from your fabulous new 'do."

"Brilliant! When did you get so fashion savvy?" Gina teased with a wink. She stepped back into the bedroom to change and touch up her makeup.

Sabella laughed, then picked up the discarded writing material and placed it on the dining room table. She bent down to inhale the fragrance of the flowers once more then wandered over to her bedroom, as Gina was putting the finishing touches on her lip gloss.

"*Voilà*," Gina exclaimed, twirling to show off her look.

"Your straight-laced financier will never know what hit him," Sabella assured.

"And hopefully we'll undo those laces a bit," Gina answered with a suggestive smile before her expression slipped to concern. "You sure you're okay with my going? I could call and reschedule."

"I'm fine!" Sabella repeated. "I have plenty of work to do and a tight deadline, thanks to this one fashion editor I know and love."

"Well you better get that done, then!" Gina laughed, heading toward the door. "Dinner tomorrow night? I'll bring Roger and regale you both with my dating misadventures," she suggested.

"Sounds like a plan," Sabella agreed as they hugged good-bye. "Have a fantastic time, and take it easy on the poor guy!"

Gina brushed her cheek against Sabella's with an air kiss and swept out the door. Sabella locked it behind her and faced the quiet apartment. *Definitely a rom-com kind of night.* She took her laptop from the dining room, flipped it open, and set it on the island, so she could watch a movie while she prepared dinner. When she turned to her refrigerator to pull out a steak and some vegetables, a few locks of hair flew forward onto her shoulder. Peripherally, Sabella noticed the purple highlights, and she smiled ruefully, shaking her head. Gina was inarguably one of a kind, and an incomparable friend.

Seven

$\mathcal{A}$ couple of weeks later, Sabella's life had, with the exception of some quiet moments when she couldn't prevent her thoughts from drifting, returned to normal. The flowers, beautiful as they had been, had withered as flowers are wont to do, and she had discarded them with only a slight twinge of regret. She had written several articles, sold a couple of those to Gina's magazine, and contacted some of the other editors with whom she maintained good connections to pitch the rest. She had even, finally, begun spinning the memories of her time with Kane into a fluffily idealistic short story, which was precisely where that unrealistic experience belonged. Meanwhile, Gina's straight-laced date had surprised her, and she had actually gone out with him a few more times, which, for Gina, meant she was seriously interested.

Sabella had just returned from meeting Gina and some others at Bartini for early drinks, to celebrate their friend Melody's surprise engagement to the extremely sweet Benny, who worked as a security guard in Gina's building. Still pondering the unlikely yet somehow perfect pairing, Sabella stopped in her building's lobby to check for mail. A padded yellow envelope roused her curiosity, and she ripped it open on the way back to her apartment. She walked through the door, absently set the rest of the mail atop the shelf to her right, then tipped the envelope to shake out its contents. An unmarked disc fell into her expectant hand, closely followed by a slip of paper. The note held two words, scrawled in an unfamiliar handwriting: *Forgive me.*

Sabella's pleasant mood plummeted, and she moved automatically through the apartment to her bedroom, to pick up the laptop she had left charging on her nightstand. She settled on the bed and slipped the disc into her computer with a mind kept purposefully blank. It could just as easily be a laborious version of spam, or a surprisingly personal message from an editor declining her work, as anything else. *Yeah. Right.* She double clicked on the icon that popped up on her desktop. The disc contained a single file. She hesitated for a few moments, blew out the breath she had been holding, and resolutely opened the file.

Music flowed through the speakers, but Sabella barely registered anything other than the heart-rending misery of the sound. When the song ended, she replayed it, paying more attention to the lyrics.

"*I just want to tell you, I was wrong, and you deserve to know...*"

Kane's words flowed around her like a hesitant caress, even through the computer speakers. Sabella played the song a third time, then set the computer aside and strode to the kitchen. She opened cabinets and the refrigerator, searching for something to distract her, but closed each door in turn without removing anything. She leaned over the sink, gazing out the window onto the artificially lit night. Eventually she returned to her bedroom, picked up the laptop, and hit play once again. The ballad was agonizingly beautiful; the emotions evoked hung in the air, enveloping her like his arms had.

It was likely to have become a sensation with his fans, she realized. She opened a browser window and quickly typed in the lyrics to discover how successful the song had been, and how long ago it had actually been written. True, she had initially thought he had written it for her, especially since she had listened to every song of his she could find before having visited Nashville, but there was no guarantee that was the case, and it was arrogant to think so. When the first search brought no results, she narrowed her entry to a few key words and added his name. Still nothing.

Sabella considered calling Gina, but she was on another date with Mr. Not-So-Straight-laced, and this gesture would absolutely not be that important. She pulled her phone out of her pocket anyway and started scrolling absently through her contacts. She could have called her sister in New York, but it was late, especially with the time difference, and Sabella didn't want to recount the entire backstory, which also ruled out any other friends, even if she had been inclined to seek anyone else's input.

An entry in the contact list caught her eye. Kane Hartridge. He had typed a heart in after his name. She put the phone down, picked it up again, then tossed it away from her on the bed. She stalked from the bedroom to pace through the limited space in her apartment—how unfortunate she had no pets to distract her—then returned once more and busied herself with hanging up the clothes she had considered wearing before going out.

When the only items left on her bed were the laptop and her cell phone, she picked the latter up again. What Gina lovingly described as being "a sucker for romance" actually meant Sabella frequently had to prevent herself from reacting with her heart instead of her brain, to safeguard against impetuous decisions which could once again leave her heartbroken. The real world wasn't romantic.

But Kane writing this song for her was.

She entered a brief message into her phone, admonished herself not to put too much weight on what came of this, and hit send.

Kane was sharing a drink with some fans during a set break when his phone vibrated against his leg. He took a swig of beer, chuckled at a raunchy joke someone had shared in an attempt to impress him, and pulled out his phone.

`The song is beautiful.`

He blinked then read the screen again.

`Bella: The song is beautiful.`

Kane mumbled some excuse and walked purposefully to the back of the club, then out the private door to a small, dark alley. He leaned against the brick wall and hit "send" a couple times until the phone dialed her number.

"Hi," he heard Sabella say after a few rings.

"Hey," he breathed into the receiver. Silence. "Thank you for, uh, well. Thanks for the text," Kane said after a few moments. He still couldn't quite believe she'd responded to the song he'd sent.

"It's a wonderful song." Despite the compliment, her voice sounded even, unyielding.

"I didn't know how else to tell you," Kane admitted. At first, he'd tried convincing himself he'd dodged a bullet. That didn't stop him from remembering their kisses, her smile, the ease of holding her against him in the park.

Soon enough, he'd accepted he'd made a mistake, jumping to conclusions. Six years ago, he never would've done that. Then again, six years ago, he probably should have. But this time, he hadn't been able to shake his regret, or his guilt. So he'd written a song. When that didn't quite help, he'd sent it to her.

"Kane!" The door to the club slammed open, sending a rush of noise into the alley. "Two minutes, man," his drummer, Steve, warned. Kane nodded then turned his back, covering his open ear.

"Sabella?" he asked, making sure she hadn't hung up.

"I'm here."

"I have to go, I'm—we're—in the middle of a show," Kane said, hoping she'd understand.

"Okay."

"I'll ca—can I call you later?" he asked anxiously, before she could hang up. Silence. "Sabella?"

"All right," he heard her say right before the line cut off. Kane took a few deep breaths to refocus on the gig. He would call her later, and he now had reason to believe she might actually pick up. He slapped the wall to shake off the nervous energy spinning within him, then pulled the door open and walked back inside.

Sabella alternated between telling herself not to pin her hopes on another call and fiddling with her phone so she wouldn't miss it ringing if it did. Logically, she knew that even if Kane did call her again, it wouldn't be for a while, since he would have to sing a full set, undoubtedly handle a few groupies, maybe pack up with his band, and who knew what else. Unfortunately, that knowledge didn't prevent her from staring at her phone.

Admonishing herself not to be so ridiculous, she slipped the stubbornly silent device into her pocket and walked to the bathroom to perform her evening ablutions. She was patting her face dry when the phone rang. Trying to calm her suddenly rapid heartbeat, she finished drying her skin and settled the towel on the ring to the right of her sink.

She walked out of the bathroom before answering the phone, intentionally without checking the caller ID. "Hello?"

"Sabella," Kane's voice cut through her otherwise silent apartment. The muted cacophony she had heard in the background during his last call was no longer there. "How are you?"

"I'm fine, Kane. How are you?" she responded politely, keeping her voice detached.

"I'm," he started to say then paused. "I'm glad you picked up," he stated finally.

"Is there something you wanted to tell me?" she asked, trying to keep the anxiety out of her voice. She noticed her nails digging into the palm of her free hand and deliberately straightened her fingers.

"I'm goin' to be in Portland again," he answered. When she didn't say anything, he elaborated, "To kick off our West Coast tour. Next Friday."

"Okay…?"

"Can I, I mean, well." He paused, and she heard him exhale. "I'd really like to see you, to talk. And obviously, if you want to come to the show, I'd put you on the comp'd list." He stopped again.

"You don't have to do that," Sabella answered, entirely discombobulated. Hadn't he been upset precisely because she enjoyed his music? Then again, that song had been an impactful admission of his mistake.

"I know." A hint of frustration tinged his voice. "Can we meet for coffee, or dinner? Somethin'?" he asked more directly.

Sabella considered a moment. Gina would tell her he had already had his chance, and he had blown it, but Sabella loathed giving up on people. "All right," she finally agreed. "Coffee. You could call me when you're in town, and we can discuss details." If she didn't hear from him again, that would be it. She supported second chances, but she had long ago learned not to be a complete pushover.

"Okay," he exhaled more than said into the receiver. "We'll talk soon," he assured.

Sabella hung up without saying anything else. There was a very real possibility she had made an enormous mistake in agreeing to see him again, but there was no guarantee he would remember to call, and even then, it was only coffee.

Eight

"You're doing what?" Gina asked incredulously over an impromptu lunch that following Friday. Kane had remembered to call Sabella that morning, and they had made plans to meet outside Stumptown Coffee Roasters' downtown location. His band was playing a couple blocks away at a club called Dante's. Sabella had immediately called Gina for some additional perspective on the situation.

"You heard that song, Gi," Sabella reminded. They were sitting on a park bench by the magazine's office building, consuming sandwiches Sabella had brought.

"It was a pretty good song," Gina acceded begrudgingly. "But that doesn't mean you should be wasting any more of your time on him!"

Sabella twirled a lock of her hair around her fingers absentmindedly. Sometimes, she thought she still saw traces of the purple highlights, though in reality those had washed out quite a while ago. "It's just coffee," she insisted, sounding weak even to herself.

Gina thought for a moment before responding. "What do you think will happen?" she asked, concern evident in her eyes and the slant of both her eyebrows and lips. She was wearing mostly gray—an unusual choice for her, especially in the summer—but a pink-and-yellow, polka-dotted scarf topped the outfit off with a splash of her customary color.

"I don't know," Sabella admitted. "But, I told him I would meet him. Maybe this will finally allow both of us to put everything in the past, and he won't send me anything else." She couldn't quite keep the depression out of her voice. Somehow, back in Nashville, she had stepped into a fairy tale. Granted, it had since gone incredibly wrong—proving that utterly romantic tales could only survive in books and movies—but she couldn't seem to let it go. The short story she had begun needed an ending, but she hadn't been able to write one, possibly because the live version continued to throw curveballs her way.

Gina threw her arm around Sabella's shoulders. "Call me if you need to," she offered, understanding she couldn't change Sabella's mind.

"Thanks, Gi." Sabella inclined her head briefly toward her friend, then they both pulled away. "Are you seeing Mr. Straight-laced again tonight?"

"Alistair," Gina corrected automatically.

"You still haven't found a good nickname?"

"He doesn't like nicknames," Gina explained. "We're

meeting for dinner after work, but I promise to slip off and check my phone a couple times, so if I don't pick up, text me."

It was unlike Gina to ignore her phone for prolonged periods of time, but apparently Mr. Straight-laced—*Alistair*, Sabella corrected herself silently—was a stickler for social graces, so she had recently gotten into the habit of dining without such distractions. Most importantly, Gina seemed happy, smiling whenever she spoke of her new beau. He treated her well, already taking her to some of the most lavish restaurants in the area and surprising her with gorgeous bouquets, and even jewelry, at the office. The diamond-and-pearl-drop earrings Gina was wearing had been a rather generous gift from him, and they sparkled elegantly in her ears. At least one of them had been lucky in love lately.

Kane drummed his fingers on his thigh as he waited in front of Stumptown Coffee. He had barely paid attention during the sound check, and everyone—his manager, drummer, and bass guitarist—had been less than thrilled when he'd announced he was taking a coffee break. He checked his phone again. No missed calls from Sabella. The street wasn't particularly busy, but it was still early on Friday night. Every time someone turned the corner, he checked to see if it was her. Not that he knew what he'd say.

"Kane." He heard her voice behind him and spun around.

"Bella," he exhaled, watching her intently. "It's good to see you."

She shifted the purse strap on her shoulder, looking uncomfortable.

"Thank you for meeting me," he added then paused again.

A couple of people came out of the coffee shop, laughing and almost bumping into Sabella. Kane put his arm out without thinking. The couple saw the motion and walked around them. Sabella looked at him, a question in her eyes. Kane dropped his arm. "Should we go inside?" he asked.

"To be perfectly frank, since you believe I had ulterior motives for our previous interactions, I'm not exactly certain what it is you want from me now."

Kane saw her lips tighten. The fact that she'd agreed to meet him had seemed like a good sign, but he could easily blow this. "A second chance," he answered honestly. "To get to know you, to, I don't know, to spend time together." Sabella looked down. "That day we spent together," he started, going all-in. Her eyes returned to his face. "It was pretty perfect."

"It was," she half agreed, half asked.

"It was," he assured. "I didn't believe that, something like that, it couldn't be real."

Some of the tension left her stance, and she watched him thoughtfully, without a word. He took courage from the fact that she hadn't yet walked away. "Let me buy you a cup of coffee," he offered.

Her exhale ended with a slight nod. "Okay."

"Okay," he repeated, his gut unclenching, then gestured for her to precede him to the door.

The smell of coffee assaulted them as they walked into Stumptown, but Sabella didn't mind. A moment later, her nose adjusted to the many scents of freshly roasted beans from around the world. Stumptown deserved their stellar reputation. The shop was filled with affable banter, markedly unlike the tense silence between her and Kane. As they stood in line, Sabella pretended to examine the board listing the shop's offerings, though she already knew what she would order. The clangs of coffee pots, hissing of foam hitting metal pitchers, and friendly calls of the baristas permeated the air.

While they waited for their drinks, one of the couches that stood on a raised dais in the corner freed up, and Kane nodded to it. "Should we grab that? I can get the coffees."

"Okay." Sabella nodded in return. She walked over to the benches and perched on the one facing both the coffee bar and the exposed brick wall behind it. Kane joined her a minute later, handing her a mocha latte. He lowered himself onto the bench beside her, and they both angled their bodies toward each other. If it hadn't been for their mutual trepidation, the pose would have appeared quite intimate. She took a sip of the coffee, letting its taste fill her mouth before flowing down her throat.

"So, how've you been?" Kane asked tentatively.

Sabella started to answer automatically, then stopped. She focused on him, the concern in his eyes, the drawn appearance of his face. With no trace of a smile, the strict lines of his jaw angled into a barely blunted point at his chin. His entire face changed when he smiled, and she suddenly longed to see that happen. "How have *you* been?" she asked rather than answering him.

"I've been thinkin' 'bout you," he responded slowly.

Sabella averted her eyes, then forced herself to look back at him. She started to lick her lips but stalled mid-motion. "I don't know what to tell you," she admitted.

Kane nodded and appeared to consider her. She met his gaze evenly, though the solemn, assessing look in his eyes made her want to hide. Whatever he saw seemed to have satisfied him. "When I first started to get noticed, known, a lot of women started approachin' me, not like they had, not like before. It took me a while, way too long actually, took a while to realize that they wanted to be with 'a musician'—the guy they'd seen on stage, or on a poster; that they wanted somethin' from me, different than normal," he told her, struggling over the words.

"I know why you would be hesitant with women approaching you," she interjected when he paused. "I mean, I can imagine that many people want something from you, the country star." Sabella stopped to gather her thoughts. Kane watched her, waiting for her to continue. She knew better than to be defensive, since it usually meant the other person attempted to prove their point offensively, but that didn't stop her from what she said next. "You found me. Even in Nashville, you literally bumped into me. You introduced yourself, and..." She trailed off, unwilling to remind them both of the remaining events of that night.

The corner of Kane's lips pulled up slightly. "You were pretty impressive up on that stage," he pointed out.

Sabella felt herself blushing, but focused on sipping her coffee, then resolutely returned to her point. "Look, in some way, I suppose I should almost be flattered that you think I am such an incredibly talented manipulator that I controlled your actions from before the moment of our meeting."

"I know. You didn't do anythin' other than be—" He cut himself off, and his throat moved as he swallowed.

"Be what?" she asked, silently scrambling to remember any moment when she may have given him legitimate reason to believe she had ulterior motives.

"Amazing," he said.

It took Sabella a second to remember where the conversation had last been.

"Ideal," Kane added.

"I'm really not."

"Agree to disagree?" he said with a faint half-smile. When she didn't respond, he continued, "I was wrong, thinkin' you were like all of them, like the others. But, I'm hopin' you'll give me another shot."

"Another shot at what?" she asked with deliberate calm. "Even ignoring everything else, we live in completely different parts of the country, and you're on tour now. It's not a question of whether I believe you, or even forgive you, or whatnot. Our worlds don't mesh, and I'm fairly certain I'm nothing like the women who normally interest you."

"Are you sayin' you don't want to see what could happen?"

She should say no, but being next to him reminded her how it had felt to be enveloped in his arms. "It's not realistic," she said instead.

"Us meetin' wasn't realistic," Kane pointed out. "We don't have to look that far ahead."

Sabella didn't say anything. Her life had become a "choose your own adventure" story that had started as a romance and spun into something else. She should have closed the book and walked away, but some idealistic piece of her needed to believe her instincts about their time together hadn't been completely wrong, again. That same piece wanted to wipe the misery from his face and return them to one of the times they had both seemed happy. In the real world, she merely took another sip of her mocha latte.

"Come to the show," he invited quietly.

She exhaled quickly then nodded, despite her better judgment. "Okay."

Kane smiled uncertainly, and the tension seeped out of his body almost instantly.

"Under one condition," she added as he started to rise. Kane stilled and looked back at her quizzically. "I am not getting anywhere near that stage."

That earned her a genuine grin. "Deal."

Nine

It was a pretty good audience. From the doorway that led to the greenroom, Kane watched people drinking and talking. He had missed half a dozen calls from Mitch, his manager, while out with Sabella. Things had been a little tense with the guys during the southern kickoff of the tour. It was his fault. His performances had passed muster with most fans and a couple bloggers, but Mitch had called them "disappointing." He'd been right, and the guys agreed. That extra connection Kane'd always had with an audience had gone missing.

"Nervous?" Kane heard his drummer's voice at his shoulder.

"Nah, man." He shifted to give Steve a better view of the room. "We got this."

"You sure?" Steve handed him a beer. "Haven't been yourself lately," he said casually.

"He just hasn't gotten laid since we left Nashville," Bobby, his bass guitarist, chimed in from behind them.

"Watch yourself, boy," Kane said with a good-natured

growl. He lifted the beer bottle to hide his agitation. He had to pull it together. For years, he'd poured everything into his music. This West Coast tour was critical. And with Sabella in the audience, there was nothing like the extra pressure. Kane turned and headed downstairs to the greenroom.

"I'm just sayin'," Bobby yammered on, trailing behind him.

They grabbed their guitars, Steve twirled his sticks, then all three circled up. "All right, guys," Kane said, praying tonight's show would bring a change. "We've worked out the kinks. We got this." He raised the beer bottle he still held.

"Relax, man. This ain't the end of the line," Steve said and knocked his own bottle against Kane's.

"Y'all are missing the point," Bobby added. "The girls out there are *hot*, and waiting for us country fellas." He grinned. Bobby was still young enough that it was all about the chicks. Kane didn't disagree, exactly, but he also needed to do the music inside him justice.

The three of them made their way upstairs and onto the stage to encouraging applause. "Thank you," Kane called into the mic as the guys got situated, then set down his beer. He caught sight of Sabella by the bar, watching him like she had the night they'd met. This time, she smiled softly. Kane launched into the energetic song that opened all their shows to claim the room's attention.

✧ ✧ ✧

Seeing Kane play in Nashville couldn't compare to tonight's show. He truly had an amazing ability to emote every song, leading the crowd's reactions. The subject matter of his songs wasn't especially unique: laments for past loves, touching ballads about crumbling relationships, and upbeat acclaims for the country lifestyle, and for country women. Still, the songs were well written, with impactful imagery and very few minor flubs in the lyrics that probably only Sabella noticed, and they were extraordinarily performed. Kane made everyone in the room feel as though they were old friends, in on every inside joke and privy to every moment, whether heartbreaking, intimate, or jubilant.

Sabella sat by the bar, with the entire room spread before her. She had never before been to Dante's, though now she thought that may have been an oversight. The darkened room, with its flickering lights, invited an intimate yet inclusive atmosphere, while the raised stage, with its red-velvet curtains, showcased the band with a faded, old-world charm. The club had also adequately adopted the literary reference of its title, with posters for "Karaoke from Hell" and flames worked into their advertising and décor.

"Enjoying the show?" the bartender asked her when there was a lull in customers clamoring for his attention.

Sabella twisted sideways so she could speak to him while still watching the stage. "I am," she admitted. He wore a black fedora and had left several buttons undone on his shirt. Kane had worn his shirt that way the night they had met, but unlike him, the bartender's attempt at appearing at ease actually felt forced. He was looking at her curiously, likely trying to judge whether she was a crazy fangirl or merely someone who had wandered in alone.

"Can I get you something?" he asked with a smile.

"A daiquiri?" She returned his smile.

"Sure thing." He patted the bar in acknowledgement and moved away to gather ingredients.

Sabella returned her attention to the stage, where Kane was singing a ballad about reencountering a past love, his eyes closed. Tonight, he wore a checkered flannel shirt layered over a gray tee with his jeans. Both the drummer and the other guitarist also wore jeans, though both with nondescript tee shirts, and neither played much through this song. Kane had let his hair grow even longer, so it now fell to his upper jaw.

The bartender slid a frosty drink in front of her with a red-and-black napkin.

"Thanks." She smiled at him automatically and reached for the purse she had tucked behind her hip on the barstool.

He cut her off with a small wave of the hand. "This one's on me."

Before Sabella could respond, someone called him to the other end of the bar with an order. Normally, Sabella would have declined his offer, but she heard Gina's voice clearly instructing her to accept the compliment. It was already a night of aberrant behavior, so she sipped the drink. *It's a harmless gesture*, she assured herself, refocusing on the stage.

Peripherally, she noticed a man in jeans and a suit jacket sidle up to the bar. He leaned on his elbows, turning his back to the stage. Sabella set down her drink, still watching Kane. Most of the time, his eyes were closed or focused on an abstract point either on the floor or above the heads of his audience, but occasionally he gazed directly at her, and the rest of the room faded away. *Way to stay practical and detached, Sabella,* she chastised, though she didn't look away until the song ended.

"You a fan?" the man beside her asked in the subsequent pause. He wore a tee shirt underneath the jacket and held a glass filled with an amber liquor. His wavy, gray-streaked hair was cut pretty short, and lines on his face marked his age.

"Isn't pretty much everyone here a fan?" she returned.

"Reckon so." He turned to survey the room, taking a gulp of his drink and wincing slightly as he swallowed. "Not all of 'em pretty as you though," he said with a thick drawl when he turned back to her.

Sabella chuckled uncomfortably at the exaggerated line. The opening chords of another song provided her with a welcome distraction, though they didn't deter her new companion. "D'you wanna meet the band?" he offered suggestively. Sabella was trying to decide how to decline when he added, "It's a good offer. I've known 'em boys for a long time."

Sabella looked back to the stage in an attempt to gather her thoughts. "I'm all set, but thanks for the offer," she refused politely.

"You sure, now? This is the last song 'fore they break."

Sabella was saved from having to answer by the return of the bartender. "You doing all right, babe?" he asked her pointedly.

The older man glanced between the two of them, then tilted his raised glass at her and ambled away.

"Thank you," she said, twisting to face the bartender.

"Any time." He grinned at her. "You were looking a little trapped." He pulled a white towel from his shoulder and picked up a wet tumbler. "Johnny," he introduced himself.

"Elle."

"You in from out of town?" he asked, ignoring a couple who had come up to the bar a few feet away. Sabella noticed a tattoo on the inside of his forearm but couldn't make it out in the dimmed light.

"No, I'm a local." Behind her, Kane announced that they would be taking a ten-minute break. "This isn't exactly my usual scene," Sabella explained.

"That's a shame," Johnny replied. He set down his latest dried glass and dropped the towel onto the counter behind the bar. "You should come around more often," he added with a wink.

"I bet you say that to all the girls who haven't tipped you yet," Sabella answered with a teasing smile.

"Why don't you come back and find out?" he suggested, flipping his fedora onto the bar in front of her. He pulled a business card from his shirt pocket and dropped it flippantly onto the hat.

Sabella kept her eyes on his face, twirling the straw in her drink.

"Yo!" someone called from down the bar, slapping a hand onto the surface to claim Johnny's attention. He winked at her again and returned to work. Sabella glanced down at the hat and the business card upon it.

"Hey," said a voice by her ear. Distantly, she registered how unusually popular she seemed to be tonight. She turned to find Kane beside her.

"Hi." Her lips curved on their own.

"Enjoyin' yourself?" he asked, subtly blocking the rest of the room from view.

She hummed affirmatively. "It's a wonderful show, not that I would expect anything less. Thank you for inviting me," she said softly, tilting her head up so she wasn't staring at his chest.

"I'm glad you agreed to come," he answered quietly enough that they wouldn't be overheard. They watched each other for a long moment, then Kane lifted his hand to brush back a lock of hair which had escaped her gold clip. Sabella considered shifting away, but he cupped her cheek and dropped a kiss onto her lips so briefly she almost thought she had imagined it. "See you after the show," he said with the slightest hint of a question before walking back toward the stage. Sabella let herself admire his gait for a moment then turned to her drink, absentmindedly fiddling with the straw.

"Miss me?" Johnny teased, popping back to her corner of the bar.

Sabella couldn't help laughing as he picked up the discarded towel and started wiping down the bar to appear occupied. She lifted the card from his hat and slipped it into the back pocket of her brown slacks. Johnny grinned and settled the fedora back onto his head as the band began their second set.

Ten

"Man!" Bobby shouted enthusiastically back in the greenroom. Steve drummed his hands against the wall. Kane grinned, watching them from the couch. He was filled with the same pulsating energy but kept it in check.

Mitch appeared in the doorway. "Congratulations, boys. That was one hell of a show."

Everyone exchanged grins. The atmosphere after a gig hadn't been this euphoric since the tour began.

Steve picked up the beers someone had brought to the greenroom for them and passed them around. "The first of many," he toasted to complete agreement.

"All right, not that I'm not fond of y'all, but I'm gonna get myself some prettier company," Bobby said, leading the way out of the greenroom.

Mitch followed after tipping his beer to Kane, who got up to follow them upstairs.

"Hey." Steve stopped him with a hand on the shoulder. "Whatever you left here, you sure got it back tonight," he commented perceptively. Steve was the only other person who knew about Kane's impromptu trip to Portland, though not all the details.

Kane nodded. "Let's hope." His thoughts moved back to the girl upstairs. They always waited until a club had mostly cleared out before they broke down their equipment, which meant they had a few hours left to mingle and enjoy the bar. "Let's get out of here, man." He grinned at Steve, pushing the willing drummer through the door.

As they rounded the stage, Steve spotted a group of girls and split off from Kane to work his magic. Kane shook his head, swallowed some beer, and wove his way through the room to Sabella. She was chatting with a bartender. Kane paused a few steps away to watch her. She had swept her hair partially back with a clip tonight, so it fell over her shoulders. She laughed at something the bartender said, leaning on the bar to get closer to her. The guy's eyes dropped to her cleavage. She didn't seem to notice. Instead, she turned to look around the room, still grinning from whatever had made her laugh.

When she saw him, her expression grew more serious, then slipped into a shy smile. The bartender tried to get her attention again, but she didn't look away from Kane. He walked the remaining steps toward her and set down the beer bottle, which made the bartender straighten up. "Jack Daniel's," Kane said to the other man.

He sized Kane up quickly. "Sure thing," he answered and moved away.

Kane leaned one elbow on the bar, facing Sabella. She was watching him silently. He wasn't sure what to say to her until he noticed her empty glass. "Would you like another drink?" he asked, falling back on bar basics.

"No. Thank you, though. I will actually have to drive home at some point."

"Right, of course."

The bartender set Kane's drink next to his elbow then turned to Sabella. "Looks like you're in expert hands," he told her, full of disappointment. "Hope to see you back sometime soon."

"G'night, Johnny," she said warmly, before he walked away.

"You know him?" Kane asked, taking a sip of whiskey with calculated disinterest. He didn't have any real claim to her. He also didn't want her flirting with other men.

"We just met," she answered easily. "I think he was mostly angling for a solid tip, since I was sitting alone."

She truly seemed to believe her theory. "Doubt it," he said.

Sabella looked at him curiously.

"But, better not to disappoint." Kane downed the whiskey and pulled out a twenty, which he tossed on the bar.

"That's nice of you." She didn't seem particularly invested, which was a relief. "So," she said, "as I'm sure you've heard, your show was amazing."

Kane smiled, putting the bartender out of his mind. "I had some extra inspiration," he admitted.

"Oh yeah?" Her laughing eyes questioned him for details. "I bet all of your shows are pretty impressive," she continued when he didn't say anything.

"Not lately. But looks like things are turning around."

Sabella smiled uncertainly. Kane was thinking about kissing her when a group of girls interrupted them, asking for his autograph. He ramped up the charm and signed the promotional posters they held. As he did, he singled out Steve across the room then sent the fans over to him for added autographs.

"Subtle," Sabella commented when he turned back to her.

"Yeah, well. I have more interesting company. You want to get out of here?"

Sabella hesitated for the briefest moment then slid off the barstool.

Kane threw his arm around her shoulders and walked her out of the bar, avoiding a few groups of people who tried to get his attention. Outside, he dropped his arm and turned to face her. "I don't actually have too much time," he told her. "Mitch'll kill me if I don't spend the night taking pictures and things like that."

She nodded. "The tough life of a successful musician."

"Successful?" he joked, earning a quiet laugh. "Can I walk you to your car?"

"Sure. Thank you." She started slowly down the street, and Kane fell into step beside her.

"It's kinda chilly," he said, angling for an opening to touch her again.

"A little bit," she agreed.

Since he didn't have a jacket, Kane wrapped his arm around her, brushing his thumb over her arm. She fit there comfortably, not pressing too close or keeping an artificial distance.

"You didn't play the song you sent me," she pointed out as they walked.

"No one's heard that song. It's private," he added when she didn't say anything.

"Isn't all of your music private?"

"Not like that." He'd written the song for her, not just about a moment or a memory.

"It's really a beautiful song. It would be a shame if no one else ever heard it."

"I didn't think you'd want it to be public."

"I'm glad it wasn't before I heard it," she admitted, pulling away to face him.

Kane didn't like letting her go, but he didn't stop her. He could see her mulling over her words. "What is it?" he asked. Seeing her under the streetlamps reminded him of their walk in Nashville. So much had happened since that night.

"I don't want to sound presumptuous, but I imagine writing that song, any song, took a not insignificant amount of effort. If you're not playing it because of me—" She paused.

"Well, don't. I mean, I genuinely appreciate that you didn't write it for your career and then simply recycle it for me…" She trailed off, then sighed. "I'm not saying this correctly."

Her concerned expression was endearing, but Kane held back his smile. "I think I got it," he assured. "I guess it is a pretty good song."

"It's a *really* good song."

"Thanks." He took in the gleam of her hair, the uncanny beauty of her eyes. Kissing her the way he wanted might be crossing a line, but he leaned down anyway. When she didn't push him away, he brought both hands up to her head and deepened the kiss, reveling in her response.

As they rounded the corner to the street where she had parked, Sabella admitted to herself that any trace of pragmatism had evaporated when she had agreed to go to Kane's show. For better or for worse, she truly was an idealistic romantic. The undeniable comfort and contentment she felt having his arm around her certainly didn't help her behave more sensibly. Kissing him hadn't either.

"So, when is your next show?" she asked when they reached her car, trying to sound casually interested. They stood by the driver's side door, but Sabella didn't make a move to unlock it. Instead, she kept her back to the vehicle, facing Kane, who shielded her from the street with his body.

"Tomorrow night," he answered. "But it's only a few hours away."

"In Eugene?"

He shook his head. "Somewhere called Bend."

There was nothing left to say, but Sabella didn't want to leave. This could easily turn out to be the end for them. *Not yet.* He was standing so close, she could feel the heat of his body warming the air between them, but he didn't close the minimal distance. She considered initiating another kiss herself, absently licking her lips as she debated. His eyes dropped to follow the movement of her tongue. She tilted up her chin, leaving her lips lightly parted. Kane looked at her as if awaiting less subtle permission. Sabella lifted one hand to his neck, barely brushing it before his head dipped down to her.

She lifted her other hand to right below his shoulder, luxuriating in the sensation of his lips against hers, of his tongue delving into her mouth. He shifted forward, pressing her between the car and the length of his body. His hands molded against her ribcage, bringing his thumbs to the outside edges of her breasts. The thin fabric of her blouse provided practically no barrier, so his palms burned over her ribs. Distantly she remembered that they were in the middle of the street, but she dug her fingers gently into his muscles instead of pulling away.

At the sound of a passerby's wolf whistle, Kane broke their kiss with a slight motion of his head. They stood there, entwined, catching their breaths. Sabella could feel her ribs expanding under his hands, his thumbs faintly brushing over her, his heart pounding under her palm.

Eventually, she looked down, breaking their eye contact, which prompted Kane to take a step back. They both dropped their hands, but Kane soon gathered hers softly in his, which brought her gaze back to his face. "It's only a few hours' drive for us tomorrow," he repeated.

"That sounds reasonable, allowing you plenty of time to set up," Sabella responded. It was a strange thing to bring up. She tried to etch every detail of his features into her mind, in case all that remained after tonight was another batch of memories. The glow of the street lamps cast a hazy light around them, glinting off the hint of stubble covering his jaw. In the dim light, the unyielding lines of his shadowed features belied the earlier softness of his lips against hers.

Kane's eyes narrowed as he considered her. Had she missed something?

"We could hang out in Portland 'til mid-afternoon and still have lots of time. I'm sure the guys wouldn' mind a few more hours here. Bend doesn't sound too excitin'," he explained with a smirk that bent the slash of his lips.

"A few extra hours in Portland," she repeated after him. Putting the pieces together felt like swimming through barely softened butter, possibly because she couldn't allow herself to hope he was indeed suggesting postponing leaving for *her*.

"To be with you," he added, as if reading her thoughts, and Sabella's breath caught.

"Me?" she echoed.

Kane watched her expectantly. "Do you want me to stay?" he finally asked outright.

Stay with me. The memory of his whispered plea stretched in the air between them. She felt strangely certain this would be his last time asking. *Time to choose, Sabella.* "Yes. Stay," she breathed, unwilling to ruminate over why the promise of those few added hours enlivened her so effectively, much less consider any potential consequences.

He squeezed her hands gently in his and smiled. "It'll be kind of a late night. But I could stop by in the late mornin'?"

"Sounds perfect."

Kane pressed a brief kiss against her smile. "Drive safe," he said, stepping away so she could open her car.

"Good night," she answered before sliding into the driver's seat.

Kane shut the door for her, ever the perfect gentleman, then crossed to the sidewalk. She glanced over her shoulder to see him raise his hand in an additional goodbye. *Bye*, she mouthed with a smile before heading home.

Eleven

*T*he next morning, after a quick breakfast that predominately consisted of coffee, Sabella tried to convince herself not to put an inordinate amount of effort into dressing for Kane. After the third outfit, she admitted that wasn't going to happen. Apparently all practicality fled her vicinity when it came to anything regarding Kane. She wanted to look nice, even though she could never compete with the bombshell fangirls who usually surrounded him.

Ultimately she decided on a flirty, pale-yellow skirt and a fitted black tank top, with a delicate floral design winding from the hem to the structured bust. Slightly heeled sandals completed the ensemble, though not her look. Next she withdrew a small box from the jewelry chest that sat atop her dresser and took out the intricate pearl-and-gold charm inside. It was strung onto a fine gold chain and had been a graduation gift from her parents. Wispy, wrought-gold earrings completed her accessories. They hadn't discussed concrete plans, but this way, she could throw on a lightweight, cropped jacket and be suitably dressed for virtually anything.

Sabella considered her reflection in the full-length mirror that hung on the back of her bedroom door, deemed the outfit passable, then moved to the armoire to deal with her hair and makeup. Carefully she lined her eyes and passed the mascara wand repeatedly over her lashes. Then, using a few tricks Gina had shown her, she highlighted the hazel of her eyes with green and gold eye shadows.

Next she pulled the elastic band from the messy bun into which she twisted her hair at the start of every morning. She dragged a brush through the waves, contemplating gathering them back into a high ponytail for the sake of ease. Instead, she pulled out a couple barrettes with false-jewel studs and pinned her hair back slightly above her ears.

She considered the final result critically, reminded herself she wasn't a miracle worker, then left her bedroom to repair the week's damage to her apartment. Most likely, Kane would spend at least some time inside, which provided the perfect motivation to clean as many surfaces as possible.

She gathered her computer from the living room, various notes she had scattered around the apartment as she worked, and stray pieces of clothing and accessories that inevitably ended up strewn everywhere. She brought everything into her bedroom, shutting the door firmly on the way out.

She briefly wished she had flowers to set on her sun-drenched dining table, but soon busied herself with various other chores: cleaning counters, washing the morning's dishes, and replacing books onto her many shelves. She was considering curling up with her copy of *Paradise Lost*, to distract herself from anticipating Kane's arrival, when the doorbell rang.

She checked her appearance one final time in the mirror in her entryway, resettled one of the hairpins, and opened the door to see Kane. He was freshly shaven with damp hair and wore an unmarked tee shirt that stretched slightly across his shoulders and the swell of his biceps.

"Hey there." He flashed her a bright smile.

Sabella stared for a moment too long, before managing to invite, "Come in." As she shut the door behind him, Sabella's gaze dropped to the two filled paper bags he held. "Should I be scared?" she joked.

"Oh, uh, no." He bent to set the bags down. As he straightened, he pulled a bouquet of mixed-color carnations from one of the mystery bags and handed it to her. "I thought, maybe, I could make us lunch."

"Thank you," Sabella said, accepting the flowers and bringing them to her face to inhale the fragrance. "Wait, lunch?" she added when Kane picked up the bags and moved toward the kitchen.

"Yeah." He set the bags onto her island then looked at her. "If you don't mind."

The startled look on Sabella's face was adorable. "No, I don't…
I don't mind," she said with wide eyes. "But, you know, maybe
I could help you?"

"Nah, I got it," Kane answered, suppressing a grin. He
started pulling ingredients from the bags and setting them on
the granite surface.

Sabella just watched him, still hanging on to the bouquet
he'd picked up for her.

"You gonna put those in water?" he teased.

She smiled, cheeks pinking with embarrassment, and
walked deeper into the kitchen to pull out a vase, giving him a
lovely view as she stretched to reach a high shelf. "You don't
know where anything is," she pointed out, filling the vase with
water.

Kane moved up behind her for the fun of pressing her
buttons. "You feel like giving me a tour?"

Her head jerked around to him, and she set the vase down
on the counter a bit sharply. Kane took another step forward,
and she abandoned the flowers.

"How about you let me do this? Promise I won't burn the
place down. You look incredible, by the way," he added, hoping
to distract her.

Sabella blushed and licked her lips. She did that almost too
often, but his eyes still dropped to the movement. She looked
so beautiful today. The colorful design on her top drew his

attention to the curve of her chest. Sunlight streaming through the windows brought out flecks of red in her honey hair and glinted off her earrings.

"Are you sure I can't help?" she asked. "You don't have to cook for me."

It took Kane a moment to snap back to his plan for the day. He stepped back so he didn't grab her right there. "I got it, so long as you don't mind me opening all the different cabinets."

Sabella returned her attention to the flowers. She ripped off the cellophane, tossed it in a bin under her sink, then plopped the bouquet in the water. "You're welcome to whatever you need," she said, still with her back to him. "But I truly wouldn't mind helping," she repeated, probably out of concern for the results, but he didn't mind.

She glanced at him then rounded the island to set the flowers on her dining table. When she headed back to the kitchen, Kane blocked the entryway with his body. She opened her mouth to speak then shut it with a sigh, settling into one hip in a challenge. Kane was thoroughly enjoying keeping her off-kilter, not to mention the fire that snapped in her eyes.

"You want a glass of wine?" he offered, goading her.

"I actually don't have any wine."

"I brought some." They stared at each other for a while. "You gonna let me do this?" he asked finally.

"So, what, I can't go into my own kitchen?"

"No. You have to stay on the other side of this island," he said, cutting off her objection. "Don't look so worried." Kane took her by the shoulders and led her to the barstools that faced the kitchen. He brushed his thumbs over her skin then dropped his hands.

"All right," she finally agreed and sat on a stool. "But, if you need help, you can ask me. Don't feel like you have to be all macho."

Kane chuckled, shaking his head, and reentered the kitchen. "Hope you like salmon," he told her. Ignoring her obvious wariness, Kane set about discovering her kitchen, pulling out the necessary pots and pans when he found them. When he found the corkscrew, he opened the Sauvignon he'd brought. Normally, he wasn't a fan of wine, but the tart white would complement the meal he had planned. Sabella perched tensely on the barstool, ready to leap into action if necessary. Kane smiled at her then turned to the cabinets that lined the wall across from the island in search of a wine glass. Keeping his eyes on hers, he filled the glass and set it in front of her. She didn't move, but he placed the bottle in her fridge, unconcerned. "So, tell me what you've been working on," he suggested.

"What would you like to know?" Sabella asked, warily watching Kane wash some zucchinis and bell peppers, which he proceeded to chop deftly. She reached absently for the wine he had poured for her, mostly to occupy her hands, so she was pleasantly surprised by the tartly fruity taste that filled her mouth.

"Anythin'. You said you'd wanted to write somethin' 'bout music? How'd that go?"

"It's actually still a work in progress."

He had brought out an array of pots, pans, and dishes from her cupboards, which he arranged on the countertops, and Sabella glimpsed a mix of vegetables, spaghetti, and two salmon fillets among the ingredients he had brought. A baguette still peeked out from one of the bags, which meant some more mystery ingredients balanced its weight from the inside.

"How come?" he asked.

"Well, it's a more in-depth piece for me. It needs to percolate, so the various parts can synthesize, hopefully into something intriguing." Sabella intended to suggest another topic, fully aware of how terribly this one had gone the previous time, but couldn't think of an alternative quickly enough.

"Go on," Kane prompted. He even seemed genuinely interested, not merely detachedly polite.

Sabella took a slightly bracing sip of wine. "Are you sure? Right now it's mostly about country."

"Please," he answered seriously.

"Well, a few months ago, when I thought, 'country music,' primarily what came to mind were singers like Carrie

Underwood and Dolly Parton, or music you would hear at a hoedown. I knew there were a few songs I liked that happened to be country, like Tim McGraw's *Live Like You Were Dying*, but I would firmly avow that, as a rule, I did not like country music."

Kane spared some of his attention to lift an eyebrow.

"That changed," she plowed on, "when I heard, well, your music. It was touching, emotional and fun, and at times incredibly well written."

"At times?"

"I'm somewhat particular when it comes to word choice," she explained, hoping he hadn't taken her comment as criticism. "But you have some extremely powerful, beautiful imagery." Kane continued preparing his ingredients, setting a skillet to heat on her stovetop. Perhaps he really had realized how unfounded his anger had been last time. "Anyway, it made me realize I may have missed the true depth of country music, which piqued my curiosity. One of the few perks of writing freelance is I get to follow my interests when they pop up, though then I'm left to hope someone in a position of power is hooked by what I write and decides to pay me to publish it."

"That sounds tough," Kane said, tossing chopped vegetables onto the skillet.

"It can be, but I write pieces on commission for a few magazines, which helps."

"Well, writin' about discov'rin' a musical culture you'd dismissed sounds pretty interestin'."

"Thanks," Sabella answered, grateful for the affirmation.

Kane moved to the cabinet that housed her spices and pulled out an Italian blend, which he sprinkled over the skillet. "How did you…" Sabella started to ask but trailed off.

"I noticed it, uh, last time," Kane explained somewhat sheepishly.

"Keeping any other secrets?" Sabella asked with mock rebuke.

"Lots." He grinned at her over his shoulder. "But I'm an open book for you," he told her, making Sabella chuckle at the cheesy line.

As he cooked, Sabella marveled at his skillful manipulation of the ingredients. The scene was incredibly homey, though she was still surprised at the sight of him moving so comfortably around her kitchen. Granted, other than a few tense moments with her, he had appeared at ease everywhere.

By the time she finished the wine he had poured for her, Kane had put all four of her burners to use. The vegetables simmered in one skillet, spaghetti boiled in a pot, salmon sizzled in another skillet, and he stirred a butter-based sauce in a second, smaller pot. The delectable smell of lemons, butter, garlic, and salmon filled the kitchen, and probably most of her apartment.

"This all smells pretty good," Sabella stated cautiously during a lull in their conversation about their high school experiences: unexceptionally filled with academics and creative extra-curricular activities for her; stereotypical life of a popular, athletic kid for him. He had been a strong safety on the football team, and his time had otherwise been saturated with a plethora of girls and occasional fights, which he had, apparently, generally won.

"Pretty good, huh?" he said without a hint of self-doubt. "Come 'ere."

"Oh, am I allowed to enter my kitchen now?" she baited, slipping off the barstool.

He smiled back at her. "You have my permission."

Sabella joined him with simulated caution by her stove as he lifted the pasta to pour the contents of the pot into the strainer he had earlier placed in the sink. She was already impressed, but everything did ultimately depend on the resulting taste. Kane dipped a wooden spoon into the sauce and held it in front of her mouth. She blew over it then flicked her tongue out to taste his creation, holding his gaze. For an instant, she noticed only the attentive heat in his eyes. Then the buttery-garlic taste filled her mouth, followed by a sharp touch of lemon, and she couldn't hold back an appreciative hum. "That's wonderful," she admitted, impressed and no longer hiding it.

"What, I'm a musician, so I can't be good at somethin' else?" he challenged with another smile then turned to dish out his creations.

"Well, I assumed you could also hit people given your superbly useful football experience, but where did you learn to cook like this?" she asked curiously, leaning against the cabinets by her refrigerator so as not to interfere with his movements. He dropped pasta on two plates then settled the salmon on top, drenching both with the sauce, and spooned some sautéed vegetables beside everything. The entire meal had taken him less than an hour to prepare.

"A local chef took me under his wing years ago. Grab the wine?"

She took the bottle from the fridge and brought down another wine glass before following him to the dining room table, where he set the plates down on her vividly colored placemats. "What prompted him to do that?"

Kane avoided her question by continuing to set the table, bringing silverware and the freshly sliced baguette. He even pulled out a chair for her before sitting down himself.

Sabella tempered her curiosity, deciding to move on from the subject, for the moment. "This looks absolutely delicious. Thank you."

"My pleasure." He filled their glasses then raised his.

Sabella clinked her glass against his, and they both took a sip. Kane watched her expectantly, so she slipped her fork into the salmon, flaking off a piece and tasting it, though now she wasn't especially surprised by its expert quality. The appreciation in her expression apparently satisfied him enough that he also delved into the food.

After only a couple bites, he paused. "I had, uh, busted up his restaurant," he admitted, reaching for a piece of baguette. "Some idiot picked a fight with me when I was out with a girlfriend. I was young, so obviously I couldn't let it go. We destroyed his place in the process, absolutely demolished it.

"So, he made us an agreement that we'd work, we'd pay off the damage in his kitchen, washin' dishes and stuff. He was smart and kept us comin' in on different days, though." Kane smiled nostalgically. "He would tell me these stories about his life, give me advice I tried to ignore, y'know. Eventually he decided I had some kinda promise, I guess, so he started teachin' me how to cook, and straightened me out in the process."

"He sounds pretty special," Sabella said quietly when he'd finished speaking.

"He was," Kane agreed, nodding pensively. He mouth twisted in a sad smile at some memory, deep in reminiscence.

"To the man who made this meal possible, then," Sabella toasted, raising her glass.

Kane's smile shifted to her, and he acknowledged her words with a tilt of his head, clinking their glasses together.

Kane waited until they had almost finished eating before bringing up the question that had been running around his mind. "So, I have to get going pretty soon," he began.

Sabella's smile disappeared, and she looked down to the table.

"Come with me," he added.

Her eyes swiveled back to him. "What did you say?"

"Come with me, us," he repeated. "You work remotely, right? So you could still work from out of town?"

"Theoretically, I could, yes," she agreed cautiously, placing her silverware back on the edge of her plate.

"I don't want to ignore this, to let this go," Kane told her. "Do you?" He hadn't stopped thinking about her since his last trip to Portland. Just the time they'd spent together before their fight had inspired several unfinished songs, not to mention the apology he'd written for her. He was probably idealizing her, but there was no way to get past that without spending more real time together.

"How would that even work? I mean, wouldn't you need to involve your manager or someone in a suggestion like this?"

Kane shrugged. Truthfully, he hadn't thought about the details, but she didn't need to know that. Still, he couldn't very well tell her he'd expected she would just be with him, literally. "I could bunk with the guys, or Mitch, or even on the bus if I had to. You could have what's reserved as my room wherever we are, if you wanted. We could work it out." Sabella licked her lips, which he was beginning to recognize as a nervous habit. Kane pushed forward. "There'd be a lot of time driving, but otherwise you would have your computer and Internet, so you could write whenever we're doing things like sound checks.

You could even write about all the special joys of being on tour," he finished wryly.

"That could be pretty interesting," she said with a tentative smile. He was making progress.

"And of course, we could spend time together. Nothing lets you get to know someone like going on tour." He could see he'd made her curious. Hopefully it was being with him, not getting a good story, that interested her.

"I can't simply jump on your tour bus with you and drive away," she stated, bringing him back to reality.

"I know," he agreed, wanting to ask why not. Sabella seemed disappointed that he'd accepted her answer. Neither one of them touched the bits of food still left on their plates. Kane hadn't had the idea too long, but he wasn't willing to give up on it yet either. "Maybe you could think about it, join us soon?"

"You know? Maybe I could consider it," she told him. A smile returned to her face, softly curving her lips and lighting up her eyes.

Satisfied, Kane smiled back then forked another piece of salmon.

Sabella laughed at him and picked up her own fork. "This really is absolutely delectable. I'm sufficiently impressed," she was saying when he heard her front door open.

"Sab?" a woman's voice called out.

Sabella darted from her chair. Kane rose to follow her.

"Gi! What are you doing here?" Sabella asked as the two women hugged.

"I wanted to check on you after…" She trailed off when she noticed Kane. "Hel-lo," she said, shamelessly looking him up and down. Kane cocked an eyebrow. The tall brunette ignored him and turned back to Sabella. She was beautiful but felt too carefully put together, not quite as wild as Sabella'd described.

"Should I come back later?" she asked pointedly.

"Don't be silly!" Sabella assured her. Kane swallowed his disappointment. "Gina, this is Kane. Kane—Gina," she introduced.

Gina threw her bag over the shelf and onto Sabella's couch without looking.

"Pleased to meet you," Kane offered politely. He vaguely remembered Sabella telling him she worked in fashion, which explained the obvious effort she put into her appearance.

"You too," she answered, looking curiously between Kane and Sabella.

Thankfully, Sabella picked up on the strange tension and intervened. "We were just finishing up lunch. Do you want something, Gi?"

"No, thanks, hon," Gina answered, still considering Kane.

He cleared his throat to excuse himself then walked into the kitchen to clean up everything he'd used.

"What is he doing here?" he heard Gina ask in a whisper that wasn't quiet enough. Sabella shushed her. Kane turned on the water in the sink to soak the pots.

"You don't have to do that," Sabella said from behind him.

"I made the mess, I can clean it up," Kane answered, quoting his old mentor.

"Exactly," she said, placing a hand on his shoulder. Kane shut off the water and turned around. "You made lunch, and it was delicious. I don't mind cleaning up later."

Kane glanced at her best friend, who was watching him intensely. He looked back at Sabella's calm face and tried to relax. "All right." He nodded.

Sabella smiled, then moved away so she faced both her guests. "You guys feel like some dessert? It won't compare to lunch, but I do have some pretty good ice cream."

Kane's phone chimed before either one of them could answer. The women exchanged looks he ignored while he checked the text. Mitch was getting impatient. "I'm sorry, Bella, but I really should get going." His time had run out, before he'd gotten her to agree to join them.

"Oh, okay," she answered. At least she looked as disappointed as he was. "Do you need a ride somewhere? I didn't even ask how you got here."

"Nope, I drove. Borrowed the car Mitch gets so we don't have to take the bus everywhere." Kane paused, wanting to say a more intimate goodbye, but not in front of her friend. "It was good to meet you, Gina," he said politely.

"Yeah, sorry for interrupting," she said insincerely as he headed to the door.

He heard Sabella follow him. They faced each other in the entryway. "So, have a good show tonight."

"Thanks," he nodded, tucking his thumbs in his pockets to keep from reaching for her. "Think about it, okay?"

"I will," she agreed, smiling up at him. At least she knew exactly what he meant.

Kane debated a second, then opened his arms to hug her goodbye. She reached forward and wrapped her arms around him. He squeezed softly before she pulled back. Right before she would have let go, she looked up, and he kissed her. She kissed him back for a few wonderful moments but then stepped away. Kane had almost forgotten that they had company.

"I should get going," he said instead of a goodbye.

Sabella nodded, and he opened the door. "Bye," she called as he stepped out. Kane looked back to see her framed in the doorway then forced himself to walk away.

"So?" Gina asked with expectant excitement.

"So what?" Sabella echoed, feigning innocence as she cleared the lunch dishes. Back in the kitchen, she speared a stray piece of zucchini from her plate, dragged it through some sauce, and popped it in her mouth.

"Did he spend the night?"

"No. Do you want some wine? It's actually pretty nice," Sabella offered, reaching for a clean glass.

"Okay, so what was he doing here?" Gina persisted, foregoing her customary perch to join Sabella in the kitchen.

"He made lunch," she answered, handing Gina the filled glass.

"Sabella! You're being intentionally difficult," Gina accused.

"What would you like to hear, Gi? He came over a couple hours ago and proceeded to prepare lunch, which was surprisingly delicious." Sabella stayed facing the sink, unwilling to face Gina's extremely perceptive eyes.

"You forgave him," she stated.

Sabella sighed. "I know it was probably idiotic."

"Okay, leave the dishes and come talk to me," Gina instructed. She plucked Sabella's wine glass from where it sat on the counter and led the way over to the living room. Having both slipped off their shoes, they settled on the couch.

"I know you think forgiving him is a weakness, Gi, but people make mistakes. He apologized, beautifully, with that song, and it's not like what he did wasn't understandable. He jumped to conclusions, and they were insulting, and I wish he hadn't, but I also think people usually deserve a second chance."

"You're right, I judge people too harshly sometimes. He was a jerk, but everyone can be, sometimes."

Sabella regarded her best friend curiously. "That's unlike you."

"Yeah, well, maybe you're finally rubbing off on me," she dismissed, taking a sip of wine and nudging Sabella with her foot.

"About time!" Sabella teased back, laughing. "Seriously, though, Gina, he didn't do anything unforgivable. It boils down to a volatile misunderstanding."

"And he apologized profusely, you're right. Sometimes men just can't control their more impulsive tendencies."

"He also handled it pretty well when I called him on his assumption. The vast majority of the time, I feel good around him; it feels right when we're together. I know I'm letting my romanticism interfere with my decision-making, but how can I simply ignore that?"

"I don't know, Sab. You've forgiven him, obviously, but so what? It's not like you could keep seeing him," Gina pointed out. "I don't want you to have your heart broken, and you're clearly invested in this relationship already, but where could it even go?" She looked Sabella over meaningfully, silently commenting on her uncharacteristic outfit, pausing on her necklace.

Sabella looked down to her yellow skirt. Gina had helped her find it years ago, but she had only worn it a few times, primarily to semi-formal occasions. The necklace her parents had given her was reserved for exceptional moments. "You're right, I should change." She nearly jumped from the couch and headed to her bedroom, though she should have expected that

Gina wouldn't drop the topic so easily. She spun back around before Gina followed her through the bedroom door. "Unless you want to go out somewhere? You look really nice today."

Gina shot her a look that said she saw directly through the attempt to shift topics. "I always dress like this. You don't."

Sabella hesitated, truly taking in her friend's pinstriped, brown slacks and off-the-shoulder tan top, accented with amber jewelry. "No, you don't. This is astoundingly monochromatic for you, especially for a Saturday afternoon."

"What happened to 'really nice'?" Gina countered, pushing past her to the bedroom, then flounced onto the bed beside Sabella's computer.

"It is really nice!" Sabella insisted as she walked to her closet. "Simply, somewhat austere, specifically for you."

Gina pouted. "I'm trying something new."

"You got tired of colors just in time for summer?" Even splayed out casually on the bed, Gina belonged in a magazine. The outfit lacked flamboyant color, but that allowed the eye to focus on Gina's features and the lines of her body. Sabella hung up her flirty skirt and pulled on a pair of jeans, then replaced her necklace in its box, removed the hair clips, and swept her hair into a ponytail.

"This is a bit autumnal, isn't it?" Gina commented meanwhile. She strode deliberately to the armoire and pulled out Sabella's meager collection of eye shadows. "You're avoiding the topic of your scrumptious chef," she pointed out, starting to draw a design on her cheek with the same green shadow Sabella had used that morning.

Sabella shifted her laptop to one of her nightstands and plopped down on the bed. "He asked me to go on tour with him."

"What!" Gina spun around in astonishment. Sabella would have been covered in makeup, but Gina was a pro.

"I know. It's ridiculous, right?"

Somewhat mollified, Gina turned back to the mirror. "What does he expect, that you'd follow him around like a groupie? Having hot sex in daring locations in between their shows? Come to think of it…"

Sabella laughed at the idea. "That definitely sounds more like you than me. Personal experience, Gi?"

"Maybe." She winked at Sabella through the mirror.

"He said I would have his rooms to myself, and he would share with the other guys, actually."

"You're considering it."

"I am. Is that completely absurd? How pathetic would it be to trail him, like a puppy?"

"Are you kidding? A summer tryst with a hot musician?" Gina shrugged. "Sounds like an exciting new experience, and all good writers need all the experience they can get, right?" Gina set down the makeup and whirled around, displaying an elaborate design that curled around her cheekbone and over her eyebrow. "Better?"

"Much." Daring and eye-catching, the design suited Gina perfectly. "Are you saying I should go?"

"As long as you're careful, and I don't just mean sex, though, you know, you should definitely use protection." Sabella rolled her eyes. Gina slid onto the bed beside her. "Seriously, though, if you can stay at least moderately dispassionate, which I know would be difficult for you, it could be a great experience. And I get the feeling you'll regret not seeing this instinct you have about him through. Just don't forget that he *is* a musician."

"Meaning?"

"Meaning girls will be throwing themselves at him, and his passion for you, even if it's real and intense, may be fleeting, although in that case he's a colossal idiot."

"Thanks for that," Sabella said with a sardonic smile.

"You can always come home, to my waiting arms. And if he does anything to hurt you, he'll mysteriously disappear between shows." The protective offer made both of them giggle.

"Maybe you're right," Sabella said eventually. "I should embrace new experiences, and this could provide unparalleled insights for my country music piece, if I ever get around to writing it."

"You will, and it will be brilliant," Gina decreed, staunchly supportive.

"Well, one question left, then," Sabella stated, watching her best friend, whose eyes widened. "Help me pack?"

"You'd be lost without me!"

Twelve

That Monday, Sabella headed out to join Kane in Medford. After helping her toss together a small suitcase filled with a mixture of flirty and practical pieces, all of which could be easily interchanged, Gina had claimed Sabella for the remainder of the weekend. They spent the rest of Saturday watching cheesy movies, eating the perishables left in Sabella's fridge, and occasionally discussing the new men in both of their lives.

On Sunday, when Gina had left to change, they had maneuvered the vase filled with the flowers Kane had brought into her car, so the carnations wouldn't go to waste. While Gina was gone, Sabella had called Kane. They chatted a bit until she had nonchalantly mentioned that she would like to join them at the next stop on their tour. Kane's excited shout had nearly busted her eardrum, but at least she knew he truly wanted her there. They had agreed that she would join them on Monday, allowing her some more girl time with Gina and giving him the opportunity to inform everyone else involved.

Sabella had no idea whether his bandmates and manager would object to her joining them, but presumably Kane wouldn't have invited her if it would cause friction.

She glanced at the dashboard clock. It was still relatively early in the afternoon, which meant Kane was likely at the promotional appearance his manager had scheduled. There was another hour or so left in her drive, which would hopefully be enough time to settle the excited nervousness that had been dancing through her since she'd left Portland. She reminded herself constantly that, if worse came to worst, she could simply turn around and drive back. She would *not* become so emotionally invested that this experience would leave her heartbroken.

She and Kane had agreed to meet by the motel where the band was staying, which had raised a whole host of other issues. It was unlikely the other band members would under-stand her presence if Kane and she didn't share a room. At the same time, she didn't want to become a groupie who followed them around to be used as Kane's sex toy when he felt like it. Still, if they shared a room, he would probably expect that to translate into a sexual relationship, and she wasn't ready for that to happen, at least not without a pretty serious conversation first.

Sabella sighed and turned up the radio to drive thoughts of all the pragmatic obstacles out of her mind. This was about expanding her realm of experience, and as long as she remained physically safe, and more or less emotionally intact, she should consider it a success. But she hoped this would be more, and a relentless part of her wished that this would turn into the great love story she had always wanted. Her one consolation laid in the fact that, if this didn't become a real love story, she could always escape into a recreated, parallel world with her writing, where she could, more or less, control the outcome.

A little after three, a freshly repainted sign directed her off the road to the slightly concealed Redwood Inn. A tour bus she assumed was Kane's covered several spots, though it considerately stood as far out of the way as possible. She parked in an unmarked spot on the gravel lot and pulled out her phone. Kane could still be occupied by his various tour-related obligations, which limited her options. They weren't playing until the following night, but she had no idea how they filled the time in between shows, other than the stray promotional event.

She'd passed a donut shop and a pizza parlor near the motel. Should she grab her laptop and walk over to one, or should she call Kane? The answer came via a text informing her that Kane, presumably with the rest of his group, was on his way back to the motel now. Sabella replied simply that she had arrived but was going to get some coffee.

She shut off the car, left the computer, and headed out to find the donut shop. The walk took less than ten minutes, though that was enough time for her to be grateful it was still early in the summer. Inside the air-conditioned, modest shop, she studied the offering in the display cases. Still nervous about the rapidly approaching encounter with Kane's band, she decided to indulge in a chocolate-covered donut. Besides, she might need the sweetness to make the coffee, which was of undetermined origin and quality, palatable.

Fully armed with sugar and reasonably pleasant coffee, Sabella headed back to the motel. For a summer afternoon, the street felt rather deserted, but then again, this was a small town, and it was Monday. She was so absorbed in the anxious prattle of her inner thoughts that she barely registered the figure leaning against her car.

When she was only a few steps away, Kane straightened up with a welcoming smile that claimed her attention. "Hey."

"Hi." She glanced around for signs of the other musicians or of his manager, but they were nowhere to be seen. Some of her tension melted away. At least she wouldn't have to meet everyone right this second. There was still time to jump back in her car and drive home, though that would mean turning her back on the gorgeous and talented man in front of her.

Kane initiated a hug, and Sabella quickly shifted the donut to the same hand that held her coffee so she could return the embrace. When they pulled back, Kane's arms lingered, seemingly reluctant to let her go. "I'm glad you came."

"You piqued my curiosity. It's a fatal flaw," she joked, unprepared for this to become an intimate scene.

Kane laughed and stepped back, ensuring she had easy access to the car. "Can I get your bag?" he offered when she opened the trunk.

It definitely didn't hurt, having a gentlemanly and conscientious man around. "Please." She rounded the car to take her laptop and a small bag with toiletries and makeup from the front passenger seat.

Unspeaking, perhaps because neither knew how to broach the topic, they moved toward the motel. Kane led her to a room, which he unlocked, then waited for her to enter. At first glance, the room appeared pretty much like any standard motel room, with a queen-sized bed covered in a dark bedspread, a nondescript wooden dresser, and a miniature refrigerator. A duffel bag rested next to his guitar case on the bed.

"Was your drive okay?" Kane asked, setting her bag down at the foot of the bed.

"It wasn't anything special." She placed the untouched donut in its paper bag and her combination toiletry-makeup case on top of the dresser, which was the nearest surface to the door, then slipped her laptop bag to the floor. For some reason, she didn't feel confident enough to enter further into the room. Upon additional examination, the signs of age and poor maintenance, including a faint trace of painted-over water damage, became more apparent. Light streamed in through the double window, illuminating stains on the floor and cracks in the furniture. Suffice it to say, she would never stay in a place like this if she were traveling alone, so she was already placing a significant amount of her trust in Kane.

"So, what's everyone else up to?" she asked in the tense silence.

"They're around." Kane stayed standing as if he, too, didn't want to bring the bed into their conversation yet.

"Are you planning on hiding me away?" she teased, attempting to lighten the heavy atmosphere of the room.

Kane's lips curved. "I'd be more than happy to keep you to myself, but you'll meet 'em soon enough. Didn't want 'em all crowdin' you."

"That's very considerate of you," Sabella said sincerely, ignoring the voice that warned her he may think she couldn't handle herself.

"That's just the kind of man I am."

Kane stepped close enough that she had to tilt her head slightly to maintain eye contact. Sabella set down the coffee she was still holding. His eyes flicked down to the hand that now rested, empty, beside the paper cup, then back to her. His intentions were written plainly across his face, and Sabella felt her cheeks heat up. He looked devilish, utterly tempting, and wholly aware of his effect on her. Right as she was sure he would lean down to kiss her, a whistle sounded from the still open doorway.

Sabella sprung away from Kane and swiveled to the door.

"Well, whadda we got here?" a blond country boy, probably a couple years younger than her, asked from the doorway.

"Bobby," Kane said with a growling edge to his voice.

"Sorry, man. Din' know you had such fine company." The boy graced Sabella with his best attempt at a charming smile. "Pleased to meet you, ma'am. If the ol' man ain't givin' you what you need, I'd be glad to lend my considerable skills."

Kane tensed, but the ambitious flirting was entertaining. Sabella could already see the boy idolized Kane and expended significant effort to emulate him. "You're a bit young for me," she answered, attempting to rebuff him kindly, yet unambiguously. "I prefer my men with at least *some* experience."

Kane let out a bark of laughter and closed the limited distance between them, placing his arm proprietarily around her shoulders. Bobby opened his mouth, evidently couldn't think of a response, then pouted the way only a rebuffed young man used to effortlessly charming every woman could.

"Bella, this is Bobby. When he's not busy skirt-chasin', he plays bass. Bobby, this is Sabella. Mind your manners," Kane warned.

Bobby was clearly unimpressed, but he joined them inside the room. Before Kane could say anything else, two more men appeared in the doorway. Had she gotten in several orders of magnitude over her head, surrounded by these four, solid, Southern men? Although, she had spent most of her time in university surrounded by male friends, and she had handled them all adeptly enough.

That didn't prevent her from tensing when she recognized the oldest man now in the room. Apparently the man in Dante's really could have introduced her to the band, had she taken him up on the offer.

"Well ain't you two just pretty as a picture?" he drawled, looking her over, then narrowed his eyes on Kane.

"Mitch," Kane greeted. "This is Sabella. And that there's Mitch, my manager, and next to him's Steve, my drummer."

The manager held back, but Steve reached out his hand to acknowledge the introduction. Sabella placed her hand in his for a light handshake.

"All right, well, we're gonna get out of here for a little while, so you guys can head on back to your own rooms or wherever else," Kane said into the subsequent silence.

"You heard 'im fellas. Kane here'd like some privacy," Mitch said, barely glancing at Sabella. Perhaps he hadn't recognized her. Steve moved to the door without more prompting, but Mitch had to gesture for Bobby to precede him.

"See ya 'round," the bass guitarist said on his way out, offering Sabella a parting smile. Mitch followed him out with only a soft nod to Kane.

❖ ❖ ❖

"So are you going to tell me where we're going?" Sabella asked from the passenger seat of her car.

After the guys had left, Kane had grabbed his guitar and asked if he could drive her somewhere. "Nope," he answered. He had no intention of sharing his plan.

Sabella sipped the coffee she had plucked from the dresser before they left. "What if I ask nicely?"

"It'd ruin the surprise. But you can keep on asking." He grinned, glancing over at her. He still couldn't quite believe she had driven down to join him. He'd never known a woman who would turn her life upside down for a man without a million promises. Now that she was here, they could try their hand at being together. Or get it out of their systems.

Kane pulled into a parking spot and stopped the car. Sabella was watching him curiously, but he just smiled and got out. Normally, he'd have gone around to get her door, but she opened it before he had a chance. He reached into the back seat instead to pull out his guitar. He'd thought about grabbing a blanket but hadn't wanted to tip her off.

"So, where are we?" she asked. Her curious impatience made him smile. Even in jeans and with her hair pulled into a simple ponytail, she was beautiful.

"You don't really get the whole concept of 'surprise,' do you?"

"I'm inquisitive," Sabella said, full of sass. She fell into step beside him as he led her around the smallish office building to a tiny park. In reality, it was mostly a big lawn, not a true park, but it'd do.

He spotted a picnic table and led her to it. He placed the guitar case on the table, but when he went to open it, she grabbed his hand. He turned back to see her smiling brightly at him in understanding. "Thought we could give this another shot," he explained anyway.

Rather than answer, she tugged on his hand and rose to her tiptoes for a kiss.

Some hours later, Kane pulled into a parking spot in the dark lot of the motel but didn't shut off the engine. His things were still in the room. He would have walked Sabella to the door regardless, but he wasn't sure how things would go from there.

They'd joked around in the park, and Kane had played some of his older songs for her. Then he'd driven them to downtown Medford in search of dinner. The day had been great, even better than the times before since they were getting to be more comfortable with each other.

Now, back at the motel, he knew exactly where he'd like the evening to go, but he wasn't sure Sabella was ready. He definitely didn't want to pressure her. She might bolt, and that was the last thing he wanted to happen.

Until that moment, they'd talked easily, but now Sabella was quiet. Steeling himself for whatever happened next, Kane shut off the car. For once, Sabella didn't reach for the door.

Kane popped his own open to avoid a silence that could easily become awkward. He rushed around the car as she bent down to get her purse, then held the passenger-side door open.

"Thank you," she said softly, with a shy smile, when she was out of the car.

"Of course." He grabbed his guitar from the back seat then returned her keys, so she wouldn't feel trapped.

Still quiet, they crossed to the room. Kane was used to the crappy rooms where they stayed on tour. But would Sabella be so accepting? Her place may be small, but it had been comfortable and well kept. The rooms held together with shoddy maintenance and usually covered in various stains were a part of his life, but they didn't have to be a part of hers. It could turn out to be enough reason for her to go home. He supposed they could try again after his tour. But it felt like, if she left, that would be it.

He unlocked the door, hit the light switch just inside, and waited for her to go in. Following her inside, he pushed the door so it didn't quite shut. Sabella put her purse on the dresser, and Kane set down his guitar.

Kane stood uncomfortably near the door, and Sabella forced herself to break the silence. "Tonight was wonderful. Thank you."

"My pleasure." His eyes flicked to the bed. "I should let you get some rest," he offered politely. He was being really careful, and she appreciated it, but some reckless part of her didn't want the flawless decorum to continue.

"Do I get a goodnight kiss?" she ventured, attempting to sound teasingly nonchalant. She didn't notice she held her breath until he moved toward her, and she suddenly restarted breathing.

The kiss started out slowly and carefully. His hands rested lightly on her hips, with hers on his biceps, as he tasted her lips. He retreated barely a few seconds later, but Sabella wasn't satisfied. She didn't want this moment to happen in the real world, filled with its sensible considerations, so she tugged on his tee shirt to bring him back closer. Kane accepted the invitation without hesitation, tightening his arms around her waist.

Sabella arched against him and lifted her hands to his shoulders for a firmer hold. He turned them so her back pressed against the hotel room door, which clicked shut. His hands traced the waistband of her jeans then slipped under her top to cover her ribcage. When she didn't protest, they climbed higher, until his thumbs rested on the outside of the lacey cups of her bra. One of his legs pressed between hers. Sabella leaned toward him rather than flattening against the door, delighting in the ravenous attention that demanded her response rather than asking permission. One of his hands moved to cup her breast, splaying over the material of the bra—the only gentle part of their embrace.

Kane was the one to break the kiss, though he didn't withdraw his hands. "If you want us to stop tonight, we should stop now," he warned raggedly.

It was the last thing she wanted, but she hadn't come there simply to sleep with him. She had always treated sex with more reverence than most people she knew, likely due to her parents' traditional influence, not to mention all of the practical concerns which *did* have to be discussed before they jumped into bed.

She nodded shakily. Kane pulled away, and her hands drifted reluctantly down from his shoulders in a last caress. He turned from her and crossed the small room, running his fingers through his hair. Sabella could still see him breathing roughly, and she tried to steady her own intake of air. She moved away from the door, clearing an exit for him, but didn't step any closer to him.

Once he had regained his composure, Kane looped the straps of his duffel bag over his arm. He watched her from his spot beside the bed, as if unsure about leaving.

Making an impromptu decision in the silence, Sabella said, "You don't have to leave." His eyebrows drew up almost imperceptibly, but the question was clear. "I mean, it's a big bed." She had shared smaller beds with more people during late nights back at university, and it had been perfectly casual. This didn't have to be different, she told herself, despite the fact that it quite evidently was.

"It is," Kane agreed.

"It's your room." She could find supportive reasoning for virtually anything, though this particular line of thinking was seriously unlike her. Apparently, the "choose your own adventure" story continued.

"I told you you could have it. It's no problem."

She knew he meant it, but irrationally she didn't want him to leave. She tried to convince herself it was due to the sketchy nature of the motel and her being wholly out of her element. "I completely believe that two adults can share a bed without anything indecorous happening. And this is a big bed," she repeated lamely.

"Hey, I'm sure you'll make a better roommate than Bobby an' Steve," he joked.

"Well, how would you know? Maybe I kick in my sleep or something."

He chuckled and dropped the duffel bag onto the floor. "Guess I'll take my chances. You're definitely prettier than either of 'em." He crossed the distance between them and bent down for a soft kiss. "You sure you're okay with this?" he asked afterward, his lips mere inches from hers. The verification was reassuring.

"You're on board with the 'nothing indecorous' part, right?"

"Scout's honor." He smiled innocently, but Sabella didn't miss the devilish twinkle in his eyes.

Thirteen

Kane woke to the sound of water running. He looked to the other side of the bed, saw the indentation Sabella'd left on the other pillow, and smiled. He'd slept in his jeans, which hadn't been all that comfortable, but it was totally worth it. They'd started out innocently enough, each on separate sides of the bed. Sometime in the middle of the night, Kane had woken up facing her, his hand splayed on her hip. Barely any light streamed into the room from the parking lot, but he could make out her relaxed features. He'd fallen asleep again watching her.

The water shut off, but Kane stayed in the bed. He figured she'd be in there a while longer, getting dressed and dealing with makeup and whatnot. She probably wouldn't be out of there until he'd heard the hair dryer switch on and off a couple times.

Sabella surprised him a moment later by coming out without drying her hair. Unfortunately, she was fully dressed. She'd twisted her hair so it was almost out of sight. Wet, it looked light brown.

Kane sat up, and her eyes moved to his bare torso before she quickly crossed the room. She kept her back to him, fiddling with the toiletry case. Kane tossed the blanket off and swung his legs over the side of the bed. "G'morning."

She glanced over her shoulder briefly. "Good morning."

He got up and covered the couple steps toward her. "Did you sleep okay?" he asked, standing just behind her. He probably shouldn't have been pressing her buttons, but he couldn't resist. Plus, he didn't want to constantly be watching what he said and how. She was much more skittish now than she'd been the night before.

"Fairly well. How about you?" She turned to face him with a carefully neutral smile.

"I slept great." He grinned at her. She kept her eyes set on his face, as if looking lower was forbidden. "Guess I should go shower," he said, taking a step back.

Her smile slipped. Her lips parted, but she closed them again without speaking. Kane flashed her another smile and turned away to the bathroom. He shut the door but didn't lock it. He doubted Sabella would come in while he was showering, but he sure wasn't going to stop it from happening. This was shaping up to be one hell of a tour.

Sabella pulled the hairband out from her wet bun so she could towel her hair dry while Kane showered. She would *not* picture him in the shower. She hadn't forgotten how great he looked without his shirt, and the image burned into her mind hadn't needed this morning's reinforcement. Previously, anger had helped her avoid the tempting mental imagery of water sluicing over his naked body, but she had no such distraction this time.

She had awoken lying on her back, significantly closer to Kane than when she had fallen asleep, despite the bed's adequate size. His arm had rested across her stomach, over the waistband of her pajama bottoms but under the tank top, which had ridden up at some point during the night. When she turned her head, his face had been so close she could have counted his many eyelashes. Naturally, she slipped from the bed as quickly as possible without waking him. In the shower, she had reminded herself of all the reasons for which she did not have sex casually, no matter how unbelievably attractive a guy was. "Positively scrumptious," Gina had called Kane. She hadn't been wrong.

When Sabella heard the water stop running, she quickly brushed her hair and twisted it back into a messy bun. Kane didn't come out immediately, which meant he was taking the time to dress. Sabella resolutely tamped down her disappointment. By the time he rejoined her, she had repacked everything she had used in the morning and was finishing up straightening the covers.

"Tour tip number one," he said from behind her, "you don't actually have to make the bed."

Sabella straightened up to see him leaning against the doorframe. His wet hair enhanced the slightly heart-like shape of his clean-shaven face. "You're so wise and learned," she answered, voice dripping with false admiration.

"Wise enough to know we skipped somethin' earlier." He pushed off the doorframe and walked toward her.

"What's that?" What did he have up his metaphorical sleeves?

He reached out to hook his fingers in the loops on her jeans and gently pulled her forward. "G'morning," he said quietly.

"You're showing your age," she joked. "You already said that."

"Yeah? Did I do this?"

His head dipped down to kiss her upturned lips. Sabella kissed him back briefly, before pushing him gently away with a breathless laugh. "Don't you have important musician duties to attend to or something?"

"Not more important than this," he answered with a charming smile then closed the slight distance between them to kiss her again.

"Oh, so this is what you do on tour all day?" she asked when this kiss ended.

"Only when you're around to distract me." He smiled and little lines appeared at the corners of his eyes, drawing even more of her attention to them. The tiny crinkles seemed to point to the alluring green of his eyes that hid golden sparks of mischief.

Sabella gave in to another languid kiss. "Seriously, what's the plan today?" she asked afterward, determined to get them both out of the motel room—and away from the bed.

"Well, we start by grabbin' some breakfast. I don't know if you're up for eatin' with the guys or not. Then, really, we have some time to kill. In smaller towns like this, we usually go over to wherever we're playin', check the place out a bit. Plus it's usually the most interestin' place around. But everythin's pretty laid-back. An' we do a show tonight."

"Sounds fairly straightforward. So, we should go meet the others? Or do they always come to you?"

"Usually, once they're up. I'm sure we could find some way to fill the time while we wait." A beguiling half-smile curved his lips.

Sabella was saved from answering by a pounding at the door. "You gonna git outta bed?" a voice she recognized as Bobby's shouted from the other side.

Kane strode across the room and yanked the door open. "You're fixin' to get whupped, boy," he threatened.

Sabella bit her lip to prevent herself from giggling.

Bobby paid absolutely no attention. "Mornin'." He grinned at Sabella, eyes slipping down to take in her fitted polo shirt and flared jeans. He lacked even a trace of subtlety.

Sabella couldn't stop herself from rolling her eyes with a smile. She plucked her purse from the dresser then joined them by the door. Bobby stepped back to let her through, and Kane followed her out. All three joined Steve and Mitch a few doors away.

"So where're we goin'?" Kane asked Mitch once everyone had exchanged pleasantries.

"Mrs. Q's," the manager answered, leading the way out of the parking lot. So far, his behavior had stayed professional, as she would expect from both a man his age and an experienced band manager. Thankfully, there was no hint of the lascivious suggestiveness from their conversation at Dante's. He didn't appear to remember that evening, and Sabella decided to ignore its occurrence, preferring to start fresh rather than judge him on a brief, likely alcohol-inspired, interaction.

They walked to breakfast with Bobby enthusiastically shifting his eager attempts to attract attention among the other men, who alternated between obliging and good-naturedly putting him in his place. Sabella drank in the fascinating dynamics of the group, trying to remain unobtrusive while filing away tidbits of information. This microcosm provided a glimpse at an entirely different world, in a way she hadn't experienced on her brief trip to Nashville. So, at the very least, this trip would not turn out to be a complete waste.

After their late breakfast, Steve returned to the motel to drive the bus with their equipment over to the 4 Daughters Irish Pub where the guys would be playing. Sabella volunteered to keep him company so that she could fetch her notebook from the room, while the others headed to the pub.

"So you're a writer," Steve stated as they walked. He had yet to speak much around her, giving Sabella the impression he preferred to observe, though he did help Kane keep Bobby somewhat in line. He was lankier than the other men and had his dark hair cut shorter than they did, and when he did speak, his voice held less of that Southern drawl.

"I am," she acknowledged.

"You writing 'bout Kane?"

"I'm sure he would make a fantastic character, but that's not really why I'm here."

"Why's that?" He kept his tone casual, but he was obviously vetting her answers.

"He invited me," she answered simply. "The whole tour experience is mostly a side-effect, though admittedly not a bad one."

"You're a fan," he stated.

Sabella couldn't fault him for being protective, but she was nonetheless irked by the hint of accusation. Didn't any of them believe in giving someone the benefit of the doubt? "If I'm going to be at one of your shows almost every day, isn't that a good thing?" she countered.

"Depends."

They had reached the motel, so Sabella split off from him to collect one of her notebooks and grab the lip balm she had forgotten that morning. By the time she rejoined Steve by the bus, she had decided to address his unvoiced concerns explicitly. "I'm not going to deny that new experiences are largely a writer's bread and butter." Steve's expression grew stonier. "But that's not why I'm here, or why I'm interested in seeing where things go with Kane. It's not about him being famous, for me. I like my life, and I don't need Kane's connections or access for a sensationalized 'inside scoop' article or anything like that."

"But you've thought about it," Steve pointed out.

"You guys do keep bringing it up."

His only reaction was a slow blink.

"I'm interested in Kane because he's Kane. All of this—the tour?—it's a part of who he is and how he's chosen to live his life. Wouldn't you want him to be with someone who supports that?"

Steve didn't answer, but she could see him considering her words as though he was weighing their truth. Sabella stood calmly under his scrutiny. Eventually, he gestured to the bus, saying only, "We should get going."

Kane chalked his cue as Sabella lined up her shot. They were playing in pairs, and Sabella was actually doing a pretty good job holding her own. She'd loosened her hair so it hung in damp waves around her shoulders. He preferred her hair down, maybe just because he remembered how it felt beneath his fingers.

Mitch had bowed out of the game. Instead he sat by the bar, chatting with the cute bartender. A few people occupied other seats, but it wasn't all that busy. Hopefully, that was only because it was early on a Tuesday. The radio show he'd done yesterday had received a bunch of calls from people looking forward to the appearance. So there was a chance they'd have a decent audience tonight.

"Yes!" Sabella exclaimed when she made the winning shot. Bobby groaned. Steve just sipped his beer, twisting his cue between his fingers.

"Nice shot," Kane told her with a grin. She smiled up at him in return, prompting him to sneak a kiss.

Bobby racked the balls for another game. A waitress brought over a fresh round of beers, and Bobby paused to flirt with her. She laughed him off, but he watched her walk away.

"Put your eyes back in your head, Bobby," Steve said idly. "Maybe that's why we lost."

Bobby grinned at him. "Like Kane always says, we got in this for the free alcohol and the chicks. And that chick brought us free alcohol."

Kane and Steve tensed. It took Bobby a minute to catch on. His gaze swiveled between the other men, then stopped on Sabella. He smiled sheepishly. "Sorry."

Sabella brushed it off with a smile of her own. "What, you think I didn't know guys start bands to pick up girls? Or are you scared you'll lose again if I don't storm off in a huff."

All three men relaxed.

"She's got you there," Kane said, further breaking the tension.

"Just thought it'd be impolite to beat her in the first game, her being a lady and all." Bobby winked.

"Well then, why're you stalling?" Steve chimed in. "Rack 'em up."

Sabella and Kane beat the guys in a few more rounds, before they all cleared off from the pool table and settled in a secluded booth. Mitch rejoined them then, choosing the additional chair placed at what would be the head of the table. Bobby and Kane occupied the corner seats, leaving Sabella and Steve across from each other on the outside ends. They ordered several appetizers, including baked artichoke dip and the bizarre culinary creation of fried pickles, as a precursor to their rather late lunch.

Sabella marveled at the rate at which everything was consumed.

"So tell me somethin'," Mitch asked casually as the others perused the menu, deciding what to have for their main meals. "How'd a guy like Kane here manage to snag a girl like you?"

It wasn't entirely clear what distinction he had made between herself and other women, other than her lack of looks, or perhaps her not being from the South. "He started out by being a gentleman," she answered, attempting to play it safely.

"Well, shoot, I can be gentle." Bobby grinned at her again across the table. He kept baiting her, but Sabella didn't fluster as easily as he expected.

"So you're halfway there. You just have to work on that 'man' part." The other men chuckled. They no longer tensed every time Bobby spoke to her, which hopefully meant they had learned she could handle him perfectly well. Bobby, however, scowled at her as if she had actually wounded his pride. "You have to stop setting yourself up so well," she told him apologetically.

"Stick to your usual, Bobby. This one's outta your league," Steve said, with an approving half-smile. Sabella took it as a compliment.

After they ordered, the conversation shifted to business. The men discussed proposed changes to their set list and potential problems with the pub's layout for keeping an audience's attention. Ultimately, they chose to cut some of the ballads, unfortunately including some of Sabella's favorite songs, but it wasn't her place to intervene.

Once everyone's plates had been nearly wiped clean, the men moved with a newfound efficiency. Mitch spoke to the owner to arrange whatever was necessary while the rest of them went to the bus for their equipment. Sabella settled on one of the pub's couches with a notebook while the musicians set up and played fragments of a few songs.

A growing stream of patrons trickled into the pub as the sound check finished up. Kane caught her eye and tilted his head toward the door. Sabella rejoined the guys, and they all headed back outside.

"The whole vibe works better if the first time most folks see us is when we take the stage," Steve explained. He had apparently warmed up to her presence after their heart-to-heart. "And this way, we get a bit of a break before the show and don't disturb their business too much. Mitch hangs around to keep an eye on all the equipment."

"Bigger places, like Dante's, have a sweet greenroom instead," Bobby chimed in.

Beside the bus, Kane asked her, "You want to take a walk?"

"Oh, well, I don't want to interfere with your guys' routine. You don't need to deviate for my sake." It wouldn't do if she disrupted some ritual, particularly on her first night with them.

"Nah, it's nice out. You'll have plenty of time to get sick of these guys." His fond smile tempered his words.

"Just get him back on time," Steve called from inside the bus.

"That was one time!" Bobby responded.

Kane grinned, slapped the side of the bus twice, then led her away through a back alley to avoid the pub's traffic.

"That sounds like quite a story," Sabella commented.

"You pretty much heard it. Last year, Bobby was off with some groupie and made it to the club almost a half hour *after* we're supposed to be on. Mitch ripped 'im a new one, he was ready to replace him. But Bobby's a pretty talented son of a gun, and he spent the next couple weeks tearin' down all the equipment 'stead of hittin' on the women after shows."

"You're like a family," Sabella noted.

Kane slanted his eyes her way, as if the remark had surprised him. "We are," he acknowledged after a slight pause. He threw his arm around her shoulders as he had many times that day, and Sabella slid comfortably against his body. They walked along, silently tracing the hidden streets of Medford, moving effortlessly with each other.

When Kane began steering them back toward Main Street, Sabella tipped her head back to look at him, and he stopped to kiss her languidly. When the kiss broke, his expression was serious and contemplative, as though there was something about her he couldn't quite decipher.

Sabella smiled back softly. "We should get you back, or your fans might find and dismember me."

Kane chuckled. "Can't have that, now can we?"

Fourteen

$\mathcal{I}$t was late by the time they returned to the motel, but nothing compared to how it'd be in big cities. It was probably best Sabella'd joined them in Medford, so she could ease into life on tour. Despite the small venue, it'd been a pretty good turnout and a successful enough show. Kane liked seeing Sabella watching him, them, up on the stage, knowing she'd be there when he opened his eyes. He'd had to remind himself a few times to look over the rest of the audience.

And afterward she'd been patient with all the women who came up to him, flirting and asking for pictures or autographs. Whenever he'd looked to find her, sitting at the edge of the room, outside most of the hubbub, she seemed calm and unflustered. Still, he'd gotten out of there as quickly as he could so they could walk back to the motel. She hadn't said anything about it on their way back, either, other than that it'd been a good show.

Back in the motel, she started across the room. Kane pulled her toward him, and she laughed. Her tongue flicked out to lick her lips—definitely a nervous habit, he'd decided—as she looked at him, a question in her smiling eyes. Kane kissed her, glad not to be alone, and even more so because she was the one there with him.

And Sabella kissed him back. When he intensified the kiss, she matched him without hesitating. Unlike many women he'd been with, she always responded smoothly and flawlessly to the different timing.

He slipped his hands under her soft top, skimming up her ribcage with his fingers. Her hands came to the bottom of his shirt and inched it up. Kane broke their kiss to pull off his shirt, dropping it somewhere on the floor. Appreciation sparked in her eyes. He cupped her head to bring her back into the kiss. Her hands traced from his waistband up to his chest. Her fingers dug slightly into his shoulders when he lowered his hands, brushing over her breasts, to slip them back under her shirt.

He walked her toward the bed as they kissed. Her head tipped back when he broke from her mouth, tracing his lips down her neck as his hands kneaded over the bra. Her breasts filled his palms, spilling past his fingers. She lowered her arms, sliding them under his and around to skim over his back. Kane kissed lower, slipping one hand to her back to unhook the bra.

"Wait," he heard her breathe. She took a small step away, knocking into the bed behind her.

Kane struggled to control himself. "You okay?" he asked, letting her go completely. He wouldn't be able to stop if he kept touching her. Sabella looked up at him nervously. Kane tried to replay the last few minutes but couldn't find anything to explain her reaction. Her lips, which she licked again, were still red from their kiss. "What's wrong?" he asked, forcing himself to focus.

She dropped her eyes. "We can't... I can't, uhm, do this," she pushed out, glancing back up at him uneasily.

"Do this," he repeated, stepping back to give them both some space. "Is it, like, a religious thing?"

She laughed, just barely, at the idea. "No. This, sex, it isn't a casual thing for me." She said it unflinchingly but still looked nervous, worried about his reaction.

"Bella, you being here isn't a casual thing for me," he said sincerely.

"That's good to know." She smiled then, but it was tense, uncomfortable. "There's just, well, a conversation that needs to happen," she told him slowly, clearly choosing her words carefully.

"A conversation," Kane repeated. He was starting to sound like a damn parrot. He turned from her, brushing his hair back, and paced across the room to distract his body. Possibilities ran through his mind. Did she want some specific commitment? Or maybe she was into something kinky? Or thought he was? He tried not to get ahead of himself like he had in Portland. "What kind of conversation?" He stopped pacing to see her formulating her next words.

"About being…safe." Kane didn't know what she meant so he just kept watching her. "I mean, about being aware of possible consequences," she explained.

"You mean, using protection?"

"That, too."

She chewed at her bottom lip, her eyebrows drawn together, almost as if she was scared of him. Kane exhaled and took the couple steps to the bed. "Okay, let's sit down," he suggested, wiping the confused frustration from his face. Sabella slid onto the bed, propping her back against the headboard. Kane settled at the foot of the bed, facing her. "What do you want to talk about, exactly?" he asked evenly.

"Well, I imagine I'm not the first person you've been with, and I'm sure you took whichever precautions you found necessary, but still, you can never really be completely sure, unless…" She broke off, licking her lips again.

Kane looked down at the motion then reminded himself to focus on what she was saying. "You mean being tested," he caught on, finally. Sabella nodded, and Kane relaxed. She was laying out the practical obstacles. She'd done the same thing when they'd met for coffee, and when he'd invited her to come on tour. "Well, I get a full physical before every tour. Including those tests. And I haven't been with anyone since before then," he added to be extra clear.

She blew out her breath and leaned into the headboard. "You haven't? What about that 'free alcohol and chicks' motto?" she teased with a faint smirk.

Kane smiled back at her. "Seems I grew out of it." She didn't need to know that'd happened right after he'd met her. "While we're talking about it, though, what about you?"

Unlike him, she understood the question right away. "I haven't been with anyone in a while, and I got tested after that relationship ended."

"Good to know," he echoed her words. Her eyes slipped down to his bare torso, and she blushed adorably before looking away. "The guys think we're sleeping together," he felt obliged to point out.

"Of course they do. I don't have a problem with that if you don't want to correct them. Protect your image and whatnot."

Her carefree response surprised him. And she'd been amazingly cool with everything else that had happened tonight, too. "Have you done this before?" he asked.

She suppressed a chuckle at the idea. "Had sex with a musician in his hotel room? Not so much." She paused. "Have you?"

"Had sex with a girl in a hotel room?" He crooked an eyebrow at her.

"Invited someone on tour with you."

"No." He'd wanted to invite Felicia Mae to his first tour. That relationship had blown up before he'd had the chance. And good riddance.

"So this isn't quite like you expected," she stated, fidgeting with the bedspread.

Pushing through the remaining haze of his need, Kane picked up on her apprehension. "It's already better," he told her. Not that he'd object to having sex, but it wasn't a lie.

Sabella didn't say anything, watching him with gently widened eyes.

"I'm beat," Kane said, though that wasn't entirely true. But he hadn't pressured girls for sex even when he was a teenager, and he wasn't about to start now. "You want to call it a night?"

A relieved smile softened her tense features. "That sounds like a good idea."

Kane rose from the bed and gestured toward the bathroom. "Ladies first."

Late the next morning, after packing their things into her car, Sabella and Kane joined the others out by the tour bus. Kane handed Mitch the motel key, and the manager went to check everyone out.

"You want to grab some breakfast from the bus?" Kane offered.

"Technically, this here's a Class A, converted-bus, recreational vehicle," Bobby pointed out.

"Is this one of those genuine tour experiences?" Sabella asked him.

"Sure is." Bobby grinned at her. As usual, Steve watched without comment, though a hint of a smirk curved one corner of his lips.

Sabella glanced among the three musicians then stepped onto the bus ahead of the guys. The bus—*recreational vehicle*—was compact but included all of the necessities. To the right of the door rested two plush seats, for the driver and a passenger inclined to act as companion. Directly ahead of her was a miniature refrigerator, adjacent to a kitchenette with three small burners and a sink. Cabinets extended above, and a drawer of sorts was visible below. Across from the kitchenette, a booth encircled three sides of a basic table. Sabella stopped by a closed sliding door that blocked the rest of the bus from view.

Cheeky as ever, Bobby offered, "How's about a tour?"

Sabella laughed. "Why not?"

He reached above her shoulder and slid the door open with his palm. Sabella stepped back and turned sideways so he could move past her. Kane and Steve started pulling out various edibles in the kitchen area.

"Behind your back, there, that's a shower," Bobby told her, feigning distant tour-guide mannerisms. He slid open another door across from the first and stepped through, then opened the door in front of her. "This bit here's self-explanatory." The revealed compartment housed a toilet and a small sink, with some extra storage space tucked underneath. "An' this," Bobby said with a flourish, "is what you'd call the livin' quarters."

He stepped into the space so Sabella could see it better. A bed, easily large enough for two people, sat slightly off-center from the entryway. A closet spanned the wall to her right, and additional cabinets were set on either side and above the bed.

"Very nice," Sabella told Bobby dispassionately, intentionally not rising to his bait, and turned back to join the others. She slid onto the edge of the booth to stay out of the way. "So this is pretty fully equipped. Do you guys actually use everything it offers?"

"Not so much," Steve answered.

"It doesn't sleep four, or anythin'," Kane elaborated. "We use it mostly to hang out before shows, on longer drives. Sometimes Mitch'll use the bed when it doesn't make sense to get three rooms."

"And our fancy duds are hangin' in the closet," Bobby added.

By the time Mitch rejoined them, the others had taken out their meager store of groceries. A loaf of bread, peanut butter, jam, some butter, and deli meats now rested on the counter that extended over the refrigerator, along with a bottle of soda and some orange juice. It was abundantly clear the men hadn't bothered to purchase more reasonable supplies and that they wouldn't be likely to make full use of the kitchenette. Surprising, given Kane's affinity for cooking.

Bobby started slathering peanut butter on a slice of bread. Watching the knife dig tan smears into the bread, Sabella asked, "Would anyone like some toast?"

Four pairs of eyes swiveled to her. "There ain't no toaster," Mitch pointed out from the other side of the table.

Sabella swallowed a smile. "I see that, yes. But if there's a skillet, we could make toast."

Kane's lips twisted to the side in a half-smile, and Bobby groaned around a big bite of his finished peanut butter and jam sandwich.

"Looks like you brought us a more inventive chef," Steve commented to Kane.

"Looks like," he agreed, still smiling at her.

"You guys never really use the kitchenette, do you?"

"Kane here's too gourmet for a kitchen like this," Bobby said. "The rest of us make do how we can. " Mitch and Steve chuckled.

"They're puttin' you on," Kane told her. "I'll make somethin' occasionally, on longer stretches. We just haven't gotten around to buyin' real supplies yet. Though I've never made plain toast on a skillet before," he admitted.

"No need," Mitch commented.

Sabella tried not to react personally to their congenial laughter, reminding herself that she felt like an outsider because she had known them for less than two days. Mitch got up to make himself a sandwich, and Bobby took his spot, sliding deeper around the table. Sabella rose as well so the men had more access. Mitch took a few plates down from the cabinet and set all but one over a burner. He pulled out a few pieces of bread and took the sliced turkey and ham to the table, sliding in beside Bobby. Steve grabbed some bread and followed suit, bringing the bottle of soda.

"Grab us some glasses, would ya?" Mitch asked no one in particular. Kane pulled three simple, oblong glasses from another cabinet and set them on the table, then brought down two more, which he placed on the counter.

"D'you want some juice?" he asked her.

"Sure, thank you."

He reached for the carton and filled both glasses. "Help yourself," he told her, nodding to the food laid out on the counter. Sabella swallowed her embarrassed self-consciousness, and soon they were also settled at the table: Kane with a mixed-meat sandwich, and her with a slice of bread smeared with butter and jam.

"It's about three hours to Redding," Mitch told them after washing down the last of his sandwich.

"How big's this one?" Bobby asked curiously.

"'Bout the same as here," Mitch answered.

All three musicians looked rather grim at the news. Taking in their expressions, Sabella decided to venture a suggestion, risking more semi-congenial ridicule. "Mount Shasta's pretty much on the way," she pointed out.

"Is it?" Kane asked.

"Suppose so," Mitch confirmed.

"I don't know if you guys would be interested," Sabella continued determinedly, "but we could take a small detour; maybe have a late lunch by the mountain? You don't have a show tonight, right? It's supposed to be quite beautiful."

For a while, no one said anything, and Sabella started worrying they were all about to tell Kane to send her home.

"The two of us could pick up some lunch and some more groceries," Kane offered, endorsing the idea.

All of the musicians looked to Mitch as if for permission. "Could be possible," he said finally, though he didn't sound particularly convinced.

"Not like there'll be lots to do in Redding," Steve added, evidently supportive of the idea. Sabella flashed him a small smile.

"Suppose we could take time to take in the sights," Mitch relented.

"Well, all right!" Bobby grinned beside her.

A couple hours later, Kane pulled Sabella's car into a spot near the tour bus, in a mostly empty dirt parking lot. Thanks to Sabella's GPS, they had managed to find a supermarket and a deli before joining the others. They'd also stopped in a nearby coffee shop Sabella hadn't been able to pass by.

After loading the groceries into the bus, the five of them headed down a marked trail, supposedly toward a vista point. Sabella had already passed out the coffees. Kane and Steve carried the rest of the food. The trail took less than twenty minutes, but it opened up onto an incredible view of the mountain.

They split around an empty picnic table. Steve and Mitch took one side, but Bobby slid in on the other side of Sabella, sandwiching her between him and Kane. Sabella set out the plates, utensils, sandwiches, salads, and fries. Easy banter passed among the guys as they ate. Sabella mostly stayed quiet, but she didn't look ill at ease.

"This is pretty nice," Mitch said once they'd finished eating.

"It was a good idea," Steve added, gathering empty wrappers and containers into one of the plastic bags.

"It was a great idea," Kane corrected.

"Glad to be of service," Sabella said. She stood and gracefully stepped over the bench. "We should get a photo of you guys, since you did make it all the way out here," she suggested.

Kane exchanged looks with the other guys.

"Photo of what?" Bobby asked.

"Of…you?" Sabella eyes moved from him to the others in turn. "In front of the beautiful mountain?"

"Not a bad idea," Mitch said. "The band, the mountain. Decent publicity shots, maybe."

Kane got up from the table. "Bobby, go get a camera from the bus," he said idly.

Bobby started to protest, but Sabella cut him off. "I have a camera," she told them, pulling a small one from her purse.

"Well, all right, then. C'mon, boys," Mitch instructed, unmoving.

With some grumbling and a little bit of direction from Mitch, they ended up standing in a triangle, offset from the mountain in the background. Sabella snapped some shots, moving around to get different angles. Luckily, with digital cameras, it almost didn't matter if she was any good at photography. At one point, she crouched off to the side of them. A wind blew just then, probably either making the shot or ruining it.

A few minutes later, she turned to Mitch. "You should join them." When he didn't move, she added, "How often will you find yourself somewhere as beautiful as this?"

Bobby egged him on, and Mitch got up to join the other men. Sabella took a couple shots with all four of them, lined up like the tourists they were. Soon, Mitch stepped forward, holding his hand out for the camera. "Your turn," he told Sabella.

"Oh, no. I'm not really—"

"Hey, if we're doing this, you are," Steve interrupted her.

"Come on," Kane said at the same time.

Faced with the four of them, Sabella caved quickly. She stood between Bobby and Kane, who wrapped his arm around her, pulling her close. A few tense, silent moments later, Bobby joked, "I've heard of more exciting funerals than this."

Everyone laughed, and Mitch snapped some more shots, which would probably turn out better. Sabella was the first to break away. She took her camera back from Mitch, and the rest of them gathered their leftovers from the picnic table. They headed back down the trail. Sabella hung back to take some more pictures before catching up to them.

"This really was a great idea," he said when she fell into step beside him.

"The detour or the photo op?" she teased.

"Both." He smiled down at her.

"Hey lovebirds! We're losing daylight!" Bobby called from up ahead, interrupting yet again.

Sabella laughed, but Kane just shook his head and laced his fingers through hers as they walked.

Fifteen

They reached the next motel a little over an hour later. Mitch quickly dealt with checking them in, and everyone split off to their respective rooms. Kane carried his and Sabella's bags, though she'd insisted it wasn't necessary. He thought otherwise. Plus, she'd packed very lightly. Then again, he didn't know exactly how long she was planning to stay. They had just over a month left in the tour.

Inside the room, she pulled out her laptop to transfer the photos they'd taken. Kane sat beside her on the bed, watching the screen over her shoulder. He was no expert, but some of them looked pretty good. Especially one with her laughing next to him.

Barely a half hour later, Steve knocked on their door. "We're gonna go out, do something. You guys coming?" he asked. Kane looked back to Sabella.

"You know what, I should really get some work done, so I might hang out here if you don't mind," she told them.

"Are you sure?" Kane couldn't tell if her hesitance

stemmed from really needing to work or feeling out of place with them.

"Unfortunately, I still have deadlines. Maybe I can join you guys later?"

"All right. Just give me a call when you're done if we're not back." Kane pulled her car keys from his pocket and tossed them to her waiting hands.

"Have fun," she answered with an open smile.

Sabella awoke the next morning with Kane's body virtually twined around her. Their legs had wound around each other, and one of his arms rested across her waist. *Too close.*

She slid carefully from the bed, making certain not to wake him, and padded to the bathroom. While Kane had been out, she had drafted an article with easy travel tips for long trips then chatted a bit on Skype. She had checked in briefly with her sister as she waited for Gina to sign on.

Predictably, Gina's first question after their greetings had been regarding Kane's prowess in bed. Though Gina knew her better than anyone, she had been astonished to learn Sabella still hadn't slept with him and admonished her to do so soon, since apparently Sabella wasn't truly touring with a musician unless sex was involved. Sabella had tried to switch the topic over to Gina, but after some basic generalizations about being "fine," Gina claimed she was being called into an end-of-day meeting, so they ended the call.

Afterward, Sabella had intended to write some more, but Kane, Steve, and Bobby invaded their motel room with playing cards and Chinese takeout. Apparently she had been too engrossed to notice the text Kane had sent her, considerately asking about her preferences, but they had brought a wide selection, and she wasn't especially picky.

They had spent the rest of the night playing various versions of poker; Bobby unsurprisingly suggested they play strip poker, but Kane had vetoed the idea. No one commented on Mitch's absence, and Sabella hadn't asked.

"Bella?" Kane called as she finished lining her eyes. Her quick shower must have drawn him out of bed. Still wrapped in only a towel, she cracked the bathroom door open. He stood shirtless on the other side, though he continued to sleep in jeans. His eyes ran over the part of her visible through the slit in the barely opened door, and he smiled in appreciation. "You want some company?" he asked her with a provocative glint in his eyes.

Sabella glanced back at the pile of clothing she had folded and placed beside the sink. She had forgotten to grab a fresh outfit. She scooped up her pajamas, schooled her expression to one of nonchalance, and stepped casually out of the bathroom. "It's all yours," she tossed over her shoulder, refusing to turn around until she heard Kane shut the door a few minutes later.

When she heard him run the water, she removed fresh clothes from her bag and dressed quickly.

Kane opened the door as she slipped her soft, V-neck top into place. "I told the guys I'd make breakfast, but then we could get away for a couple hours," he said.

"That sounds nice." He hadn't shaved. Apparently he did so only once every few days, at least so far. A few stray drops of water on his bare chest caught the light. "I'm going to go for a walk," she said abruptly, tearing her gaze away from his torso. "Meet you by the bus?"

A lazy, knowing smile crossed Kane's face. "I just need five minutes," he called after her, as she grabbed her cell phone and rushed out the door.

After breakfast—some fairly decent French toast, considering the equipment he had available—Kane drove Sabella over to the Turtle Bay Bird Sanctuary Mitch'd told him about. He'd brought his guitar but left it in the car for now. She'd hear him play tonight. Listening to the same songs over and over would probably get old all too soon. They wandered around the sanctuary at an easy pace, taking in the occasional wildlife.

Sabella seemed lost in their surroundings. Had the guys' banter gotten to her last night? She'd held her own without a problem. Still, Kane could tell she was more skittish about the whole topic of sex than she liked to let on. The guys hadn't been subtle in their ribbing.

"What's up?" he asked her.

"Hmm?" She switched her focus to him. "Oh, I'm just thinking," she said with a smile and squeezed his hand in hers.

"'Bout what?"

"Transience." Kane didn't say anything, watching her to encourage her to go on. She looked away before continuing. "All of your songs, about past relationships, past loves, they're all so intensely, genuinely passionate."

"All relationships are, in the moment. The passion is real."

She nodded at the ground. "And then it dissipates. The relationship ends."

Kane pulled her to a stop near a fairly secluded grove. "Most relationships end," he told her. This time she stayed silent. "People change; they grow up. Life gets in the way, or you realize the passion—it isn't love, isn't permanent."

"Exactly."

She was watching him calmly, without any blame or expectations. Kane still felt pressure to drive his point home, to make sure he'd gotten it across. He had a bad tendency to misspeak unless it was through song lyrics. "It's not like you went into each relationship you've had thinking, 'This is the one,' right?" He pressed on when she nodded. "It was a possibility. You thought it had potential, thought it might become permanent. But circumstances, they changed, and they, the relationships, they ended."

"So what happens if our circumstances change?" she asked evenly.

Kane tried to read her expression before answering. It didn't seem like she was asking for a guarantee of happily ever after. He couldn't give her that even if she was. He did need to give her an answer.

"Well, when our circumstances change," he started, paying close attention to each word, "maybe they'll change in a way that lets us, gives us a chance to bring our lives together, for real, not for a couple weeks like this." Her thoughtful expression didn't change. "And if not, well then, hopefully, even if not, we'll have pleasant memories of the time we spent with each other, with someone who cares deeply."

She smiled, finally. "You know, that's a pretty perfect answer."

Kane's shoulders unclenched. Sabella's tongue flicked out over her lips. He bent down, and they shared a slow, unhurried kiss. By the time they continued back to the car, they were both breathless.

Sixteen

When they arrived in Sacramento, they drove directly to the Firedance Lounge, to set up and do a sound check before the evening rush. Settled in a booth with her laptop, out of the way of all the equipment and instruments, Sabella alternated between trying to write another one of her previously pitched articles and taking notes on the bustling activity that seemed to fill the club despite a scarcity of patrons. A busboy collected strewn-about dishes, while dancing to music only he could hear; a few college kids studied at a table masked by a layer of books; a waitress and bartender played cards by the bar in between mixing and delivering drinks; and another waitress argued with someone in hushed tones over the phone. At one point, Bobby slipped in beside Sabella. He started asking about her work, but a shout from Steve called him back to the stage.

Like true older brothers, Kane and Steve made noises about Bobby slacking off, but in reality the equipment was set up swiftly, and soon they all headed out to free the club for the patrons. They had ordered off the club's menu before leaving, and a busty waitress brought their orders out to the tour bus, which was taking up most of the employee lot. It took her a few trips to bring everything out, but her smile lit up to mega-watt status whenever Bobby spoke to her, so she had likely forgotten specifically his drink order on purpose.

Mitch checked in with them as they were finishing up, but he soon left again, to "get a feel for the crowd." Steve and Bobby pulled out their deck of cards, and Kane sprawled on the bed in the back of the bus. He had left both separating doors open, so they could hear him strumming a melody Sabella didn't recognize.

Sabella moved to the driver's seat, swiveling it around so she could observe the scene. The entire setup felt casually habitual, as if the men had done the exact same thing dozens of times before, and they probably had.

Eventually, despite the dubious protection of her laptop, Steve noticed her watching him and Bobby. "You wanna play?" he invited.

Bobby twisted in the booth so he, too, could see her. "Yeah, c'mon, Sabella. If I gotta lose, might as well be while lookin' at you," he added with his customary grin.

Sabella shut her laptop and stood, setting the computer on the counter before joining them. "That waitress might mind if she catches me near you," she teased Bobby, who actually blushed.

Steve chuckled, and the continuing banter drew Kane out to join them. They played a rowdy, prolonged game of Egyptian Ratscrew, which Sabella hadn't played since summer camp many years ago. Bobby was trying to slap back in when Mitch rejoined them.

"Showtime," Kane said. Efficiently, the cards were swept off the table, Kane and Bobby gathered their guitars, and Steve picked up the sticks he had left on the seat beside him. Instinctively adhering to ingrained manners, all of the men waited for Sabella to leave the bus first. Once they entered the club, Sabella and Mitch headed over to separate seats at the bar, as the guys filed onto the stage to a welcoming surge of applause.

Sacramento was the first of a sequence of shows in the Bay Area, and it was a huge success. The audience had been captivated by their performance. Kane had even played a couple encore songs. All three of them were set upon by fans as soon as they left the stage. The crowd didn't even begin to thin out until two in the morning.

At one point, Sabella'd slipped in between groups of fans. She handed him a fresh beer and cupped his neck, pulling his head down to whisper, "Happy Birthday."

When she dropped her hand, Kane pulled back, losing himself for a moment in her cheerful expression. "Thanks." He smiled back and briefly considered ditching the crowd to find a secluded spot with her.

"Who's she?" a woman hissed from a few feet away.

"Cheers," Sabella said, tilting her glass in his direction, before she slipped back into the crowd.

The spot where she'd been was soon filled by a co-ed in a see-through tank top. Kane searched the room between posing for pictures but couldn't find where she'd gone. He was soon distracted with extricating himself from the clingy grips of giggling fans who hadn't let go after taking their photo. Mitch helped him out by bringing through a "VIP," who was thankfully satisfied with a photo and an autographed flyer.

When they left, Kane spotted Sabella in a corner at the edge of the bar. As usual, she tried to fade into the background, observing the activity around her. But to him, she may as well have been under a spotlight. He bee-lined for her, blocking her from view of the room when he reached her.

"Need a break?" she asked, eyes smiling.

"Just rather be with you."

"I bet you say that to all the girls," she joked.

"Only one per show," he teased back. "Tonight's your lucky night."

She laughed and pulled him closer by his shirt. Kane ducked his head to kiss her.

"You're like a drug," he whispered when the kiss ended.

She looked up at him questioningly. "Destructive?"

"Addicting."

Bobby called out for him from somewhere else in the room just then. Kane flashed Sabella an apologetic look then made his way to the group of girls gathered around Bobby.

By the time they finally left the lounge—with the waitress glued to Bobby, and the "VIP" chick hanging off of Mitch—and made it to their room, both he and Sabella didn't do much more than fall into bed. Unfortunately not in the good way.

He woke up to the sound of her moving about the room and glanced groggily at the alarm clock by the bed. It was only nine. "Why're you up?" Their next show was in Davis, which was pretty close. They didn't have to be up for at least a couple hours.

"Shh, go back to sleep," she said softly.

Kane tried to clear his head. She was fully dressed and held her car keys. "Don't go."

She came to the bed, bending down to place her palm lightly on his chest. Kane grabbed her hand. "I just need to run an errand," she murmured. "I'll be back." She dropped a kiss on his lips. "Go back to sleep," she repeated before leaving.

Kane sat up enough to see her suitcase still tucked beside the dresser before letting himself drop back to unconsciousness.

When Sabella stepped out of her car, back at the Comfort Inn, voices emanated from the tour bus. She pulled out a plastic bag with some birthday supplies, left her other purchases in the trunk, and made her way toward the commotion. Bobby appeared in the doorway before she could step aboard.

"You can't come in here," he told her sternly then glanced behind him at the sound of a crash.

"What do you mean? What's going on?" she asked, trying to see around him.

"It's, uh. Wait, where's Kane?"

"I think he's still asleep." When Bobby didn't budge, Sabella shook the bag she held for emphasis and added, "I thought we could decorate the bus a bit for his birthday." Hopefully the reminder of Kane's birthday would inspire Bobby to get the waitress out of the bus and the bed cleaned up, if nothing else.

"Oh, uh, yeah."

"Dammit, Bobby!" Steve yelled inside the bus, following up with a string of expletives.

Bobby considered for a moment then backed up, unblocking the doorway. "Maybe you could help us?" he asked, with a hopeful half-grin.

Sabella stepped tentatively onto the bus. Inside, Steve stood by the kitchenette, splattered with whatever mixture had started out in the bowl in front of him. An opened loaf of bread lay on the counter, along with scraps of mutilated slices. Her mind tried to make sense of the pieces as if they were an abstract painting. One piece of bread somewhat resembled an upper-case letter *B*.

"What are you doing?" she asked. Steve fixed her with a glare, but she laughed in response as the pieces clicked. She extracted a string of letters from the plastic bag and held it up so the guys could see. "This might be an easier way to get the message across." Steve continued to look grim, and Sabella stifled her laughter. "You could make a French toast number instead? For his age?" she suggested.

"That'd be easier," Bobby agreed.

Steve looked like he would rather skewer Bobby with the knife he held, so Sabella quickly interceded. "Why don't you get some of this cleaned up while Steve and I finish?" she told him.

Pretty soon, a pile of French toast lay stacked neatly on a plate, with the top pieces cut into two threes, and the banner hung from the cabinets above the kitchenette. They had also placed candles in thirty-three of the cupcakes Sabella had bought and positioned those into a rough pattern of a guitar on the table. She stashed the extras in a cupboard and surveyed their work.

"Not bad," Steve commented approvingly, clearly in a much better mood. He looked down at his speckled shirt and scowled again. "I'm gonna go change. You should get Kane up," he told her.

"You did most of the work, why don't you call him over after changing?"

He lifted an eyebrow but didn't say anything before leaving the bus, which Sabella took as agreement.

"This's sure better'n last year," Bobby told her as she washed the dishes they had piled into the small sink. "We came in the bus, me and Steve, to try and figure somethin' out for 'is birthday, right? And this girl comes out from the back, wearin' nothin' but Kane's shirt, and she lets out this yelp! We tried to shush her, so she didn't do nothin' to spoil it, y'know? So I tell 'er it's his birthday, and she starts gushin'. So Steve tries to shut 'er up, but Kane comes out with all the noise, and she throws 'erself right in his arms! She starts makin' all these plans like it's *her* birthday not Kane's…" Bobby finally noticed Sabella's lack of response and stopped the flow of words. "Er, sorry," he added after a moment of uncomfortable silence.

"Don't worry about it," she told him, keeping her voice light. She had known Kane had a past that included sleeping with his fans, she reminded herself sternly.

Bobby came up beside her and placed his hand on her shoulder, prompting her to look at him. "I did say they'd just met the night before, right? At our gig. I mean, it wasn't like with you, or nothin'."

He looked genuinely concerned, so she shut off the trickle of water and turned to face him. "I know. Thanks," she assured him.

"Guess that's why they're always tellin' me to shut up, huh?"

"Don't worry about it, Bobby. I'm tougher to scare off than they think."

"Good," he answered, completely serious for once.

Steve led both Mitch and Kane onto the bus before she could question the deeper meaning behind that one word.

Laughter and easy banter filled the combination kitchen-dining area as they lit the candles, which Kane blew out with one breath thanks to his singer's lungs, and everyone partook in a sugary birthday breakfast.

Afterward, with some less-than-subtle urging from Steve, Bobby volunteered to do the dishes, and Kane led Sabella outside. A subtle wind ruffled his hair, dropping it over one eyebrow, and he smiled at her. "Thank you."

Sabella removed a spot of chocolate frosting from below his lip with her thumb. "The guys did most of the work."

"Like your errands?"

"Well." She shrugged instead of finding an answer.

They watched each other, smiles slowly slipping away, until Kane stepped closer and kissed her as if he would have rather devoured her than the toast and cupcakes. Sabella met the passion of his kiss, running her fingers through his hair with a soft pressure.

When they came up for air, Kane stared at her with an intense, penetrating gaze. His thumb shifted directly beneath the clasp of her bra, and he was nearly vibrating with tension. She dropped her hands from the base of his skull to his shoulders.

The sound of shoes hitting pavement snapped their eye contact. "Not to break up the party," Mitch drawled, "but there's somewhere you gotta be." When they didn't move, he added, "You do got twenty minutes before we leave."

Kane nodded. Mitch raked his eyes judgingly over Sabella. She dug her nails into her palms to prevent from backing away, exhaling when he stepped back onto the bus.

"I didn't realize you had something before tonight's show," she said to fill the resulting silence.

"Mitch might've added somethin'," Kane answered nonchalantly.

"Maybe you're taking part in a reenactment in Old Sacramento."

"Don't even joke," he growled, but a smile tugged at his lips nonetheless.

"I'm sure you would make an exceptional cowboy," she teased.

"I'd make a better bandit," he countered. His gaze flowed over her suggestively, but Sabella pretended not to notice, spinning away from him so he couldn't see her cheeks warm.

Never one to miss an opportunity for publicity, Mitch had planned a promotional event for their afternoon in Davis, with Kane's birthday as the hook. A solid group had gathered in a local park, near a burger joint which provided basic catering. Toasts, jokes, and good fun abounded. Unlike after their shows, most people didn't scramble for his attention, since they already felt included in a "private" event. Women flirted but not as shamelessly in the light of day. The upbeat energy was invigorating.

On occasion, Kane glimpsed Sabella laughing with the locals. He wouldn't have minded spending his birthday alone with her, preferably in bed. Then again, since they hadn't had sex yet, that could have proved to be more torture than pleasure. He could barely keep his hands off her as it was.

When most of the food and quite a bit of drink had been consumed, Mitch climbed on a bench and called for attention. "Just wanted to thank y'all for joining us out here today," he said, raising the cup in his hand. "None of us would be here today if it weren't for Kane." Cheers followed. Steve slapped Kane on the back, and Bobby whooped from across the park. Kane grinned back at them all. "We hope you'll continue celebrating with us tonight, over at the Graduate, and make this a very happy birthday for our boy."

People laughed at the shameless plug. Kane admired Mitch's smooth manipulation of the crowd. He hadn't played an empty room once since teaming up with the older man. After Mitch stepped back down, Kane wove his way through handshakes and pats on the back until he reached Sabella. Before they'd left Sacramento, she'd changed her shorts for black pants that clung to her hips beneath a bright purple top that made her hair shine in the sunlight.

Kane clenched his hands to prevent from reaching out for her. An integral part of his image was, as Mitch put it, "unattainable availability." So, he and Sabella mostly kept their distance in public.

When he reached the group she stood with, she turned toward him with one of her bright smiles. "Hey there." A silver charm nestled between the tops of her breasts. Kane probably would've kept staring, but the guy to his left held out his hand.

"Hey, happy birthday, man."

Kane shook the offered hand, taking in his goatee and sagging pants. The guy's entire demeanor felt a little weak, like he couldn't hold his own in a fight against a twelve-year-old. The short, redheaded girl hanging off him didn't seem to mind.

Kane turned up his passive smile. "Thanks. It's nice of y'all to make it out."

"Oh, we just love your music," the girlfriend added.

"I can't believe we're actually here, having this conversation with you," Sabella chimed in. Secret knowledge sparkled in her eyes.

Kane almost choked on the sip he'd taken. The couple didn't catch her sarcasm. "I'm mighty glad of the company," he recovered. Sabella arched an eyebrow at his word choice but then looked at the ground. She tightened her lips to keep back a laugh.

The couple didn't notice that either. The redhead started commenting on some of his lyrics, and Kane tried to focus. He knew he was nothing without his fans, and he genuinely appreciated their support. He just also couldn't get his mind off Sabella when she stood so close.

Many had left the park soon after Mitch's speech, but a few more people joined his group. Eventually, so did Bobby and Steve. Together, they fielded questions about their music, touring, and occasionally their personal lives.

"Have you met anyone special?" one fan got up the courage to ask.

"Kane loves nothing as much as his music," Mitch answered for him, having joined the group after settling things with the caterers. Kane kept a good hold on his personal finances, but he liked knowing he could trust Mitch to take care of the details on tour. The crowd laughed, accepting the answer. "Sorry to break this up folks, but the boys've gotta get ready for tonight's show." Mitch added, subtly weaving in another plug.

The remaining fans took the cue, drifting off with a couple more calls of, "Happy birthday!" and, "See you tonight!"

"Hey, can we buy you a drink tonight?" the redheaded girl asked before walking away.

"You bet," Kane told the couple with a nod. Once they'd headed off, he turned to Sabella. "Any chance I can buy you a drink tonight?" he joked.

"I'll think about it," she teased back with a sweet smile.

"I can be quite persuasive."

Sabella opened her mouth to answer, but Steve interrupted wryly, "Break it up you two."

Laughing, all of them made their way to the bus.

That night's show went extremely well. Kane liked the Graduate, and he'd played there on every one of his West Coast tours so far. There were more than a few familiar faces from earlier, and he made sure to acknowledge them. One woman called out a birthday greeting in a lull between songs. Bobby encouraged her by playing the tune. The crowd chimed in, and the whole room sang to him in a humbling gesture. Kane raised the beer bottle he always brought on stage in a salute. He deviated from the set to play an upbeat foot-stomper, to laughter and cheers. Then, seeking out Sabella, he switched to one of his favorite ballads.

A soft smile graced her lips and touched her eyes as he played. Like a few times before, he felt her eyes on him even when his own were closed. A momentary hush filled the room when he ended the song, telling him he'd succeeded in reaching the audience in a rare way.

An enthusiastic rush of people surrounded him after the show. People asked for photos and autographs but also offered to buy him drinks. Much of the time, Kane declined politely, keeping tabs on his consumption. Certain people insisted, and Kane was unusually glad for his high tolerance. Already, this was shaping up to be a long and fun night. He was damn lucky.

Soon after the show, Sabella slipped into a group he stood with by the bar. She took advantage of a strangely heated argument about whether he'd written a specific song to tell him, "I'm going to head back. I'll see you back at the hotel, okay?"

Kane let the argument continue for the bit of privacy it afforded. "You all right? You want me to take you back?"

She shook her head. "I'm fine. I'll see you soon?" she half-asked.

Kane nodded automatically. Should he try to change her mind?

One of the people arguing must have realized there was an easy way to end the dispute and asked Kane directly. In the minute it took Kane to settle the debate, Sabella had disappeared from the club.

Seventeen

Sabella gathered the bag she had placed in her trunk that morning before returning to their room. The Comfort Inn was probably the nicest place they had stayed so far, possibly as a gesture for Kane's birthday, though it wasn't likely that had swayed Mitch when making reservations.

She had been thinking about the right time to elevate her and Kane's relationship since her first day with them on tour, with Gina's enthusiastic encouragement. Kane's birthday turned out to be one week after the lunch he had masterfully prepared for her—one week since he'd invited her to join them.

When she thought about it in those terms, it didn't seem like enough time, but nothing about their relationship had matched her mental guidelines, and time almost flowed differently on tour. In that week, they had spent more time together than some couples would have in months of dating. Their conversation the day before had tipped the scales for her. Kane hadn't attempted to convince her he loved her—she would never have believed him if he had—but his words had felt genuine. Similarly, the time *felt* right.

Sabella pulled out the extra candles she had bought that morning and placed them strategically around the room. She grouped several candles on the dresser in front of the mirror, so the reflection would amplify the resulting glow. Forcing herself not to fidget with their placement, Sabella turned to her suitcase. On her last day in Portland, Gina had insisted on them going negligée shopping. As usual, she had been right, and Sabella was grateful her friend had convinced her to pack two slinky options, one of which would hopefully augment her fledgling sexual confidence tonight. She chose the sapphire baby doll and also pulled out a box of condoms Gina had not-so-subtly tucked into the suitcase.

Sabella opened the box to place several condoms on the bedside table, laid out the vibrant baby doll and matching panties, and stripped so she could shower. She twisted her hair up and out of the way, clipping it into place, and turned the squeaky knob to run the water. It wasn't entirely clear how much time she would have before Kane returned, but she should have at least an hour given their post-show obligations.

Still, Sabella rushed with anxious anticipation. She shaved with particular care and then stepped out of the steamy shower. Lotion she had bought months ago as a birthday treat was then slathered over her skin, and she stayed wrapped in the towel while touching up her makeup.

First, she relined her eyes, then she added some purple and gold shadows and a rose lip gloss. Finally, she couldn't put off dressing any longer. After patting her skin absolutely dry, she slipped into the negligée. The baby doll provided support for her cleavage with underwire, solid cups, before flowing down into a silky yet sheer lace with a solid trim. The draping helped hide the fact that she absolutely never worked out her abs, but the sheer fabric still hinted at her passable waistline. Despite Gina's urging to experiment with a G-string, and the dirty double *entendres* that followed given Kane's occupation, Sabella had selected a matching string bikini which helped her feel sexy rather than uncomfortable.

Finally, she removed the clip and shook out her hair. Slightly dampened waves fell over her shoulders. She took one last look in the bathroom mirror then slipped the strappy heels she had worn that day back on.

Self-consciousness forced her to survey the result once again in the bedroom mirror. Overall, she didn't look half-bad, she persuaded herself. She would have liked to have had time for a manicure, but presumably Kane wouldn't notice that her nails were bare.

She circled the room with a lighter before switching off the overhead light. The candles washed the space in a soft, romantic glow, and the lack of lighting would help the baby doll hide her too-plump tummy from Kane's sight, if not his touch. All she could do now was await Kane's imminent return and hope she wouldn't chicken out before then.

❖ ❖ ❖

Kane left the Davis Graduate as soon as he could, taking the rental car. He'd extricated himself from the fans fairly early and promised the guys he would make his bailing, again, up to them. It was the first time Sabella had left a gig before him. Maybe she wasn't feeling well, or maybe the tour schedule was starting to get to her. There was also the chance she would pack up and leave, fed up. A voice in his head whispered that she might be planning some birthday surprise, but he tried to ignore it. It was never good to get his hopes up.

When he got to the room, he saw only a dim, flickering light inside. He forced down his disappointment as he carefully opened the door and set his guitar down, moving as quietly as possible so he didn't wake her. The tour schedule was pretty tough, and she had gotten up even earlier than necessary that morning, just for him.

"Kane?" His head snapped up, ready to apologize for disturbing her. But Sabella wasn't in bed.

She stood in front of him, wearing only a sheer blue negligée and heels. Stunned, Kane didn't move. In the back of his mind, he realized the shimmering light was coming from candles she'd lit around the room. If this was an alcohol-induced hallucination, he was okay with that.

The candlelight flickered over her features, highlighting first her eyes, then her lips, then her eyes again. It shimmered over her bare skin and loose hair, which curled over her shoulders to brush the tops of her breasts. The light taunted him, touching her everywhere he wanted to feel, to taste.

"Happy Birthday," she murmured timidly when he still didn't move.

Kane snapped out of it and kicked the door shut without looking, then closed the distance between them. "You look unbelievable," he said quietly. He stood inches away but didn't touch her, still partly afraid to shatter this image.

She smiled softly, relaxing as if she'd thought he could have ever turned her down. Her tongue passed over her lips, and Kane swallowed roughly, watching the motion almost despite himself. This was about to become an unforgettable birthday. "You sure?" he whispered.

Sabella smiled more brightly and tilted her chin up in invitation.

Sunday, Sabella awoke enveloped in Kane's arms, entirely ensconced in his warmth. For once, she didn't spring out of bed but rather relaxed into the embrace. She was drifting back off to sleep when the alarm rang a few minutes later. Kane open his eyes and kissed her through a smile.

"We have to get going," she whispered, before rolling away from him reluctantly. Kane's groan followed her to the bathroom, and Sabella smiled. Last night had been amazing, and they hadn't spent much time sleeping, which didn't change the fact that they needed to check out and move on to the next tour stop.

After a lightning-fast shower, she opened the door, wrapped in only a small hotel towel, to see Kane standing on the other side, still gloriously naked. He blocked her path and kissed her again, and Sabella sagged into his body, though some part of her acknowledged that they didn't have time.

A pounding on the door forced Kane to pull away. He reached past her to grab a towel, which he wrapped around his waist before opening the door barely enough to see the person on the other side. Sabella tightened her towel around herself and remained out of sight until he had shut the door again.

Kane slowly raked his eyes over her, lips curling in a mildly predatory smile, then sighed. "You were right, we gotta hurry up." Regret saturated his words.

"You should probably jump in that shower then," she answered.

He dropped the towel obediently and headed toward her, the suggestive smile still across his face. Memories of the night before flashed through her mind, and Sabella stepped away from the bathroom, face flushing.

"Care to join me?" he invited from the doorway.

"That doesn't sound like it would be fast."

Amusement joined the heat in his expression. "Definitely not."

✧ ✧ ✧

Once they'd made it to San Francisco, Kane and Sabella split off from the other guys. He couldn't stop thinking about how she'd felt last night, and his palms itched to touch her. He'd been right—she was addicting.

He was in such a good mood after last night, even Bobby noticed a change. The unbearable sexual tension between Sabella and him had turned into a more comfortable, constant awareness.

They wandered through Golden Gate Park. It was a sunny day, though being San Francisco, it was also nicely cool outside. Bits and pieces of possible lyrics floated through his mind. When the wind picked up, Kane automatically brushed his hair from his face. Sabella tied hers back. Kane wouldn't have minded watching the wind whip it around. It hadn't taken long last night for her hair to become wonderfully tousled as a result of their passion.

After a quick lunch at Crepevine, they headed back. It was still early enough in the afternoon that they had a few hours before they needed to set up. Kane wanted to make some sense of the song pieces in his mind. Since Sabella hadn't had time to herself yesterday, he figured she also needed to write. At least, she hadn't objected to them heading back after lunch.

Once in the room, Kane tried to find a way to tell her he needed to be alone with his guitar, but she spoke first.

"So, I wanted to make some calls, and maybe work. Do you want me to go find a coffee shop or something? That way you can write or play in peace. Or nap," she added, biting back a smile.

She'd almost read his mind. "Nah, I can go out to the bus or something. It's out of the way, and that way you can stay here or go out. Your call."

She nodded, watching him. "Okay."

Unwilling to pass up the opportunity, Kane tugged her closer for a kiss. Slowly, they tasted each other, first with only lips, but soon more deeply, tongues twisting together. Kane held her close, and she melted into him. Her hands played over his chest, slipped up into his hair, skimmed over his arms. Beneath his palms, he felt the soft swell from her waist to her hips.

They took their time, letting the kiss draw out with the knowledge that tonight, it would be more. Finally, both of them pulled back. Heat filled every spot where her body brushed against his. Maybe they should take a different kind of advantage of their free time.

Sabella stepped away, sensible as always. When she licked her lips, he almost covered the minimal space between them again.

"You wanted to go write," she reminded him.

"Maybe I need some more inspiration," Kane countered.

Other women he'd known would have found a nonexistent insult in his words. Sabella just laughed and walked deeper into the room. She removed her computer from her suitcase before turning toward the bed. "You're still here?" she asked him with mock surprise.

Kane shook his head with a smile, picked up his guitar, and left, whistling the start of a new tune.

Eighteen

When Kane left, Sabella sent a text message to Gina, asking her to go on Skype, and settled back with her laptop. As she waited for a response, she answered some emails, including a fairly promising message from an editor about her "Art of Writing" article, and one from her parents, who were loving their well-deserved, extended European adventure.

The ringing that indicated an incoming Skype call interrupted her idle Internet browsing. She answered the call and smiled at the image that popped up. "Hey, Gina."

"Hey, pretty lady. What's going on?" On the other end, Gina sat in her living room, looking stylish as ever. Her uneven cut was growing out beautifully, but today she had her hair pinned back on each side, which masked the cut, creating an entirely different look.

"Well, that sapphire negligée was a big hit," Sabella told her.

Gina let out a small scream of surprised approval. "You

slept with him! Tell me everything. Was he magnificent? Or is he more looks than lover?" she asked, scrunching her nose.

"Slow down!" Sabella interjected, laughing. "Oh, Gi, it was amazing. He was… Well, suffice it to say, if I had ever had sex like this before, I would have had a much more difficult time abiding by my moral convictions until now."

"Wow. I mean, I know you have a pretty low standard here, but so, at the very least, he's good for something!"

"He's good for a lot of things!" Sabella defended then blushed. "But he's definitely pretty fantastic at this, too."

"Well, look at you," Gina commented with a proud smile.

"Oh Gina, I can't even describe it. He's so considerate, and protective, but in that comforting way, and funny, and sharp—so smart…" Sabella trailed off. Gina was watching her with a thoughtful expression. "I think I really like him," Sabella finished, almost pleadingly. She needed Gina to talk this through so her diving in emotionally didn't feel so premature, or perhaps to talk some sense into her.

"Sounds like it," Gina agreed. "But, you know that's okay, right? He's not Riley."

Sabella sobered at the mention of her first college boyfriend. Like an idiot, she had believed from early on not only that she would marry him one day, but also that she was, as he had insisted, truly everything he had ever wanted and more. He had claimed she meant everything to him and that he would never hurt her.

After she had lost her virginity to him one awkward night, he had apparently found a girl who meant even more, or maybe she was simply better in bed. Sabella had been naïvely idealistic in that relationship, but she liked to think she wasn't a complete idiot, and she had learned quickly from her mistake. Practical considerations had swiftly replaced idyllic dreams. The few guys she had dated after Riley had been kind, attractive, and interesting—perfect on paper, and the relationships had mostly been pleasant enough. Ultimately, though, Sabella hadn't been able to discard her dream of a deeply romantic, passionate love, so she had found reasons to end the relationships. Most importantly, she hadn't allowed her unruly emotions to have more than a modicum of control over her behavior, until this story with Kane had swept her along with an atypical series of choices.

"Sabella, listen to me," Gina continued sincerely when Sabella didn't respond. "Riley was a jerk. He wasn't your Prince Charming, but that doesn't mean there isn't one out there. You're allowed to care, even deeply, about the man you're with. In fact, I'm told it's kind of encouraged. Your instincts are better honed now; you can't keep yourself pleasantly closed off from real emotions anymore. And if Kane's the one to break through that impenetrable shell of yours, and he's also rocking your world in bed, then count your lucky stars and enjoy it."

"But what if his feelings, whatever they may be, or even mine, what if it's all temporary? Transient? You've heard the unfettered passion in his voice when he sings songs based on girls from his past. If he feels so fervently for every girl, doesn't that ultimately make his feelings somehow less?"

"People have baggage," Gina countered. "He used his experiences, probably heightening them for effect, for his music—and that's completely normal. What he felt for a past love may not have lasted, but that doesn't make it any less real. Sometimes, you need to let right now be enough. Let the future play itself out. You say you can't even always control the characters in stories that you make up; you have no hope of trying to control or predict real life. And if this ends, you'll have great memories of a unique experience."

"Kane said something similar," Sabella admitted, contemplating the advice.

"Plus, you'll have had some outstanding sex," Gina added, lightening the mood.

"When did you become so wise?" Sabella teased.

"Hey, I may not be the poster child for committed relationships, but only because I rarely find someone worth caring about. That doesn't mean I don't believe in romance. Kane's made some grand gestures for you, and quite frankly, if all he wanted was a girl in his bed, I doubt he'd have trouble finding one in every city on his tour. He's choosing to be with you, and that means something. If he's making you happy enough that you're opening up emotionally, so much the better. Not much beats an ardent summer fling," she finished with a wink.

"Speaking of," Sabella said, steering the topic away from her dubious, though admittedly exhilarating, relationship, "how is Alistair? Are you still seeing him?"

"Yes, actually."

"Has he whisked you away to some fabulous location on a private jet yet?"

Gina smiled at the idea, and her eyes dropped pensively. "No, not yet. He's actually spent the night a couple times, though."

"And you haven't kicked him out in the middle of the night after being sufficiently satisfied?" Sabella asked disbelievingly.

"What can I say? Maybe it's time for me to settle down in a more solid relationship, too."

"As long as he continues to make you happy," Sabella agreed. She observed her friend a bit more closely on the screen. "I keep catching you when you're wearing gray." At the moment, Gina wasn't even wearing a vibrant scarf to offset the sleek shell, but there was probably an ambitiously patterned skirt hidden from view.

"Sometimes sedate colors are more becoming, and more appropriate," Gina answered uncharacteristically.

Sabella laughed. "Did you just hear yourself? You're a torchbearer for outstanding and striking vivacity in a woman's wardrobe."

"Ostentatious looks aren't always the best idea." Gina shrugged off her comment. "I'm diversifying my style."

"Okay. Well, you're the fashion mogul," Sabella backed off, seeing she had inadvertently upset her. "Far be it from me to question your decisions." Gina barely smiled, so she added, "I miss you."

Excess tension seeped out of Gina's posture, and she smiled more genuinely. "I miss you, too, Sab. Sounds like you're having a great adventure. Don't be afraid to experiment if Kane suggests something," she advised, waggling her eyebrows.

"What in the world do you mean?"

"I mean, sex doesn't have to happen in a bed," Gina stated bluntly.

Sabella blushed despite herself. "I know that!"

"Well, maybe now you'll have a chance to experience it in real life. Just follow Kane's lead. If he doesn't introduce you to some alternatives, I'll be extremely disappointed," she said with mock severity.

Sabella wrinkled her nose, her mouth twisting to one side. She had absolutely nothing appropriate to say in response to that. Insofar as she had understood, Kane had already suggested one alternative—shower sex—earlier that day. She had played off her refusal as an issue of timing. In reality, while the idea of shower sex wasn't at all shocking to her—since her friendship with Gina, she had been introduced to significantly more outrageous theoretical possibilities—neither was it an existing part of her repertoire.

Gina's doorbell rang, and her head snapped in the direction of the sound. "Oh! Sab, I have to go. We'll talk soon, okay?" she said hurriedly.

"Thanks for the perspective and advice," Sabella started to say, but Gina ended the call before the sentiment was out. It wasn't like her to rush goodbyes rather than allow whoever stood on the other side of the door to wait, but she probably had exciting plans with Alistair, and Sabella certainly couldn't begrudge her a blissfully exciting relationship.

Things fell into an easy pattern after Kane's birthday. Sabella found time for her work, got along with the other guys, and didn't seem to mind either the bizarre schedule or the flirting that went along with his image. Kane was nearly done fiddling with a couple new songs, inspired by her.

Most days, they found a few hours to be on their own, which somehow never became strained or boring. They continued to get very little sleep, but Kane sure didn't mind. Sabella's open and enthusiastic approach to sex was intoxicating. She read his responses so well and was so willing, Kane almost couldn't believe it.

Her suggestions in their down time made them all see more of every city than the club, hotel room, and tour bus, as they'd done on other tours. Monday night, after their promotion at Stanford, they all explored downtown Palo Alto. Tuesday, before their show at Club Rodeo, they spent a lazy afternoon on outdoor couches in the Santana Row district, though Steve and Bobby took off pretty quickly.

Wednesday, they left the Bay Area and drove down to San Luis Obispo. The return to a smaller setting at once offered a nice break and promised a boring evening. But, at Sabella's urging, they detoured to visit the mission before heading to the Los Padres Inn.

As they finished dinner at Pappy Macgregor's, Bobby pulled out a deck of cards. They played a couple rounds of BS, at which Sabella failed pretty spectacularly because she licked her lips every time she bluffed—an easy tell, which Kane found both reassuring and endearing. The other guys didn't seem to notice.

"What's next?" Bobby asked after a third round.

"Crazy eights?" Kane suggested.

"Are you guys up for going out tonight?" Sabella asked.

"Go where?" Steve asked. Bobby started dealing the cards again.

"We could go out dancing?" Outright laughter met her idea, drawing a few patrons' eyes.

"This kinda dancin's not exactly our style," Bobby felt the need to explain.

"What about country dancing? I'm betting you fellas know how to lead a girl around the floor," she fake drawled with a touch of sarcasm.

"Where?" Mitch asked. He'd begun giving in to Sabella's suggestions, seeing how much the guys enjoyed them. The promo shots turning out well hadn't hurt.

"Actually, at the SLO Brewing Company. Their page says they're having a country dance night."

"Well you just might be on to something," Mitch said thoughtfully. Bobby and Steve watched him warily. Kane wouldn't have minded, if there was decent music. "It'd be an okay way to get some extra bodies back tomorrow night," Mitch decided.

"Oh well, I didn't intend to make you feel like you have to work," Sabella protested, glancing apologetically at Kane. He placed his hand on her thigh reassuringly, and a bit to cop a feel.

"I think you boys can handle dancing with some beautiful women," Mitch said. Once he caught onto a publicity idea, he wasn't likely to let it go. And it really didn't seem like a bad way to build the audience for their show tomorrow night.

When they arrived at the club, all the men flanked Sabella, drawing more than a few jealous eyes her way from the single women who took note of the group's entrance. The attention prickled along her skin, following their movement from the doorway, around to a table with an impromptu "reserved" sign. Once the idea was out there, Mitch had called the club's manager to arrange their visit. Sabella truly hadn't intended for this to become a publicity stunt, but the guys didn't seem to mind too much.

The brewery had old-fashioned architecture, with wooden pillars and exposed brick walls, which featured a mosaic-style pattern. Most of the floor was kept bare, though it was filled with swaying bodies, and some basic, polished-wood seating had been placed around the room's perimeter. The slightly raised stage was empty, except for a disc jockey who selected a variety of country tunes with differing beats.

Before they even got settled, Bobby held out his hand to her with a customarily cheeky grin. "The cutest one gets the first dance, right?"

The other men exchanged mildly exacerbated glances, but, as usual, Sabella simply laughed. "Since you're the youngest, sure. Wouldn't want to keep you out past your bedtime."

"Don't you worry," he countered, gaze circling the room. "I plan to be in bed mighty soon."

They danced a two-step that mostly consisted of Bobby trying to avoid stepping on her feet as she flailed in her attempts to follow his lead. A few times, Sabella tried to pull him off the floor prematurely, but he stuck with her until the song ended then led her back to their table quite courteously.

"Well, now. Reckon it's my turn," Mitch said at their approach, standing up.

The disc jockey played a waltz, and Sabella scrambled to find a reason to back out.

"Don't you worry. These ol' feet can take it," Mitch cut her off, leading her to the floor.

Surprisingly, Sabella didn't trip over her own feet as they danced. Mitch held her in a solid frame, directing her as if he frequently danced with neophytes. Come to think of it, for all she knew, he did. It was peculiar, dancing with him, especially a relatively intimate dance, since he primarily avoided acknowledging her presence altogether.

"You seem to have quite an effect on Kane," he commented as they danced.

"How do you mean?" Sabella asked, making every effort to remain detachedly polite. Mitch was an important and trusted member of Kane's world, and she had no desire to alienate him.

"Your joinin' us has helped his music, added somethin' to his performances."

"That's kind of you. I'm not sure I have quite that impressive an impact on his work."

"Don't underestimate the value of your...talents. I bet you've had quite the—impact, did you say?—on many a man."

Sabella tensed, not missing the implication but fumbling several steps. Mitch subtly lowered his hand to below her waist, but she tried to ignore the inappropriate movement, acting as though it was a natural part of his guiding her around the floor, though she knew otherwise. She silently reminded herself that she had been raised to handle any situation with aplomb, though she would have preferred to emulate Gina and slap him, whirling off the floor. Still, upbringing and a deference to their inevitable continued contact won out. "I'm sure I don't know what you mean," Sabella told him.

Thankfully, the song ended soon afterward, and she pulled away from his hold. She headed toward the table where Kane sat, nursing a beer, and Mitch stepped in beside her, acting the part of a genuine Southern gentleman. Bobby and a bright-eyed brunette in a handkerchief-style top that was held on by two thin straps around her back beat them to the table, providing a welcome addition and distraction, as far as Sabella was concerned.

She slid onto the bench beside Kane, who placed his arm around her and offered her his beer, which she accepted to fill her mouth and prevent any ability to speak. Bobby's chatty companion filled the conversational gap without hesitation.

When a West Coast swing came over the sound system, Kane stood and held his hand out to Sabella. She placed her hand in his with an almost automatic ease. Kane took a last sip of his beer then led her to the floor. He started with some basic steps, making sure to direct her movement. West Coast swing was tricky to lead, mostly because partners spent most of their time connected only through their hands. Not for the first time, Sabella surprised him. She followed his leads quite easily, only hesitating occasionally.

"You're pretty good at this," he told her sincerely.

"I might kind of be cheating," she admitted, with a semi-concerned smile. Intrigued, Kane waited for her to explain. "I took dance lessons when I was younger. For a few years, actually. Not this kind of dance, obviously, but following is basically the same."

"Well, then. Let's see what you can do," he challenged. He led her in some of the more complicated steps he knew, and she followed almost seamlessly. Back home, people would've seen that the steps weren't familiar to her. Kane was impressed anyway. She held her own up until the last step, when he turned her into a dip that ended up tangled somehow. He brought her out of it, both of them laughing.

A ballad played next, and Kane gathered her close. He wrapped one arm around her waist, holding the other bent between them. Her free hand rested on the front of his shoulder. He kept their steps to an easy box, enjoying the relaxed familiarity of their eye contact. He wanted to pull her even closer, to dip his head for a kiss, but kept a respectable distance for the sake of appearances. Though, at this point, he probably wouldn't have cared if his fans found out. Still, Mitch was right. Kane didn't want to risk alienating any of the women who were pretty much the basis for his success.

At the end of the song, both of them hesitated a few moments before separating. A small group gathered for a line dance, and Kane led Sabella out of their way. Bobby and his latest companion had disappeared somewhere, but Mitch and Steve were back at their table. Steve stood as they got closer.

He nodded at Kane then said to Sabella, "Save the best for last."

"Oh, I really don't know this dance," she said uneasily. "Next one?"

"You look like a fast learner," Steve assured her, taking her back to the floor. Kane watched them for a while as Steve talked her through the basic figures.

A pair of women came up to their table, asking Kane and Mitch to dance, and they obliged. Mitch talked up their show the entire time. The women promised to come back the next night, casting flirty smiles Kane's way.

All in all, they spent a couple hours at the club, dancing and drinking. Soon after Bobby disappeared with the enthusiastic brunette, Kane suggested to Sabella that they head out, too. He half expected her to ask for a couple more dances, but she agreed easily.

"Are you tired?" she asked as they walked outside.

"Not exactly."

Amused heat filled her eyes when she realized his meaning. "So, we're not heading to bed?" she asked, feigning innocence, unsuccessfully.

"Didn't say that, now, did I?" Even in the dim light of the street lamps, he could tell she blushed. A quick lick of her lips followed. "We could skip the bed if you'd rather," he added casually, mostly to goad her.

She saw right through him, laughing at the suggestion. Truthfully, Kane was perfectly content in bed with her. But he wasn't opposed to trying other locations either. Sabella was still shy, tentative at first, but she usually relaxed quickly enough. He'd have to find a way to entice her to try some other options.

Nineteen

As the tour continued, Sabella found a comfortable rhythm for her sporadic bursts of writing, and the musicians all appeared more comfortable with her presence. Someone had snapped photographs of her and Kane together when they had gone out dancing, and speculation abounded, though his fans generally responded supportively. Kane hadn't appeared perturbed. He now acted with less calculated restraint after his shows, frequently seeking out Sabella and publicly acknowledging their relationship with unmistakable body language they hadn't previously permitted themselves. She hadn't minded before, but the change was surprisingly nice.

The photos they had taken at Mount Shasta had also been met with overwhelming approval once posted on his website. Sabella particularly loved one shot when the wind had begun playing with Kane's hair, gently puffing it around his face, with Steve and Bobby standing offset behind him. All three men appeared solemn—pensive yet solid—and they were not the least bit overshadowed by the magnificent mountain behind them. Even Mitch approved.

In private, her and Kane's nights continued to be filled with fairly spectacular lovemaking. Kane was at once demanding and considerate in bed, subtly expanding her realm of experience. Sabella wasn't completely naïve, having read an abundance of detailed scenes in a variety of romance novels that provided an outlet for her idealistic views on relationships, but being with Kane exposed her to new heights in real life, some of which matched literary scenes she had previously believed to be completely fictitious—fabricated for enhanced effect. They virtually always fell asleep naked, bodies intimately entwined.

Despite this new physicality of their relationship, Kane still insisted on a few hours alone for the two of them during the day, which continually reassured her that her value to him was more than as a physical convenience.

In Santa Barbara, they chose the beach over another park. They strode through the sand at the water's edge, with the waves occasionally lapping at their feet. On a secluded out-cropping of rocks near their parking spot, he played her a new song, ostensibly inspired by her, about the intoxicating, metaphorically mind-altering effect of even their relatively innocent behavior. *Addictive*, he had called her once.

On her end, Sabella knew she hadn't remained as emo-tionally detached as she had intended. Each day that they spent together gave Kane more pull over her heart, though her perfected denial usually protected her from acknowledging her exponentially increasing affection. She had become so accustomed to his company that she barely registered his light accent anymore.

On their first day in Los Angeles, the guys had an understandably hectic schedule. Sabella tagged along to their radio interview, but, at Mitch's suggestion, she didn't accompany them for their dinner plans with some consequential executives, which ended at a bar-sponsored whiskey night.

Kane brought back a bottle of Jack Daniel's for them to share. Sabella greeted him in the second negligée she had packed. This one was black silk, with curving lace panels that traced from below her bust, in toward her waist, and down to mid-hip. The look seemed to receive an ardent vote of approval from Kane. He responded so enthusiastically that their first time that night happened with her pressed against the wall, her legs wrapped around Kane, who discarded his shirt but still wore unzipped jeans. Thankfully, they both somehow nevertheless had the presence of mind to use a condom. Later that night, he traced the marks his jeans had left on her thighs with his tongue.

Occasionally, Sabella checked in with Gina, but their schedules had become largely incompatible, so the conversations stayed short. Overall, the impression she had was that Gina was content, though she appeared to be particularly stressed, by work or something. Hopefully, she was able to turn to Alistair for solace, though he was likely so professionally driven himself as to lack the appropriate compassion for Gina's ranting version of stress relief. Sabella once proposed Gina take an afternoon off with Roger, but Gina brushed away the suggestion before needing to end the call.

A week after their night out dancing, they drove the longest distance between shows since Sabella had joined them—from San Diego, where they had all spent an afternoon exploring the world-renowned zoo, to Phoenix. It was a six-hour trip, the first of many from there on out. They stopped a little over halfway through for a quick, yet delicious, lunch that Kane whipped up in the tour bus' kitchenette. Sabella offered to drive the second leg of the trip, but Kane declined, politely yet decisively, the same way he declined when she offered to pay for the gas they frequently poured into her car.

From Phoenix, they went on to Las Vegas, where they were scheduled to remain for five full nights, with two shows over the weekend, and undoubtedly some publicity promotions or business meetings. Everyone seemed excited about the opportunity to stay settled for an extended length of time.

Late Saturday morning, Kane and the others left to see the space for that night's show, which required some creative setup as it was significantly larger than the majority of the tour's other venues. Despite her lack of personal affection for Mitch, Sabella privately admitted he had lined up some tremendous opportunities for the musicians this weekend.

Rather than spending the alone time writing, Sabella took advantage of being unoccupied at an unusually reasonable time of day to catch up with Gina. "Hey stranger," she greeted when Gina answered the Skype call.

"Hi, Sabella," Gina answered. The collection of old-fashion sketches of European cities that hung in her bedroom showed behind her, though choosing her bed rather than her extraordinarily comfortable couch was uncharacteristic. Come to think of it, so was using Sabella's entire name in greeting.

"What's going on, Gi? Are you not feeling well?" Sabella asked, concerned.

"Oh, no. I'm fine!" Gina rushed to reassure her. "Where are you guys now?"

Sabella accepted the change of topic but expanded the video so it filled her screen. Gina's hair was slicked back into a ponytail, though a few strands had escaped, and she wore no noticeable makeup, not that she ever needed it. Still, both choices were unlike her, as was the white scarf knotted haphazardly at her neck.

"We are in Vegas. We're actually supposed to stay here until Wednesday," Sabella told her.

"Wow. Make sure to stay away from any corrupting influences," Gina advised without a trace of humor. Sabella's brows inched toward her hairline, and Gina added, "You know, don't go so full-out with new experiences that you end up in a dangerous situation."

"Of course not," Sabella agreed. "We always talk about me lately. Tell me how things are going with Alistair."

Gina's eyes widened for a second, and she bit her bottom lip. A forced smile flashed briefly before she pressed her lips together. "Oh, things are fine," she answered with a pleasantly wiped expression. "We talk about your life because you're the one off on a once-in-a-lifetime adventure."

Something must have drawn Gina's attention to the window because she turned her head. With the motion, lighting in her room shifted over her face, and Sabella could have sworn she saw a faint mark on her cheekbone, but Gina turned back to the screen before she could be certain.

"So, have you had any more fights about his fame?" Gina asked, fiddling with the scarf around her neck.

Sabella squinted at the screen; something seemed off about the shadows covering Gina's neck as the scarf moved.

"Uhm, no…" Sabella answered, barely registering the question. She wrested her attention back to the conversation. "Things have been great, actually. Some fans found out about me, and there wasn't a backlash like they, well mostly Mitch, had apparently expected. We've gotten to a pretty comfortable place, and I'm actually really glad I did this."

"That's wonderful," Gina said with her first genuine, though subdued, smile of the conversation. In the background, Sabella heard the front door shut loudly. Gina's smile dropped, and her eyes jerked to gaze over the laptop's camera as though she could see through the wall separating her bedroom from the entryway. The computer tilted on Gina's lap. The movement must have thrown off the small camera, since her face seemed to empty of its color.

"I have to go, I'm sorry," she blurted, shutting her computer before Sabella had a chance to respond.

The bizarre conversation replayed in Sabella's mind to utter distraction. Something was definitely wrong with Gina, but she didn't want to jump to any conclusions. Moments from their recent talks whirled in her mind, pieces of a puzzle she couldn't place.

She was still replaying the conversation when someone knocked on the hotel room's door. Sabella heaved herself off the bed to answer it.

Mitch stood on the other side, wearing his habitual jeans, faded shirt, and dark jacket. "Oh, did Kane forget something?" Sabella asked him absently.

"Well, now, you could say that," he said, brushing past her into the room. His eyes flicked over her, and Sabella fought the urge to cross her arms in front of herself. She remained by the door, keeping it open.

"Can I help you find something, then?"

"Well, darlin', I figured you an' me, we might talk. It's about time, don't you think?"

His words took her aback, especially considering how infrequently he had acknowledged her presence, which generally happened only when Kane was around to notice. "Talk?" she echoed.

"You've taken to this life, to tourin', mightily. Kane's fans have taken to you, too. I've got a proposition for you." He hadn't said anything inappropriate, and yet discomfort from being alone with him crawled along her skin.

Someone spoke outside, and Sabella recognized the voices as those of the returning musicians. "I'm a little hungry, actually, so, if you'd like to talk, perhaps we should have some lunch," she suggested to draw him out of the room. She picked up the purse she had thankfully left right inside the doorway and stepped through the opening, leaving Mitch little choice other than to join her outside.

Kane saw Sabella leaving their hotel room with Mitch. She smiled when she noticed him, though it looked a bit superficial for her. "What's going on?" he asked her once they'd met.

"We were just discussing getting lunch. How was the space?" She tilted her face up for a kiss.

Kane brushed her lips with his before answering. "It's pretty great. Big. We've got a lot to do to set up."

"You can take a break to eat, though, right? Have lunch?"

He looked from her to Mitch, who stood a few feet away. He wasn't an idiot, and he'd picked up on the tension that sparked between them now and again. He hadn't made sense of it yet. He did know Sabella could take care of herself, not that he believed she needed protecting from Mitch. They probably just needed some more time to shake out whatever wasn't gelling between them. "Sorry, Bella. We really have to get back."

She licked her lips, gaze dropping for a moment. "Please?" she murmured. "It could be a super quick lunch."

"Don't you worry, Kane. I'll take care of her. You boys should probably get the gear and head back, else you might miss dinner, too," Mitch joked.

Kane cupped Sabella's shoulders, brushing his thumbs over them reassuringly. Sure, she and Mitch had yet to get along, but she seemed particularly upset. "You all right?" he asked quietly.

"Yeah, yes," she answered, visibly shaking her head as if to clear it.

"If you don't have to work, come by after lunch. There's a casino across the hall. Maybe you'll get lucky."

"Oh, is that not guaranteed today?" she asked with more of her usual mischief.

Kane laughed, dropping his head down for another kiss. Bobby's call from across the parking lot tore him away.

Steve caught up to Mitch and Sabella as they headed toward one of the many nearby all-you-can-eat buffets. "Thought Kane should do his time, babysitting Bobby," he said as explanation.

"You're lettin' 'em handle your drums?" Mitch asked.

"No way. I'll have time after lunch," Steve answered easily.

It was unlike him to leave the others to set everything up, but Sabella was grateful for his presence. She was likely being paranoid, but it was nonetheless best to avoid the risk.

Their lunch conversation mostly centered around work, commentary about that night's space and some logistics for the rest of their time in Vegas. All in all, it was the most vocal she had ever heard Steve be.

After their first round of food, Steve excused himself from the table. Sabella twirled her fork in the remaining lobster salad on her plate. The buffets weren't particularly expensive, considering the reasonable quality of the wide variety of foods they offered. Presumably, they served mostly to keep visitors contained in the buildings that housed the casinos, which everyone acknowledged as the true moneymakers, though that apparently didn't prevent people from wasting hours in front of machines or, for the more adventurous, at gaming tables.

"This tour, it won't last forever," Mitch commented soon after Steve's departure.

"That is the nature of tours, as far as I am aware," Sabella acknowledged, keeping her tone neutral.

"A girl like you, you may be mighty interested in continuin' on with other bands, other tours."

Sabella set down her fork. "Why would I do that? What purpose would I serve?"

"Pretty much the same one you do now," he answered. Despite his somewhat lecherous behavior when Mitch was near women, preferably those close to half his age, intelligence gleamed in his eyes. This tour couldn't have been organized by someone poorly acquainted with both the business and music worlds, and he clearly thought, confident in his acuity, that he had figured out some vital part of her personality—one he apparently intended to exploit.

Playing dumb, Sabella pointed out, "Now, I spend time with Kane. It doesn't seem likely that that would provide any opportunity for continuing on tours, unless or until he chooses to have another."

"Kane will always choose to go on another tour, though that's not too relevant. If you wanted it to, somethin' could be arranged. The excitement of this tourin' life, it's worth a lot to girls like you."

Catching on, Sabella inquired, "And what exactly would I have to do for this to be…arranged?" She already had more than a vague idea what he thought about her, but she wanted him to be explicitly clear.

Mitch smiled as though the final piece to a perfect plan had fallen into place, and he had won the prize.

Steve returned then, coming to their table with a blank face. "Kane just texted me," he told them. "Looks like they need me back." He nodded vaguely in their direction before heading across the lavishly decorated dining room.

Sabella returned her attention to Mitch, prepared to put him firmly in his place.

"Darlin', all it'd take is you switchin' from Kane's bed, to mine," he told her, with a straightforwardness born of utter confidence. "I'm sure you're gettin' tired of the same meal every night. With more experience comes more, shall we say, flavor. An' more variety."

She'd thought she was prepared for it, but Sabella was still unable to respond to his blunt proposition. Instead, she rose without a word and followed the path Steve had taken to the exit. The consumed lunch sat heavily in her stomach. This day had already been filled with conversations previously unimaginable even to her creative mind, and it wasn't even half over.

It was a good thing Steve had waited to talk to Kane until after the sound check, because he was furious. How was it he kept finding himself with women more interested in latching themselves to fame or power than having real relationships? He'd actually started to believe Sabella was different enough that that wasn't the case.

At the start of their dinner break, he pulled Sabella out to a private alley most tourists would never want to know existed. She followed him without question, apparently still sure of her act. He blocked her against the wall, hands braced on either side of her.

"This? This is why you came out here? I mean, wow. You sure had me fooled."

Her brows drew together as confusion filled her expression, but Kane refused to be swayed.

"Back up, please," she breathed.

Kane didn't move. He wasn't going to be taken in by her any more. He knew she could hold her own. "I can't *believe* I actually fell for your act in Portland!" he growled, slapping one hand against the wall.

She flinched at the sound and directed her eyes away from him. "Please, back up. Please," she repeated.

She'd played him expertly, plucking his strings until he'd sung whatever tune she wanted. Still, Kane didn't have it in him to bully her. He took a couple steps back but stood directly in her path, arms crossed over his chest.

"You still don't trust me," she stated, holding his gaze.

Kane forced himself to ignore the hurt and gathering tears in her eyes. "Steve told me what you and Mitch were discussing," he spat out.

"So, he told you a snippet of an overheard conversation, and you assume the worst. About me, anyway."

What had Steve actually said? Despite everything, Kane searched for a way he may have misinterpreted. Like before, Sabella didn't simper or try to convince him he'd misunderstood. "You came out of a hotel room with him, and headed to lunch when you saw us. How unfortunate for you I asked Steve to join you."

"I practically *begged* you to come with us!" she snapped at him. She closed her eyes for a few seconds and blew her breath out before speaking again. "I don't know what else I could do to show you that you can trust me," she said, keeping her words even.

"Nothing," he answered, realizing it himself. She looked crestfallen but kept herself from crying, proving even more he had once again gotten it all wrong. Coming on tour hadn't even been her idea. How could he be so stupid? "I do trust you," he started to say.

She exhaled sharply, eyebrows drawing together in disbelief.

"I just… There are these moments, when I can't, I just can't stop worrying that it's, that none of this, is true." Kane paused, hearing himself. "It's not your fault."

Sabella watched him without a word. He was paying such close attention to her reaction that he could see her swallow.

"Being with you," he continued, laying all his cards on the table, "it's been unbelievable for me. It's been, I wish I had a better word, but it's been pretty perfect." He stopped, hoping to see some small sign that she believed him. "After everything, I keep, well. I just keep waiting for the other shoe to drop."

She didn't move, but her stance eased a bit.

Kane dug his fingers into his arms to prevent himself from reaching for her. He couldn't think about the possibility of never holding her again. He didn't want to believe this had all been a lie. His phone started ringing, but he didn't move either. "I'm sorry," he stated. "You're already, you're so much more than I deserve."

She broke their eye contact, looking to the ground.

"Don't leave," he whispered. He could have sworn his heart and lungs stopped working as he waited for an answer.

Her gaze flew back to his face. "Okay," she agreed, moments later. "Not right now."

Twenty

Sabella berated herself mentally for the duration of the show, which somehow felt filled with more loving ballads than its predecessors. Despite their distressing argument, Kane's music enthralled her as always, making it nearly impossible to think of anything else. The packed audience definitely didn't seem to mind, and a detached part of her was thrilled for Kane about this undeniable success. The rest of her was coming to realize it didn't matter which choices she made; this adventure would always end the same way.

The exuberant applause that followed their final song intensified when Kane stepped back on stage. When he spoke, he repeated parts of phrases as he did when slightly nervous, most frequently on stage. "Thank you. This next song, well, this is a song I wrote for, uh." He looked directly at her for a moment before continuing. "I wrote it for the woman I, well...y'know," he faltered, breaking their eye contact.

Sabella reminded herself to breathe rather than speculate about how that sentence had been intended to end, but a voice in her mind whispered that she knew exactly what he hadn't said. She didn't know, however, whether it was a ploy in response to their fight.

Unlike the rest of his performances, as Kane sang this song—the one he had played for her so recently—he focused on his guitar and the spot in front of him, rather than the audience. Where the song had initially been enthusiastically animated, this time he sang it almost wistfully. A hush fell over the entire room as mesmerized fans listened raptly.

"Don't wanna come down," he repeated to end the song. As Sabella surveyed the room from her spot on its side, it seemed as though the sole movement was the slow turn of her own head, until the remnants of his last chord dissipated, and the room erupted.

She had agreed not to leave, and she didn't want to run away from the rest of their conversation—well, argument—but she couldn't stay for the imminent hours of small talk and watching Kane flirt with his fans. In addition to their fight, her conversation with Gina still played on a loop inside her mind. She was progressively more certain of what was going on back in Portland, and the picture that had formed was devastating.

Sabella made her way to the slightly concealed corridor that led to the backstage area, weaving through chatting groups of delighted fans. From a few steps away, she glimpsed Bobby rushing out to mingle with the crowd, heading specifically toward a group of women with cheap tiaras perched on their heads. As she turned into the darkened entry, she nearly ran into Kane.

"Woah, there." His hands on her shoulders steadied her automatically, lingering for a moment when their eyes met, but Sabella dropped her gaze, and Kane slowly lowered his hands.

She took a deep breath and forced herself to look back at him. "I wanted to tell you I'm going to head out, back to the hotel."

His expression remained impassive, its lines grim as he considered her. "Let me grab my guitar. I'll come with you."

Sabella glanced to the crowded room behind her. "They're all waiting for you."

Kane followed her gaze but answered with only the tiniest hesitation. "Let 'em. Two minutes." He fixed her with a stern look, silently instructing her to wait. Sabella nodded barely, stepping further into the recess and out of sight of the club's patrons as Kane left.

After he rejoined her, they returned to the hotel, maintaining a tense silence. Kane set down the guitar, and Sabella conscientiously ensured the door remained open, standing near it, still apprehensive after everything that had happened today. Kane's jaw clenched, but he didn't comment on her precautions.

"I know it's not easy, bein' with me," he ventured, breaking the silence.

"This whole day has been anything but easy," Sabella commented under her breath before returning to the pertinent topic. "Being with you isn't the problem, for me. But you don't trust me, and I don't think there is anything more I can do about that." She had been forthcoming with him, wholly honest, and more emotionally exposed than she had allowed herself to be in years.

"It isn't you." Kane stayed unmoving, directly across the room. "I have a complicated... I've told you, there've been women, who tried to become a part of my life, but only to have an in. A way to make their own careers, or access to money they thought I had, or just 'til something better came along. Some weren't subtle, but I still fell for it, early on. I haven't let anyone matter, not in a long time."

"You can't perpetually wait for some hidden motives to come to light. Someday, with someone, you won't want to."

"I don't want to now," he insisted, before she had a chance to continue. "What Steve heard, it made me question..."

"Me," she finished for him as he searched for the conclusion to his thought.

"No," he contradicted fervently. "Me. I felt, I was up in the clouds, with you. Flying high. Steve, he said, he told me I'd missed something, and it—I—crashed."

"I don't even know what he told you," Sabella admitted, unsure what else she could say.

"That you asked Mitch what you'd have to do, to keep going on more of his tours."

Sabella took a moment to process, focusing on drawing air into her lungs. In an echo of the last time she had stood by this same open door, the other men's voices carried to them from a ways off. It was early, but there was a chance they had been forced to cut the evening short after Kane's departure. Breaking her own rule against being defensive, Sabella decided to lay out her side of the situation. "Mitch suggested I had only joined you all for the excitement of life on tour. My response, which Steve overheard, was intended to be sarcastic. It's a bad habit of mine. Do you want to know what Mitch said? After Steve left?"

Kane's eyes narrowed, and his jaw clenched again, but he nodded once, sharply. Laughter floated into the room but did nothing to dissolve the tension arcing between them.

"He told me," Sabella recounted deliberately, maintaining an unfaltering eye contact, "all I would have to do is switch, from your bed, to his."

Kane froze in an eerily predatory way. Without a word, he sprang forward, speeding past her through the door. Sabella turned in time to see him vault over the rail that separated the rooms from the parking lot. His fist collided with Mitch's jaw before any of the other men had a chance to respond. Mitch rocked back on his heels, into Bobby, who caught him reflexively. Kane stalked back toward the room as everyone watched, thunderstruck.

Sabella wanted to be heartened by his visceral response, but mostly she was saddened that her presence in his life may have torn apart his close relationship with his manager, and possibly with the others as well. Maybe she should have never accepted Kane's invitation.

Steve was the first to move, taking off after Kane. He jogged to catch up to Kane's ground-eating stride, and they reached the doorway where Sabella still stood almost at once. Kane barely glanced at the other man. "Better ice that hand," Steve told him.

Kane looked down, wincing almost imperceptibly as he tested the function of his fingers. Still, he looked to her rather than heading toward the ice machine. "You really should," Sabella agreed with a small nod.

"Looks like I got it wrong," Steve ventured after Kane walked off. "I'm sorry."

Sabella shrugged, though it was nice of him to apologize. "You were protecting your friend."

Steve nodded contemplatively. They both ignored Mitch and Bobby, who remained in the parking lot. "Bobby still jokes, running around with every woman he meets, but this's only his second year out with us. Kane and me, we've been doing this a long time now; we've learned better. Kane especially." Sabella didn't respond, unwilling to interrupt but mostly unsure what he expected her to say. "Women have thrown themselves at him, of course, but that's not the worst. Girls he got close with, all too soon, they asked for introductions to his connections, or slipped him demo tapes. A few ditched him soon as they met someone more famous, with better connections. The girl he was with before our first tour, she was a piece of work, selling an interview filled with their private life to some trashy tabloid. When I heard what you said, I had to tell him. Better he found out sooner." His tone was explanatory, solemn, though unapologetic.

Truthfully, Sabella didn't hold him responsible for the misunderstanding, or the fallout. They were virtually strangers; this conversation was the most intimate they had had. Kane, however, should have given her the benefit of the doubt where his friend couldn't.

"He really cares about you," Steve added when Sabella didn't respond. "I hope you can understand, accept how it's messed with him."

She didn't have an answer for him, or for herself. Privately, she wanted to forgive Kane; she yearned for everything between them to return to how it had been as recently as that morning, but unrelenting pragmatism made her question if that would be the right decision, especially considering Gina's apparent situation.

Kane held a bag of ice on his knuckles as he walked back to the room. Everything seemed to be slipping away. Steve still stood with Sabella inside the doorway but excused himself at Kane's approach. Whatever they had said to each other must've been charged, but it didn't feel hostile.

"Is your hand okay?" Sabella asked. For the first time since she'd joined them, she looked worn out.

"It'll be fine," he answered. They both walked further into the room. This time, Sabella shut the door. Neither one approached the bed. "Are we? I know I'm stretching the limits of anyone's patience. But, bear with me." *Please*, he added silently, unable to plead more openly.

Tension twisted her lips. She parted them to speak, but didn't, licking them instead.

"Will you stay?" Kane forced the words out. If she just didn't leave, he could find a way to fix this.

"I have to leave in the morning," Sabella exhaled more than said.

Kane steeled himself against his own doubts. Her words didn't mean she was leaving because she couldn't get what she had actually wanted. He had never known how long she planned to stay. Her eyes stayed trained on his face, unwavering.

Kane thought through their conversation. She had been genuinely willing to talk things over. So she probably wasn't running from a botched plan, or because of the fight at all. *This whole day has been anything but easy*, she had murmured earlier. "Did something else happen?" he asked, fighting every instinct to stay controlled. Part of him was sure he'd been played. The other was willing to beg, so long as she didn't leave.

"I think, maybe," Sabella started to say but cut herself off. She looked away, swallowed, and licked her lips again.

Kane ground his teeth to prevent from pressing her.

"I think Gina might be being abused," she whispered, pausing before the last word, as if not saying it kept it from being true.

Kane would've been less shocked if she'd said she was leaving to accept the Nobel Prize. He dropped the ice and moved to her. He lifted her hand in his. When she didn't pull back, he tugged her into his arms. She resisted for a brief moment but soon wrapped her arms at his waist. Kane stroked her hair, steering her to the bed, which was the only decent seating in the room.

"Tell me what happened," he instructed.

She did, haltingly describing the hidden bruises, the subtle changes in behavior, and the tight, anxious look that didn't seem to leave her friend's face lately. A look she hadn't placed until today.

As they talked, Kane kicked off his shoes. Sabella copied the movement, and they settled on the bed. Kane wrapped his arms around her, willing the universe to give him a way to erase this day for her. A day he'd only made worse.

"It'll be okay," he assured. Sabella stayed quiet, but a slight shift in her shoulders showed she didn't believe it. "It will be okay," he repeated, promising silently that he'd *make* it okay. Somehow.

Something must have convinced her, and she relaxed into his arms. Kane kept running his fingers through her hair until she fell asleep.

At some point in the middle of the night, they must have undressed, because Sabella awoke wearing only panties and a bra, curled against Kane's bare torso. She vaguely remembered kicking off her jeans. One of them had apparently also maneuvered the blanket so it no longer lay beneath them. She had heard people describe waking after difficult days as a moment of peace, before reality rushes back, but Sabella experienced no such reprieve. She remembered the day before, not to mention everything she now had to do, in unambiguous detail. Then again, she also remembered Kane comforting her, sheltering her in his arms, assuring her that, somehow, it would all be all right.

Last night, nestled against him, the idealistically hopeful part of her had believed him. Now, faced with the prospect of returning home, to deal with a situation she could barely imagine happening, much less knew how to handle, she was far from sure. Amidst everything else, there was no opportunity to consider what future, if any, lay ahead for her relationship with Kane.

With an almost mechanical efficiency, they both showered and dressed, and all too soon, Sabella was completely packed.

Her small suitcase stood by the door, staring at her, as she waited for Kane to finish shaving, so they could go through the motions of an inevitably uncomfortable goodbye.

When he reappeared from the bathroom, Sabella rose from her spot on the corner of the bed. Kane strode toward her and wordlessly wrapped her in a hug, the heat of his palms seeping through her thin tee shirt. For a few blissfully impractical seconds, she allowed herself to cling to him, appreciating the solidly physical support. He didn't quite let go when she did, keeping his arms loosely looped at her waist.

"D'you want to get some breakfast before you get going?" he asked. Since she had told him about her suspicions, he had been wholly understanding. Not once had he questioned her resolve to leave or attempted to revert the topic to the status of their own relationship.

She had once dreamt of being with someone perceptive enough to see which situations were game-changing for her, and which, despite their relative importance, could be discarded by the wayside. As with most pieces of this fairy tale, however, his discernment hadn't come to light how she would have expected. Their argument the night before had brought their continued relationship into question, but it was her situation back home which ultimately altered their circumstances, putting an abrupt end to this summer fling. He understood she couldn't stay, but, irrationally, she wished he wouldn't let her go.

"It's a long drive," she responded, slightly shaking her head.

"At least grab something from the bus," he insisted.

"Sure. Thanks."

They broke apart, and Kane picked up her suitcase. Sabella lifted her purse from a small lacquered table by the door and patted her pockets, ensuring her phone and car keys were in place. Kane held the door open with one hand, and she slipped past him, heading to the opening in the blue railing and out to the parking lot.

Before climbing into her car, which had been loaded not only with her belongings, but also with a brown paper bag filled with all manner of snacks and a couple of water bottles appropriated from the bus, Sabella paused, searching for something she could say to resolve the cliffhanger spanning between them. Inches separated her from both his body and the car behind her.

"Drive safe," Kane said in a low voice.

She forced a smile from the protesting muscles in her face. "I will."

Kane brought one hand up to cup her face, his thumb brushing over her cheek. Sabella's breath caught from the painful reality of their goodbye.

"Let me know you got back all right, okay?"

She nodded, feeling her jaw press against his hand with the motion. Kane hesitated, then dipped his head down for a brief kiss which restored her ability to breathe. A soft brush of his lips on the tip of her nose followed, before he dropped his hand and stepped out of the way, so Sabella could slide into her car. Kane watched her drive away.

Twenty-One

By the time Sabella arrived back in Portland, it was almost three in the morning, so she did little more than send a text message to Kane and fall into bed. The nearly eighteen-hour drive, not counting a few indispensable breaks, had provided more than ample opportunity to think. The one benefit to her fight with Kane was that it afforded an opening for her newly designed strategy. Hopefully she still knew Gina's schedule well enough for it to be successful.

Early on Monday morning, which Sabella adamantly refused to acknowledge came only a couple hours after her arrival, she drove over to Gina's apartment, aiming to catch her before work. When the girls had first moved to Portland, they had shared an apartment, until both had become financially stable enough to live on their own, though in Sabella's case that label sometimes still seemed optimistic. Gina's current place was closer to downtown and about a ten-minute drive from Sabella's.

Atop the private, outdoor stairs that led to Gina's apartment, Sabella steeled herself and slipped out the keychain that held her spare key to Gina's place. She had decided on this course of action quite intentionally, with plenty of time to contemplate it, she reminded herself. With a deep breath, she unlocked the door and walked into the familiar apartment.

A tall man in an obviously expensive charcoal suit, with a carefully selected, patterned, lilac tie, sat drinking a cup of coffee at one of six chairs that accompanied a round dining table. He glanced up in surprise as Sabella entered.

"You must be Alistair," she said with calculated politeness, crossing through the living area toward the table. Everything about him looked deliberately assembled, from his close-cut, blond hair, to his dark eyes and thin lips. Undoubtedly, if she could have seen his feet, his socks would have been color-matched to an expensive pair of loafers. For the briefest moment, Sabella felt somewhat bedraggled by comparison in her tee shirt and jeans. Then she remembered why she had come.

Alistair set the coffee cup silently on a saucer. "And you are?" he asked with cold civility.

"Call me Elle." She determinedly strode further into the apartment. Since her last visit, Gina's uninhibitedly colorful throw pillows had disappeared from the L-shaped couch and matching armchair to her right. All of the surfaces, from the oval coffee table to the sleek buffet that hugged the wall beside the dining table, stood polished and cleared of their customary trinkets. Sabella forced herself not to dwell on the changes. "Is Gina around?" she asked pointedly.

"Gina," Alistair called without raising his voice or moving from his seat.

One of the coolest aspects to Gina's apartment, and the most influential selling point for her, was the walk-in closet that connected the bedroom to the bathroom with private doors, though the architect had appropriately planned for guest access to the bathroom as well, through a nook beside the dining area. Immediately after Alistair called, Gina emerged from that nook, lip gloss in hand. She wore herringbone slacks with a navy turtleneck, cinched with a wide black belt.

"Sabella!" she exclaimed with a small shake of her head. "What, uh—what are you doing here?"

Sabella shrugged, drawing on her very limited acting abilities to mask her ulterior motives. "We had a fight. It was pretty awful." That was actually true, even if it wasn't the point. "So I'm back." She dropped her purse onto the edge of the dining table, across from Alistair's seat. A tic jumped at the side of his jaw.

Gina plunged the lip gloss's wand back into its container. "I'm so sorry," she said compassionately, rounding the table to scoop up the discarded purse. "Are you all right?"

"No, not really," Sabella answered honestly. Under normal circumstances, it would have been wonderful to discuss the situation with her friend. "Think you can play hooky today?"

Gina eyes flicked over to Alistair's stern expression before she answered. "No, I, uh, I really can't."

"You can't?" Sabella repeated, overplaying the accusation in her tone.

"I have many responsibilities at work, Sabella. I can't simply take off with no warning," Gina admonished as though the very idea appalled her. Her chin lifted a notch in defiance, but her eyes involuntarily flicked back to the man at her table.

"Well, what about tonight?" Sabella asked, unwilling to challenge this newfound resolve. She herself had occasionally commented on Gina's less-than-professional attitude toward work.

Another glance at Alistair. "No, I don't think I'm free tonight," she answered. Sabella didn't have to fake the shock and hurt in her expression. "Maybe we can plan a lunch, now that you're back," Gina suggested noncommittally and held out Sabella's purse in a gesture that was unquestionably dismissive.

Sabella was taken aback but nowhere near ready to give up; she had come prepared to do whatever it would take. "I can't believe you!" she exclaimed, snatching the outstretched purse. "So much for always being there for me, I guess." Had this been spontaneous drama, Sabella would have stalked out of the apartment. Given the current scenario, she remained rooted to the spot, staring at Gina and pointedly ignoring Alistair.

Gina faltered, turning her head toward the seated financier, eyes shifting from him, then back to Sabella, before finally dropping to stare at the table. Alistair unfolded from the chair and carried his dishes to the sink behind him. "We can skip our dinner," he said, walking back to join Gina, though he maintained a decorous distance. "If you want, you should comfort your"—he assessed Sabella—"friend," he finished with obvious distaste. The scene was clearly too messy for his controlling sensibilities.

Sabella licked her lips nervously before she could stop herself. "Don't do me any favors," she stated venomously. When Gina didn't respond, she whirled around and headed for the door in a final gambit.

"No, Sabella, wait," Gina called, finally. Beside the coffee table, Sabella turned back to face both of them. "I'll come by after work," Gina murmured, with a soft nod.

Behind her, Alistair's jaw clenched. He shook the sleeve off his wrist and lifted his arm to expose his silver watch. "We're going to be late," he stated, unmistakably intending for Sabella to leave.

"I'll walk you out," she offered instead, unwilling to leave Gina alone with him for even a second longer. Everything about this morning confirmed her suspicions, including Gina wearing a turtleneck of all things in the middle of summer.

Wordlessly, Alistair lifted the briefcase that stood by the armchair, and Gina ducked into the bedroom for her bag.

"I'll see you tonight, then," Sabella confirmed in the parking lot with Gina, who nodded, averting her gaze from either of her companions. "Sorry to interrupt your morning," she added to Alistair, attempting not to arouse any misgivings. A distraught friend was one thing, but a completely impolite, overly dramatic woman may be seen as unbelievably over-the-top.

Alistair didn't respond, and all three of them split off toward their respective cars. In her front seat and out of their sight, Sabella focused on controlling her breathing, waiting for the trembling of her hands to subside before she started the car to drive home.

Back in her apartment, Sabella fell directly into bed to catch up on some sleep before the undoubtedly long evening ahead. A call from Kane woke her several hours later. His concern was sweet, especially given the shattered state of their relationship, but she had no idea what to say, so she ended the call relatively quickly. Dwelling on a relationship that could only ever have been short-lived wouldn't change anything.

Since she hadn't left any perishable ingredients before joining Kane, lunch consisted of pasta smothered in a canned marinara sauce. A quick survey revealed a woeful lack of edibles, which would undoubtedly be a necessity later that night, not to mention for the rest of her return to reality. That and the cold, somewhat unwelcoming feel of her empty apartment prompted Sabella to drag herself out for a shopping trip.

Once she returned with sufficient supplies, there was little left to do besides wait for Gina. She tried to write, but the sole ideas floating around her mind centered on avoiding situations and relationships like the one in which her best friend now found herself. The trouble was, she had no idea how Gina—smart, beautiful, confident Gina—had gotten there in the first place.

That morning's scene kept playing through her mind, different details standing out with each replay. Late in the afternoon, she finally gave in to her guilt about the morning's drama and sent a text message to Gina.

Gina didn't respond. Hopefully, she would show up later regardless. Nonetheless, Sabella began concocting an alternative plan as she lay on the couch, watching cheesy movies.

Partway into her second movie, Gina burst through the door. "What the hell was *wrong* with you this morning!" she demanded without preamble, striding into the living room.

Sabella shut her laptop and jumped off her couch. "What was wrong with *you*? Did you *hear* yourself this morning!"

"What are you talking about?" Gina asked, some of the initial fire melting away, breaking Sabella's heart and fueling her resolve to see this through.

"'*Maybe* we can schedule lunch now that you're back'?" Sabella quoted.

Gina opened her mouth to defend herself but exhaled instead, switching modes to compassionate. "Tell me what happened with Kane."

"We had a fight. It was pretty ugly, and I think it's over," Sabella admitted. "But, that's not the main reason I came back."

"So you lied this morning?" Gina asked incredulously, seizing onto the excuse to turn the situation around.

"Really? You're upset that *I* wasn't honest? What's under the long sleeves and the concealer, Gina?" A professional would likely have been aghast at Sabella's approach, but all the stress and fear of the last couple of days had simply boiled out into the accusation.

"Nothing," Gina replied quickly, stepping back and wrapping her arms around herself. "I don't know what you're talking about."

"Gina. What happened?" Sabella implored.

Gina shook her head slightly, as if rejecting something inside her head. "It was an accident."

Sabella stepped around the coffee table that still separated them. "What was?"

Gina hugged herself tighter, shoulders coming up defensively. "He...grabbed me," she whispered, tear-filled eyes pleading with Sabella to understand. "He was just too strong. It was an accident," she repeated.

"What about your face?" Sabella pointed out softly.

Gina's gaze dropped, her brows and lips pinching together. Painful memories flitted over her expression. Sabella waited silently.

"He backhanded me," Gina admitted finally, her voice lower than a whisper. When she looked up, Sabella attempted to draw her into a hug, but Gina shifted away. "It's fine. I'm fine," she insisted. "He apologized, and you said yourself, 'people make mistakes,' and they deserve a second chance."

"That was different," she claimed, holding back her own tears. She had said exactly that about Kane, but the situations weren't comparable. "I also said some mistakes are unforgivable." Gina didn't budge. "Like *hitting* you. You know that isn't acceptable, Gi."

"He loves me," she insisted, begging Sabella to accept the claim. "It was just a 'volatile misunderstanding.'"

Sabella winced at Gina quoting her own description of her first fight with Kane, but she wasn't convinced. The circumstances were absolutely not the same. She stifled the nagging guilt that it was *her* arguments that paved the way for Gina to fall into Alistair's trap. "Look at what you're wearing in the middle of summer," she stated simply. "Think about the changes you've made to your apartment. What happened to all the throw pillows you loved? To the Gina touches? To your daring fashion choices? Even your nails are beige now. Or wait, no, it's that you put your friends first, right? That you're always there for people like you have been for me during our latest phone calls? What about *you*, exactly, does he love?"

"That's not fair." Gina backed even further away.

"What did he do to you?" Sabella murmured, following as her heart broke further at the sight of the wrecked shell that remained of her friend.

"He's helping me be better," Gina answered. Sabella couldn't respond, struggling to find her next move. "Sanding the rough edges," Gina soon added into the quiet, with the first hint of resentment. "That's what he calls it."

Sabella silently claimed the small victory. "You want some ice cream?" she offered, buying time to figure out how to proceed.

"I can't," Gina answered, sliding her hands over her flawless waistline. "He, uh. He checks my weight."

Sabella couldn't do more than blink at the statement. "Do you weigh him...?" she asked eventually, flabbergasted enough not to monitor what she said.

Gina glanced down, plucking uncomfortably at her top. "You think I could maybe change into something? While I'm here?"

Sabella nodded. "You know you don't have to ask. Let's go find you something." She gestured for Gina to precede her into the bedroom.

Gina stopped in the middle of the room, and Sabella moved past her to the closet, automatically pulling out some of her more vibrant tops and a soft pair of shorts with a drawstring waistband. She placed the options on her bed, and Gina lifted off her blouse. She reached to the pile of tops, but Sabella couldn't hold back a gasp at the revealed sight of a nasty, multicolored bruise that covered most of Gina's side.

"Gina!" Sabella exclaimed. She had steeled herself to expect the faint purple rings around Gina's wrists, but not this.

As if unsure what had surprised her, Gina followed Sabella's gaze down to her ribcage. She sank onto the bed, defeated, clutching a top in front of her to hide the bruising. "I guess... I just wanted to believe someone like him, who really has his life together, could want to be with me. I know most people find me unbearably over the top. And everybody has their flaws, right? If he could put up with all of mine, I should be able to handle his only one."

Sabella pushed aside the pile of clothes and settled next to her. "First off, I never thought I'd say this, but your biggest flaw right now is not having faith in yourself. You're an incredible woman. So vivacious, and generous, and supportive, not to mention brilliant and beautiful. He's clearly too insecure to be with someone so amazing, so he tried to stifle you, turning you into a watered-down version. Second, all flaws are *not* created equal, and there is absolutely no excuse for him hitting you!"

"You're probably right," Gina finally admitted. "But it's not like I can just put an end to our relationship. He wouldn't let me."

Her hopeless expression fed Sabella's gnawing guilt. "Gi, I'm sorry I wasn't around to help stop this sooner, but I am here now. We'll figure something out, starting with you spending the night here."

Gina leaned into her for a moment before turning to sift through the clothes sitting beside them.

Sabella stood to give her more room. "So, pizza or Chinese?"

Gina began to protest, out of her newly formed habit, but stopped herself. "Pizza," she answered with a smile. "And cheesy breadsticks," she added a moment later.

By the time the pizza arrived, a batch of their signature, über-chocolate brownies—originally concocted during one sleepless night during finals week—stood baking in the oven. Sabella paid the delivery boy, and the two of them settled in the living room with the boxes of cheesy goodness, Sabella's laptop, and a stack of DVDs.

When most of the pizza, all of the breadsticks, and a few slices of brownies had been consumed—and Cher had just unintentionally picked a fight with her protégé, Tai, over her stepbrother, Josh—Gina's phone rang. Dread replaced the peaceful lethargy of her food coma.

"You don't have to pick up," Sabella told her, pausing the movie. Gina continued to stare at the phone as if it would explode if she didn't answer. "Or, you could tell him that I'm too much of a mess and need you to stay here."

Jaw clenched, Gina nodded and answered the call. The conversation was peppered with too many apologies but nevertheless ended with the understanding that Gina would spend the night at Sabella's.

When she hung up, she deliberately slid the phone onto the coffee table beside the computer. Rather than restarting the movie, however, she leaned back on the couch. "You haven't really told me what happened with Kane."

"Pretty much the same thing as last time," Sabella answered. Gina watched her expectantly, prompting her to continue. The conversation could have waited, but if this helped Gina, even as a distraction, so be it. "After everything, he still doesn't trust me, my reasons for being with him."

"How do you know?"

Sabella picked up another brownie, fiddling with it to delay speaking. "His manager, Mitch, suggested not-so-subtly that I may enjoy other tours of his. You can imagine my answer, but one of his bandmates overheard, and misunderstood, and told Kane, who proceeded to accuse me of using him, again. He was almost…feral." She sighed and dropped the brownie down onto a napkin. "I guess I was coming to believe, after our rather idyllic time together, that this could truly be something good between us, but how could it be, if even after everything, he still didn't give me the benefit of the doubt in a situation like that?"

Gina regarded her with overly perceptive eyes. "Yeah, I understand. I mean, *your* trust issues are more than sufficient for any one couple."

The allegation was irritating, probably because it was true, but it was nevertheless heartening to hear the insight. Despite everything, Gina was still Gina. "What do you mean?" Sabella asked anyway.

"You might not throw it in his face, but you don't trust him either—don't trust him to be on your side. You seize the slightest excuse to support your fear that your relationship isn't going to last. In that way, you're not so different from him."

Sabella stared at her friend, stunned.

"You were happy with him; I could see it when we talked. Maybe you've even found your fairy-tale love," Gina added. "But if you both keep running away from the possibility, then it definitely won't last."

"How could I ever love someone who doesn't trust me?" Sabella asked miserably.

"How could he?" Gina countered.

They watched each other for some minutes, until Sabella said, "That's incredibly insightful, even for you."

Gina shrugged and shifted her attention to their leftover food, searching for a distraction as Sabella had earlier. "You used to love the comparison that falling in love is like leaping off a cliff." She looked back to Sabella. "I think you're right, and if you jump together, with the right person, you act as each other's parachutes. But ultimately, you still have to jump."

"That's beautiful," Sabella commented. "I'm not really sure we're there, though." Given how things had ended between them, she wasn't even certain whether she would ever see Kane again. She was definitely not in love with him, though.

"Oh please, Sabella. You were standing at the edge of that cliff before the first time you slept with him, or you wouldn't have done it."

Gina was right, but the unusual use of Sabella's full name reminded her that Kane wasn't actually why she had returned home. "You know, Alistair may have shoved you off a cliff," she said, taking Gina's hand and squeezing gently, "but I'm always here to catch you."

"I know," Gina breathed after a moment, squeezing back. "I'm glad you're home."

They smiled at each other, both secure in at least this one relationship in their lives, then Gina leaned forward to restart their movie.

Twenty-Two

Early the next morning, Sabella plucked her phone from her nightstand and quietly slipped out of the bedroom so as not to wake Gina. She curled into the blue chair in her living room and dialed Roger.

"Well look who decided to remember the little people," Roger greeted after a couple rings.

"Hey, Roger," Sabella answered, smiling despite herself.

"What's up, buttercup?"

"I wanted to let you know that Gina won't be in today." On the other end, she heard Roger move to a quieter part of the office.

"Are you sure about that? She's been pretty...focused, lately," he said seriously, a hint of concern evident in his tone.

"I'm sure. She's spending today with me. If anyone asks, you can tell them we're working on a new series of articles." It wasn't necessarily a lie. Eventually, she would likely write a few pieces related to abusive relationships, though she wouldn't pitch them to Gina.

"Ooh, so can I take this to mean you're back, and order will be restored?" Roger asked with a mix of sarcasm and anticipation.

"Here's hoping," she answered, unable to match his optimism.

"What about your sexy adventure with the cowboy?"

Good question. "He wasn't a cowboy," she corrected. "I'm where I should be; you know that."

"That bad?" Roger asked. Sabella didn't answer. "Well, we've missed you, Elles. And I'm looking forward to some vicarious cowboy love in one of your fabulous stories," he teased, reverting to his habitually upbeat tone.

Murmured conversation sounded from his end of the line, and Gina appeared in the entrance to Sabella's living room, so Sabella hung up without saying anything more.

"I told Roger you wouldn't be at the office today," she explained.

"Thanks." Gina nodded and moved further into the room, wincing as she settled on the other chair. "Do you have Tylenol or something?"

"Sure." She went to bring the pills and a glass of water from the kitchen. "I think maybe we should get you to a doctor, though," she suggested, handing Gina the supplies.

Gina threw back a couple of pills and cushioned the half-filled glass in her hands. "I'll be fine," she protested.

"That bruise over your ribs looks pretty nasty," Sabella

insisted. "It may be good to ensure it's not more serious than it seems."

Gina might have responded, but the doorbell rang, and both girls twisted to stare at the door. Sabella glanced back to see her once vivacious friend pale with fear, her eyes wide and lips tightly drawn.

"Go in the bedroom," Sabella whispered. Gina's eyes snapped to her face, filled with a blend of despair and resignation that forced Sabella to reason rapidly through their current options.

The door was locked, and she had her phone. Alistair probably wouldn't force his way into her apartment, and it was inconceivable that she would let him in. If he was out there, she could call the police. First, she needed to find a way to be certain it was him. If she called out, he would know she was home and assume Gina was there as well, which meant he might stay there, out of sight of the peephole, until they ventured out of the apartment. *The peephole!* She could verify who stood on the other side, without making a sound.

Resolved, Sabella whispered, "It's ok," and moved carefully toward the door. She waited until Gina had softly shut herself inside the bedroom, stilled her body as much as the adrenaline pumping through her would allow, then glanced through the tiny circle.

She recognized the man on the other side but in that moment couldn't be certain of what she had seen. Two deep, quiet breaths later, she checked again then sagged against the door in relief. With unsteady fingers, she flicked the lock and twisted the knob.

"Hey, Bella." Kane stood opposite her, holding a carrier with three hot beverages Sabella assumed were coffee and, as always, his guitar. His rumpled clothes and tensed eyes showed he probably hadn't slept, but adrenaline still coursed through her, and Sabella was too relieved to see him to worry about the impracticality of his presence.

He stepped through the doorframe, set down both the carrier and the guitar case, then hesitated before finally reaching for her. Sabella nearly fell into his arms, forgetting for that moment every unsettled issue between them.

Before Kane's arms had completely closed around Sabella, she pulled back. With brows drawn, she exhaled, "Gina," and twisted away. Seconds later, she disappeared through her bedroom door. Muted voices flowed from the other room. Kane grabbed a coffee from the carrier and walked over to one of the chairs in the living room. By now, he was running pretty much only on the cheap coffees he'd bought on the long drive up, but he took another bracing sip anyway.

After Sabella'd left Vegas, he'd tried to keep to himself, but it hadn't really been possible.

Steve had apologized during their sound check. Kane appreciated the gesture, but he didn't really blame the drummer.

Oblivious as always, Bobby'd asked, "What happened to Sabella?"

"She left," Kane told him flatly.

"Out of your league after all, huh?"

"Bobby!" Steve snapped, cutting him off.

Kane leveled a stare at the younger man. "She had an emergency at home."

Mitch sidled up to the stage then, and Kane fell silent. Hitting the manager the night before hadn't done nearly enough to diffuse his rage at the betrayal. He'd trusted the man who'd taken an interest in his music all those years ago. Apparently, he'd taken an interest in more than just that.

Steve spoke quietly to Bobby, probably explaining the situation. Bobby'd seen the punch but missed everything else. Mitch chose that moment to come up to Kane. "Let's talk outside," he suggested.

Kane set his guitar down on the stage and crossed his arms over his chest. "You want a matching pair?" he asked, pointing out the purple bruise covering the other man's cheekbone and reaching up toward his eye.

Mitch cocked one hip, widening his stance, but didn't back down. Kane had caught him by surprise the night before, but if it came to it, the other man could probably still hold his own in a fight. "C'mon, Kane. I was just making sure she wasn't another one of those fame-seeking gold-diggers who always try to latch onto you."

It was a desperate defense. Kane narrowed his eyes, losing even more respect for the man he'd once considered family. "Don't do that."

Mitch shifted his jaw, tightening his lips. "You've known me a long time, boy. I've always been there for you, believed in you."

"And you got paid well for it." Kane had been Mitch's first client to make it through more than one tour. The partnership had opened doors for both of them. Kane hadn't really thought about all the ways Mitch had benefited from it before.

"True enough," his manager admitted easily. "Still, I've been there for you, a long time now. This one girl—who's gone, now, by the way—this one misunderstanding, it's not—"

Kane cut him off. "After Seattle, we're done."

By then, both Steve and Bobby'd been watching the quiet conversation.

"I've always done right by you and your music, Kane. Even those boys, I'm the one who brought y'all together."

Kane didn't respond.

Mitch's eyes narrowed. "Back in Portland, that girl of yours, she was with the bartender." He paused, watching Kane closely. "When she was there, at Dante's, she was *with* the bartender."

Outwardly, Kane didn't react, but his mind raced back to that night. She'd told him they'd just met. Before, he wouldn't have thought Mitch would make something like that up. Before, he'd trusted the man without question. But Steve had overheard Mitch's blatant offer, and Sabella'd been right. He couldn't keep searching for some hidden motives in her actions. He didn't want to. Sabella wasn't like the other women he'd been with.

He desperately hoped he was right.

"You misunderstood," he told his manager.

"Maybe I did. But from what I saw, when I saw *that* was the girl you'd met in Portland…" Mitch stopped, considering his words under Kane's stare. "I thought you'd learned, that you were just having some fun. But I know you, Kane. I saw you falling for that girl, and hell, that's great for your music, but she'd been with someone else days before. Maybe I was wrong." He threw his hands up. "Maybe it was something else. But I had to make sure she wasn't another Felicia Mae."

Out of the corner of his eye, Kane saw Steve stand straighter, ready to break up a fight if he had to. Kane had met Felicia Mae soon after signing with Mitch. She'd been beautiful and feisty, and she'd loved animals. She'd even owned honest-to-goodness pearls. Kane had thought that meant she was both ladylike and compassionate. He'd thought she was everything he wanted. He'd ignored the fact that she was only sweet to people when they could hear her, or that she hadn't liked his friends. He'd even mistaken her interest in his music for support. Until his first tour.

She'd claimed she'd done the tabloid story to help him, get him more attention. She'd actually done it for a meeting with a music producer the reporter knew. Then she'd sung the guy a few songs Kane had been working on. A mutual friend had sent him a link to her breakout video.

Sabella was nothing like Felicia Mae, not in any way that counted. But he'd once made the same assumptions Mitch claimed to. Kane uncrossed his arms. "We'd met before Portland," he corrected the other man.

Mitch nodded. "I was only looking out for you, like I always have," he said eventually.

Kane didn't answer. He hadn't known how to. Mitch stayed out of his way the rest of the night, and Kane had focused on performing for the crowd.

After the show, Bobby pulled him aside instead of making a beeline for the most giggly group of girls. Unusually serious, he'd said, "She's special—even I see that. Don't let any of us ruin her for you, man."

Kane had faked his way through the rest of the night. He'd also grit his teeth the next day and made it through an important lunch meeting. Afterward, he'd assured the others he'd be back for the next show, jumped in the truck, and driven straight to Portland.

Mitch hadn't been pleased. Kane didn't care. If Gina was actually being abused, her and Sabella going up against whoever this guy was alone was *not* an option.

✧ ✧ ✧

It took Sabella longer than she would have preferred to calm Gina down, assuring her it had been Kane at the door—*not* Alistair—and that they were safe in the apartment. She forewent mentioning that they were likely safer now that Kane had arrived, unexpected as his presence was. With broader shoulders, bigger muscles, and simpler clothes, Kane appeared rougher around the edges than Mr. Straight-laced. It was therefore completely unsurprising, though no less distressing, that Gina would be skittish at the thought of being enclosed in a small apartment with him.

Eventually, after the initial panic subsided, Sabella managed to convince her to take a soothing shower. Hopefully the combination of steaming-hot water and the opportunity to put herself together visually would help Gina regain some sense of control before she actually needed to acknowledge Kane's presence.

When Gina went into the bathroom, Sabella veered into her living room, looking for Kane. She stalled in the artificial entrance. He had dozed off, splayed out on one of her armchairs. He looked slightly worn around the edges in his jeans and a long-sleeved, gray Henley shirt, with his head propped on one fist and a cup of coffee held loosely in his drooping other hand. Sabella was sufficiently self-aware to admit she was relieved to have him there, even if only for moral support. She considered brushing back the lock of hair that had fallen onto his forehead, down over his eye, but didn't want to wake him, knowing first-hand how harrowing the drive from Vegas to Portland was. Instead, she reached for the coffee he was about to drop, working it gently from his lax grasp.

The slight movement turned out to be enough to rouse Kane from his barely alert state. Before Sabella could move away to set down the coffee, he wrapped his now free arm around her hips and pulled her gently onto his lap, steadying her startled body with his other hand. Sabella rested the cup on her thigh, balancing carefully on his lap, and swept the lock of hair she had previously noted back from his face.

"Hey," he whispered hoarsely, a smile curving his lips despite the fatigue etched into his face.

"Hi." She couldn't quite manage to smile back. "Thank you for coming."

Kane's expression hardened, mouth dropping into an unforgiving line as his eyes, suddenly alert, examined every detail of her condition. "Did you find out what's goin' on?" He kept his voice low, either due to his own fatigue or to prevent Gina from overhearing when she came out of the shower.

Sabella broke their eye contact, unable to answer unemotionally. Kane brought one hand up to stroke her hair. "I think her ribs may be broken," she murmured, straining to keep her voice steady. "I'm hopefully taking her to see a doctor after we have some breakfast."

Kane's hand gently pressed her head onto his shoulder in an attempt at a supportive hug, though the tension nearly vibrating through his body countered his intentions. Even his seething anger, however, ultimately comforted her with the protection it seemed to offer. Regardless of their uncertain personal future, at least he cared enough to want to help.

The opening of the bathroom door broke the silence, prompting both Sabella and Kane to rise. Gina soon stood uncertainly beside the entrance to the kitchen, arms wrapped around herself, keeping a sizeable distance between her and Kane.

"I'm going to jump in the shower really quickly, okay?" Sabella asked, directing the question predominately to Gina, who nodded tensely.

Kane followed her out of the living room and offered, "I could make some breakfast, if you'd like."

Before Sabella could answer, Gina jumped in nervously. "Oh, no, I can make you something, if you just tell me what you would like to eat."

Kane's eyes flicked to Sabella, who stood at a loss for how to diffuse the situation. Apparently Alistair had strong opinions on gender roles. "Really, I don't mind," Kane insisted. "We don't get many real kitchens on tour. If you don't mind me invading yours again?" he asked Sabella, doubtlessly already aware of the answer.

"Breakfast sounds lovely. Really, Gi—Kane's a pretty great cook. He could probably whip up whatever you want, assuming I have the ingredients."

"It'd be my pleasure," Kane chimed in.

Gina didn't appear particularly convinced, but she didn't protest, pressing her lips together. Sabella stepped closer. "I'll be super fast," she assured in a low tone.

"Not if you keep babysitting us," Gina answered, equally low, with a tight smile.

After one last wary glance between the two of them, Sabella headed for the shower.

"So, what're you in the mood for?" Kane asked the obviously skittish Gina. She stood keeping the island between them, in her gray pants and dark-blue top. Kane hadn't missed the faint purple smudges on her face, but he stuffed down his anger so as not to scare her. Outwardly, he focused instead on looking through the ingredients in Sabella's kitchen.

"Isn't a famous star like you used to having people doing this kind of stuff for you?" Gina ventured, making Kane chuckle.

"My career isn't quite there, yet. And I actually enjoy cooking." He turned back to face the brunette, who stood slightly hunched, as if waiting for him to go after her. Kane spoke as if he didn't notice. "Looks like we could go for French toast or eggs any way you want 'em—scrambled, omelets... I could probably also find the fixings for pancakes. What would you like?"

Her shoulders lifted in a small shrug. "Whatever you'd like to have."

"That's not really the question," he pointed out gently, stepping toward the island. She bristled and nearly jumped at his movement. Kane stopped himself and moved backward until he hit the stove. The two considered each other silently. Kane's eyes narrowed when they fell once again on the shadows over her face.

Gina's hand flew to her cheekbone, covering the bruises. Her sleeve slipped, revealing more marks around her wrist. Kane gripped the counter behind him as a reminder not to clench his hands into fists. "A man who hits a woman is nothing more than a piss-ant," he stated.

Gina's hand dropped. Her chin lifted a notch, and her arms crossed. "What if she deserves it?" she asked, blinking back tears.

"Did you beat a kid?" Her brows drew together, but she didn't answer. "Did he hit you literally to stop you from beating on a child? Or a little old lady?" Kane clarified.

"No," she said, with a small shake of her head.

"Then you didn't deserve it."

She stared at him, trying to read his tone. Finally, she sank down onto one of the barstools. Kane took it as a good sign. He didn't move, giving her a chance to process.

"Everyone has their flaws," she stated a couple minutes later.

"Yeah. And whoever this guy is, he's got more than most."

"You don't know that," she insisted. "He's successful, respected, refined."

"What would you say if he was dating Sabella? Treating her the way he treats you?" Kane gripped the counter harder for a second, then forced himself to relax so she didn't notice.

"He wouldn't. Sabella, she's more elegant, more demure. He wouldn't have to—" She cut herself off.

"Have to what? Hit her?"

Gina pursed her lips in response.

"Someone like that, he'd find a reason, something to be unhappy about. So he could control her. Eventually, he'd hit whatever girl he's with." Kane paused, searching for a sign of acknowledgement in her expression. "It's not about you, about there being something wrong with you," he continued. She rolled her eyes, dropping her gaze to the granite. "He needs to feel strong, and that means he needs to make you, or whoever else, needs to make them feel weak."

"Maybe I was just weak to start with."

Kane's own lips tightened. "I met you before, Gina."

"So?"

Kane took a deep breath and let it out, pushing off from the counter. "So maybe it's time to show him how strong you really are." Her eyes snapped back to him. Kane held her gaze for a long moment. "You decide what you want to eat?" he asked eventually.

Gina exhaled, relaxing slightly into the back of her barstool. "An omelet sounds good, if you're sure you don't mind."

"I definitely don't."

Sabella chose that moment to leave the bathroom, covered only by a yellow towel. The water had shut off a while earlier. She'd probably overheard their conversation and let them finish. "You want an omelet, Bella?" he called.

She stopped beside the door to the bedroom and nodded. "That sounds great. Thank you," she said with a meaningful smile before ducking into the doorway. Unfortunately, the towel didn't slip.

After they had cleared the breakfast dishes, Sabella turned to Gina, who had marginally relaxed around Kane. "We should probably get going."

Gina nodded her agreement.

"Do you want me to make up the couch for you? So you can get some rest?" Sabella asked Kane.

"Nah, it's fine as is." He shook his head for emphasis. "Thanks, Bella."

By the door, the cups of coffee Kane had brought sat untouched. "Mind if we grab these with us?" Sabella asked sheepishly, having completely forgotten about his sweet gesture.

Kane arched an eyebrow. "They're prob'ly cold." Beside her, Gina stiffened. Kane promptly added, "But suit yourself."

"Should we heat them up?" she asked, looking up at Gina.

"It's hot outside," Gina pointed out, avoiding looking at Kane.

"Oh, you're right, as always. Ice cubes?"

Gina's eyebrows and shoulders lifted in timid acquiescence. Kane watched the exchange, bemused. Sabella taking the coffees into her kitchen and pulling out a tray of ice cubes didn't seem to assuage his confusion. "Iced coffees," she explained, though it really should have been clear by that point.

Kane's mouth curled into a smirk. "That's such a fancy West Coast thing."

Sabella smiled back at him. "Yeah, well. They're delicious."

With their drinks filled with adequate amounts of sugar, milk, and ice cubes, the girls finally headed out.

"Drive safe," Kane called after them before shutting the door.

The first stop on their impromptu itinerary was an urgent care center, where Gina's injuries could be adequately assessed.

"It's going to take forever, and I'm *fine*," Gina protested yet again during the drive.

"Gi, I'm driving you to the clinic. I can't force you to go inside, or to get checked out, or to say the word *abuse* if you do get checked out. But that bruise on your ribs looks absolutely awful, and I'd feel better if a medical professional made sure you're going to survive the injury. Be grateful you're dealing with me and not Gerardo." Gina's brother would have dragged her to a doctor kicking and screaming upon seeing the bruises, likely doing more damage—accidentally—in the process, before going on to commit some justifiable yet nonetheless prosecutable crime involving Alistair's welfare.

Gina's silence prickled along Sabella's skin like thousands of needles. "So we don't say anything about Alistair," she stated finally, allowing some of Sabella's anxiety to dissipate. "At the clinic or to my family."

"If you're sure that's what you want," Sabella agreed. She spoke carefully, unwilling to do or say anything that could resemble bullying. The Sabatinos would be at once devastated and furious. Worse, they would almost certainly feel as guilty as Sabella did, which would hurt them further. "At the same time," she continued, still hoping to convince Gina, "having official documentation—even if you don't do anything with it—could be smart."

By that point, they had almost arrived at the urgent care center. "Don't leave me alone with all the doctors, okay?" Gina said once Sabella shut off the engine. "They'll just keep asking all those questions."

Sabella nodded, placing her hand over Gina's. "I'll be right there with you."

After a barrage of photos, x-rays, and subtly prying questions, both the medical staff and Sabella were satisfied with the diagnosis and documentation of Gina's injuries. Luckily, nothing was physically broken.

"So," Sabella asked with false cheer as they left the clinic, "how about lunch and some shopping?"

Gina slanted a look her way and sighed dejectedly. "I don't know, Sabella."

"Oh, come on," she persisted. "I'll even let you choose the restaurant."

A wan, half-hearted smile met her needling. "You always let me choose the restaurant."

Sabella shrugged. "You have great taste. I bow to your incomparable expertise," she teased.

Gina didn't answer as they crossed the parking lot.

"Are you not hungry?" Sabella asked when they reached the car.

Gina considered her over the roof. "If I say no, you're going to drag me back to the doctors aren't you," she accused with a wry twist of the lips.

Sabella suppressed a smile, shoulders and eyebrows lifting simultaneously with feigned innocence.

Gina shook her head and opened the passenger-side door. "You know," she said, sliding into the seat as Sabella followed suit, "you didn't have to remember every trick my ma tried to teach you."

Sabella flashed her a grin. "You flatter me by the mere comparison. Your mom is worlds out of my league." She started the car, ignoring Gina's exasperated stare. "So where are we eating?"

Twenty-Three

$\mathcal{F}$ollowing a revitalizing lunch at Kenny and Zuke's in downtown, the girls paid a visit to some of their favorite boutiques on Tenth Avenue. At first, Gina shied away from the daring choices that had previously defined her style, considering only options that even Sabella, under her tutelage, had come to consider too mundane. She did purchase a cute, albeit gray, dress with long sleeves and a handkerchief hem, which she would hopefully wear accessorized with the vibrant colors that would transform it into a standout piece.

Eventually, the energetic options surrounding them seemed to soak in, and Gina selected a light-pink tee with a multicolored pattern of circles, which she layered over her navy top. Another boutique provided some thick, iridescent hoop earrings that completed Gina's new ensemble and a matching, twisted variant that was deemed suitably outside Sabella's comfort zone. By the time they stopped for manicures, Gina outwardly resembled only a slightly subdued version of her former self.

Despite the pampering, however, a weighted silence hung over them both as they returned to the car. When Sabella pulled out into traffic, Gina popped the muted bubble. "Thanks for doing all this, Sab."

"Of course," Sabella murmured.

"But, it doesn't actually change anything," she continued meekly. Sabella glanced over, waiting for her to go on. "And I don't know how to. I don't know what I can do."

Sabella blew out the breath that had stilled in her lungs. "Well," she said cautiously, "you could start by calling him—ending the relationship."

"Over the phone?"

"Yes," she answered, keeping her voice unemotionally steady to sound certain. "It's a controlled environment, so you know he can't hurt you, and you can prepare what you'd like to say ahead of time so it's unequivocally clear."

"Clear or not, what if he doesn't let me end things?"

"It takes two people to be in a relationship. He may *want* to control you, but he can't actually compel you to stay." She glanced over to verify the efficacy of her words, but Gina, who gazed despondently out the window, seemed unconvinced. "There is nothing he can do to you as long as you're not alone with him, and he can't force you to be alone with him."

"He has a key," Gina whispered so quietly Sabella almost didn't trust having heard it.

"We'll change the locks," she responded evenly, starting a mental "to do" list. *Number one: buy a replacement lock, and maybe an extra deadbolt.*

"What would I even say?" Gina asked a few minutes later.

"That he's scum?" Sabella proposed sarcastically, without thinking.

"I'm not sure that's 'unequivocally clear,'" Gina answered wryly.

Sabella drummed her fingers on the wheel, focusing for a while on navigating the streets. "You could tell him that it's time for the two of you to go your separate ways," she suggested eventually.

"Go our separate ways?" Gina snorted. "Only you could say it like that, Sab."

"What? It's direct and definitely clear."

"It's a little impersonal. Is that how you broke up with all those guys?"

"They got the message," Sabella answered defensively. *Number two: help Gina convincingly break things off with the calculating jerk.*

Gina laughed outright, and, despite her discomposure at the needling, Sabella smiled.

Kane woke to the sound of a door closing. He opened his eyes in time to see Gina disappear further into the apartment and Sabella smile at him. The curve of her lips eased his tension better than the nap. Kane sat up as she came to stand by the couch.

"Did you get some sleep?" she asked softly.

"A little." He tugged her onto the couch beside him. "How'd it go?"

She licked her lips, nodding quickly. "Okay." Her hand smoothed the concern from his face.

He took in hers. She had her hair pulled back and wore earrings he hadn't noticed before. He traced the curve of her ear before thumbing one of the colorful coils. She ducked her head, blushing. "They're, uh—"

"They're nice," he cut her off. A little flashier than he'd seen her wear, but somehow still subtle on her.

Sabella's eyes jumped back to his face. She parted her lips to answer, but Kane leaned closer, and they shared a gentle kiss.

The sound of Gina clearing her throat ended it. Everyone traded uncomfortable glances.

"Mind if I grab a shower?" Kane asked to break the silence.

"No, of course. Let me get you a towel." Sabella stood, and Kane followed her, past Gina, to the bathroom.

Sabella pulled a towel from the cabinet by the door before he stepped inside. She faced him with it in her hands. Almost no space separated them in the small bathroom.

"You want to join me?" he asked softly.

Heat filled her cheeks and her eyes. She swallowed, tongue flicking over her lips again, then pushed the towel silently at his chest. Kane stepped reluctantly to the sink so she could leave.

"So, after he showers…" Gina started to say but cut herself off. They were sitting on the bench in Sabella's dining room, enjoying the evening sun. It was absolutely evident whom she meant, but Sabella was beginning to wonder if she avoided Kane's name intentionally. There were more immediate issues, however.

"I was thinking, we could ask him to go find you a good, solid lock? And maybe a deadbolt?" Sabella suggested, opening the discussion Gina didn't feel comfortable starting.

"Oh, I wouldn't ask him to, I mean, he really doesn't have to run errands for me."

"I'm pretty sure he wouldn't mind."

Gina shot her a pointed look. "I don't think that's quite why he drove up here. Maybe I should run out to find locks, give you guys some time alone."

"I imagine he came up here to help, Gi. I know you're anxious about it, but you do need to call Alistair," Sabella insisted, though carefully. Gina watched her without commenting. "If you'd like Kane out of the apartment when you do…I doubt he would mind. He could probably even help us put the new locks on tonight. You still have the toolbox your dad left, right?" Gina nodded her confirmation. The two of them weren't entirely self-sufficient when it came to tools and construction, but both could manage the basics.

The bathroom door swung open before Gina could protest again. Kane strode out, his wet hair finger-combed back from his face, but stopped with his arms crossed, on the other side of the dining table. The rivulet-shaped mirrors on the wall behind him reflected the sunlight streaming through the windows, so it sparked over the dampness of his hair only to echo again in the mirrors.

"What's the plan, ladies?" he asked in the face of their stares. Now, no hint of his charmingly irresistible smile graced Kane's features. Even attempting to seem harmless, he looked formidable—steadfastly protective.

Sabella glanced at Gina then asked him, "Have you eaten lunch or anything since we left?"

Kane's brows drew together, angling up at their outer edges. "I'm fine."

Sabella licked her lips and looked over at Gina again, who faintly shrugged her shoulders. "We were, well. We need to get some new locks, for Gina's place, so, that has to happen at some point," Sabella told him.

Kane lifted and dropped his chin in a single, contemplative nod. "Do you want some help putting those in?" he asked, looking to Gina.

Sabella started to respond but bit her lip instead.

Not that long ago, Gina would have sweet-talked any guy into helping her with whatever may have needed doing, but she was obviously hesitant even to accept the offer. "That would be nice of you," she ultimately agreed with a slight stammer, barely making eye contact.

"It's not a problem," Kane confirmed. "Anything else I could do?" he directed to Sabella.

"Well, honestly, I've never had to buy locks. I guess, we would simply have to go to a hardware store?" Sabella couldn't bring herself to contradict Gina's previously affirmed preference, regardless of her personal belief that it was a perfectly acceptable means of having Kane leave the apartment for a while, especially since the errand had to be done either way.

Kane wasn't lacking in the intelligence department, however. Even if he couldn't somehow tell they wanted privacy so Gina could make that phone call, he knew she didn't feel particularly comfortable around him, and the tension building among the three of them was nearly unbearable. "I could go buy some," he suggested nonchalantly. "Save you the trip."

Sabella waited for Gina to reply, attempting—and likely failing—to maintain a similarly unconcerned posture.

"All right," Gina agreed, pressing her lips together into a tight curve resembling a smile. "Thanks."

"Sure. Any, uh, any color preferences or…?"

The girls exchanged a mystified look. "I think the one you have now is kind of tarnished silver?" Sabella commented.

"Yeah, probably. So, silver, I guess?"

"Do you want to add a door chain or anything?" Sabella asked. Even though Alistair may be able to break through the door regardless, it would be an additional deterrent, or at the very least, proof of violent entry, though Sabella fervently hoped the situation wouldn't progress to such extremes.

"Yeah, I guess that'd be a good idea. If you wouldn't mind," Gina added hastily, eyes flicking across the room to Kane.

"Not at all." Kane started toward the door, and Sabella rose to follow him. He paused to lift his jacket from the couch, patting the pockets before pulling out his wallet and keys.

Sabella wanted to reach for him, to wrap her arms around his waist, both in gratitude for his willingness to help and for the comfort the touch would provide. Instead, she told him quietly, "I think there's a hardware store nearby. Would you like me to write down directions for you?"

"I'll find somewhere. There's GPS in the truck." He spoke as softly as she had, the raspy tinge to his voice underscoring the tension evident in the stern lines of his expression.

"Thank you," Sabella mouthed.

"See you in a bit," he answered, heading out the door.

Sabella blew out her breath between puffed cheeks before turning back toward the dining room.

It was growing late, so they decided to call Alistair as soon as Kane left. Sabella brought out her laptop since she could type faster than she could write, and, after several rounds of pacing and some minutes of deep breathing, Gina placed the call.

"Gina," his voice came over the speaker, calm and confident.

"Hi," she responded.

Sabella nodded in encouragement.

"How is your friend?" Alistair asked into the ensuing silence, his distaste plainly evident even through the phone.

"She's…better." Sabella waited for her to go on, but Gina froze. Sabella started typing in bold text on her screen as Alistair confirmed their dinner plans. Gina took another deep breath then spoke resolutely. "Listen, Alistair—"

"Don't tell me you're cancelling again because of some drama," he interrupted.

"No, that's not it," Gina murmured. She swallowed then continued with a clenched jaw. "I think it's time we go our separate ways." She struggled but managed to complete the sentence, prompting a small smile from Sabella.

"What are you talking about, Gina?" he asked, seemingly still unflustered.

Gina stood from her seat by the dining table and strode toward the door and back. "Exactly what I just said. Our relationship isn't working, so it's over."

"Gina, you know I care about you deeply. Whatever is bothering you, I'm sure we can find a logical solution," he said calmly.

Gina stalled back beside Sabella, who typed, *Unforgivable.*

Alistair resumed speaking, but Gina nodded sharply and cut him off. "There isn't a way to fix this, Alistair. We're done." Her fists clenched in the stunned silence that followed.

"All right," Alistair finally stated smoothly. "I'll come by tonight to pick up my things."

Gina glanced at her, so startled and scared her eyes seemed to double in size, and Sabella typed furiously. "Don't worry about that," Gina told him, reading the screen. "I can pack up anything you may have left and drop it off in the lobby at work."

"I'd like to talk to you in person," he protested.

"There's nothing left to say." She seemed to be gaining confidence as his imperturbable demeanor slipped. "We're done," she repeated.

Hang up, Sabella typed. It wasn't the superb breakup that Gina's past suitors had likely experienced, but she had successfully ended their affiliation.

Gina sank back onto the bench, her cell phone hanging weightily in her hand. Even the bright sunlight streaming in behind her couldn't alter the somber moment, as though the rays glanced off an impenetrable bubble around her. Sabella silently waited for her to process, and recover.

When Gina set the phone down beside herself, Sabella noted quietly, "You did it."

Gina's gaze flew to Sabella but dropped back to the floor in front of her after a couple blinks. "I don't want to go back to my apartment," she whispered. "It's just so filled with him."

"Well, you don't have to." There was no question that Gina could stay with her, until she felt comfortable going back or found another apartment. Simultaneously, though, that would be another thing Alistair would have stolen from her. Gina had loved that apartment once. "Or we could change it," Sabella suggested. "Make it all you again."

"Change it?"

"An apartment makeover." The idea was teetering between stupid and brilliant, but Sabella plowed on. "A splash of color can make a huge difference, or we could switch up the décor."

Gina regarded her as if she was unrecognizable. "I can't paint my place; my landlord would kill me."

Sabella shrugged. Their roles had certainly reversed. "We'll paint it back if you ever decide to move out."

A smile tugged hesitantly at Gina's lips. "It'd be a lot of work," she pointed out.

"I think we can handle it." Sabella smiled at her. "We could try to do a mural or something if you wanted."

Gina laughed in mock horror. "Neither of us knows how to paint."

"That's a minor obstacle," Sabella agreed.

"We could use stencils or something?" Gina suggested, still somewhat hesitantly, though the idea was obviously growing on her.

"Yes! That is definitely a smarter plan." A tight smile rewarded the statement. "We could do it tomorrow."

"There are lots of things to take care of, though," Kane heard Gina saying as he returned to Sabella's place.

"All we need to do is choose colors, buy supplies, and get the furniture out of the way," Sabella answered.

Kane closed the door and set the replacement locks down.

The two of them came out into the hallway, still chatting. "That'll take a fair amount of time, and I do have that little thing called work, Sab," Gina said.

"You could skip one more day, right? We'll convince Roger to help. He's always making noises about feeling left out. Plus, he probably has more experience stenciling than either of us."

"Oh, yeah. Can you imagine Roger moving furniture?" They both laughed. It was a great sound.

"Maybe Kane could help out with that part," Sabella suggested, looking at him. "Hi, there," she added with a smile that was less about humor.

"Hey." Kane walked to them. "Help move furniture?"

"We're discussing painting her apartment," Sabella explained.

"You want to move things tonight?" he asked. Like it or not, he had to leave tomorrow so he could make it to Reno.

"We don't have any supplies or anything," Gina said. She

still didn't look completely comfortable, but she didn't shrink from him, either. "Or colors, for that matter."

"What about a yellow? It's cheerful, and it's supposed to make you subconsciously happier or something," Sabella told them, moving into the living room.

Gina followed, and both of the girls settled on the couch. Kane kept his distance just in case and chose an armchair, as Sabella went on.

"Or blue? It's a calming color, I think. Red is supposed to be infuriating, or something."

"Really?" Gina asked, actually interested.

Kane just let them talk.

"Or passionate? I don't remember, but we could look it up. Or you could just choose the colors you want."

"Oh, we could do some really bright trims if we don't use stencils?" Gina seemed timidly excited about the idea.

"Whatever you want, Gi. It's your place," Sabella told her, a bit more seriously.

"We'd have to buy a lot of stuff," Gina pointed out.

"We can go tomorrow morning," Sabella said. "We'd need to remember to buy tarps to cover everything. But we can measure everything when we change the locks tonight?"

Gina nodded. The bright earrings she wore looked less out of place now than before he'd left.

"And since we're going to head over anyway, we could move the furniture tonight as well. Kill two birds?" Sabella added, looking between them with a falsely angelic expression.

"Let's do it," Kane answered, seeing right through her.

They both looked at Gina for the final decision. She nodded unevenly, focusing on something other than the room in front of her, and smiled.

Twenty-Four

Sabella and Kane followed Gina to her place to initiate the process of eradicating everything Alistair-related. Kane impressively managed to be simultaneously unobtrusive and indispensable.

As he, with some minor help from Sabella, moved the living room furniture, Gina created a pile of Alistair's things by the door. When they switched to the bedroom, Sabella ducked into the spacious closet in search of a box they could re-appropriate. The majority of Gina's vivacious garments had disappeared from the hangers—some replaced by a couple of suits, men's shirts, and a few ties—though hopefully the clothes had been moved rather than discarded. A big box stood tucked into the corner of the walk-in closet, and Sabella nudged it out into the bedroom, where Kane and Gina were discussing her bookshelves.

"I guess we could keep that wall white," Gina was saying. The tall bookshelves covered most of the wall, other than a small patch of space beside the door.

"That'd make it, well, it'd be easier to move all the other furniture out of the way then," Kane agreed.

"We could still stencil that area by the door, if you want," Sabella suggested.

Gina agreed, so Kane shifted her dresser toward the bookshelves and away from the adjoining wall.

"Hey, Gi, what's in this box?" Sabella asked meanwhile.

"That's just some clothing," she answered, barely glancing over her shoulder.

Sabella snatched some scissors to open it. Vivid fabrics reached out of the box as though seeking air they had long been denied. Sabella clenched her jaw and emptied the box onto the bed, barely containing a verbal response to this new sign of Gina's recent suppression.

When all the furniture had been repositioned, Kane set about replacing the locks, while the girls sorted through Gina's clothes and finished gathering Alistair's things, the majority of which they dumped unceremoniously into the freed box. Gina insisted on treating the expensive suits with more care, and Sabella refrained from commenting, focusing instead on the minor victory of the revitalized closet.

It was dark outside by the time Kane finished putting in the new locks. Sabella had gone out to pick up color samples and takeout. Gina hadn't objected to being left alone with him, which Kane took as a good sign. She sat in her recliner with her laptop. They didn't bother with chitchat, which suited him just fine.

Kane tested the chain then replaced the tools in their small box, leaving the door unlocked for Sabella. He still needed to move the entertainment center before they left, but besides that everything was set.

"Any chance you'd look at the loose shelf in my closet?" Gina asked when he turned to her. She swallowed nervously but didn't look away.

Kane smiled at the improvement. All in all, she was bouncing back quickly. "Sure," he said. He grabbed the tools and went into the bedroom. Fixing the shelf was a bit more complicated than tightening a screw, but Kane wasn't phased. He hummed a new melody quietly as he worked.

When he heard Gina's voice from the other room a while later, he assumed Sabella'd come back. Until a man's voice answered.

Kane made it out of the bedroom in time to see a slick man in a suit backhand Gina. Instantly, Kane pulled the man away and slugged him.

The suit backed away, hand on his jaw, and turned to Gina, who stood with her arms wrapped around herself, by the fridge. "Is *this* why you tried to break things off?" he yelled. "Him? You thought you could cheat on me? You think you can humiliate me like that! You ungrateful whore!" He made another move toward Gina, but Kane blocked his way.

"Get out," he growled, trying to stop himself from more violence.

"Get out of my way," the other man said with a sneer. He tried to shove Kane.

Kane grabbed the outstretched arm and punched him again. Fury drove his blows. The other man fought back, even landing a few shots, but Kane was better, stronger. He drove the fight across the living room, managing to avoid most of the furniture. The consideration let a solid punch connect with his own jaw.

Kane retaliated with a hit to the solar plexus. He'd been in enough fights to know how to take a hit, and do a lot of damage. And those'd been with real men, not this pansy who got his rocks off hitting women.

Kane shoved him out the still open door and onto the private landing. The bruises around Gina's collar drove him to press the other man over the railing. Kane kept hold of an arm, twisting it behind the scumbag's back, and pressed his free arm into the man's neck, dangling him over the parking lot. It was only a one-story drop, but it'd still do some damage.

"You stay away from her. You understand?"

The suit continued to struggle. Kane shoved him harder into the railing. For a moment, he considered letting the man fall. He deserved worse than the broken leg it'd give him.

"Kane?" He turned his head to see Sabella standing at the foot of the stairs with some shopping bags. He forced himself to let go of the other man, making sure to block the door to the apartment.

The pansy wiped at the blood seeping from his nose. "You're crazy!" he accused.

Kane clenched his jaw and his fists. He kept a wide stance in case the idiot decided to charge him.

"You'd better leave, Alistair," Sabella said evenly from below.

Alistair tried to size up Kane again but decided not to press his luck. He was obviously used to targets who didn't hit back. He stumbled down the stairs. Kane followed partway, in case he was dumb enough to try hitting Sabella.

Instead, he sneered at her. "You think she's better off with him? Look at how far she's come with me! *No one* will be as good for her as I was, especially not this pugilist trash! With those uncontrolled violent tendencies, you'd both better watch out. Who knows whom he'll attack next?"

Sabella held her ground without answering or correcting the assumption. Alistair looked again at Kane before skulking off. Sabella spared Kane a glance he couldn't quite read before rushing past him up the stairs.

Kane gripped the railing, regaining control. A few breaths later, he walked stiffly inside the apartment. Sabella sat on the kitchen floor, hugging a crying Gina to her. She looked at Kane with eyes at once devastated and determined, resolutely protective.

Kane couldn't move. *Uncontrolled violent tendencies...* The scumbag's words rang in his head. *Watch out.*

He'd *never* hit Sabella, or Gina, or any woman. He could only hope, after what she'd seen, Sabella would believe that, despite also seeing him hit Mitch just days earlier. But even if she did, that wouldn't change the harsh part of him.

Growing up in the country, fighting hadn't been a rare part of his, or anyone else's, life. The women he was used to expected it, understood it. But Sabella came from a more delicate, more refined background. In his world, men settled things with their fists. In hers? They probably talked or something. Maybe the pansy'd been right, and the violence in him couldn't be truly controlled. It had no part in her world.

When Gina fell asleep, Sabella slipped out of her bedroom as quietly as she could. Kane sat by the island, an ice pack absently pressed to his face.

It had taken significant comforting and enticing, but she had ultimately managed to persuade Gina out of the apartment and into the car. Kane had left first, scooping up all the bags she had dropped in the living room, and taken Sabella's car.

She still didn't have a clear picture of what had happened. Thankfully, Kane had been there and had intervened before Alistair had done any further physical damage. The image of Kane wholly dominating the other man, lit by the moon and a distant street lamp, was laser-etched in her mind. He had been fierce, almost ferociously protective. Now, he appeared more introspective, with an undertone of despair.

"You want to come in the bathroom? Let me try to patch you up?" she murmured so as not to disturb Gina through the thin walls.

Kane rose without a word. Sabella went into the bathroom and pulled out a first aid kit, trusting him to follow. He leaned against the counter and dropped the ice into the sink.

Sabella surveyed the damage as unemotionally as she could. The knuckles of his right hand, already bruised from the altercation with Mitch, were pretty banged up. Another bruise was forming over his cheekbone, and a small cut with dried blood damaged the line of his lips. Kane seemed to try to shrink into the corner under her scrutiny. Sabella shut the door, noticing a new tightening around his eyes.

She gently cupped the side of his face that wasn't visibly injured. "Are you all right?"

Kane's expression didn't soften, and he avoided eye contact. "Maybe I should stay somewhere, in a hotel or somethin', stay somewhere else," he said stonily.

Sabella dropped her hand, struck by his words. She busied herself with opening a bottle of hydrogen peroxide and pouring some on a clean face towel. When Kane didn't object, she dabbed at the dried blood beside his lip, then at his scraped knuckles. She worked in silence, and eventually his gaze returned to her.

For a moment, she returned his regard but then diverted her attention to his shirt. She hadn't been present for enough of the fight to know whether Alistair had landed any blows other than those on his face, but she needed to check, especially considering the horrid bruising on Gina's ribcage. She began to inch his shirt up, but Kane gently grabbed both of her wrists. Sabella looked up at him, silently questioning.

"You heard what he said," Kane told her.

Sabella was temporarily at a loss, caught in his fervid scrutiny. When understanding dawned, another piece of her heart broke away, replaced with a deepening ache. With a perverted yet perfected skill, Alistair had used a few effective words to slice deeply into the man before her.

"Kane." He freed her wrists, and she immediately yearned to touch him, to comfort him however she could. "You are absolutely nothing like that piece of garbage," she assured. He diverted his eyes once again. "You use your strength to protect people, not control or demean them."

"Does that really matter?" he asked. The pain she had seen in his eyes belied the calm of his voice and stiffened her resolve.

"Of course it does. There is nothing inherently wrong with being strong, or even with using that strength." She cupped his jaw carefully with both her hands. He no longer looked away but rather stared at her, as if drinking in every detail of her expression. "You are a good person. You stood up for someone who couldn't do it for herself, and that is honorable and noble. And this concern? This questioning? It only proves that. Terrible people don't worry about the morality of their actions. Only truly good people, who are forced by circumstance to act, do."

Kane continued to watch her, completely unmoving.

Sabella tilted her face closer to his but paused to add, "You did a wonderful thing tonight. Don't let his spiteful words destroy you because of it."

Hopefully her words had registered, because he dipped his head the meager distance between them to kiss her, extraordinarily gently.

Sabella's lips pressing against the cut in his hurt, but Kane ignored it. He'd had worse injuries. Her soft hands brushing over his bruises had been torturous but for other reasons entirely. When he kissed her, those hands slipped to their usual spot on his shoulders. He brushed his thumbs over her cheeks then slipped the band from her hair. The soft waves fell over his battered knuckles.

Sabella pulled back, barely breaking their kiss. Her hands slipped down to lift his shirt. This time, Kane didn't stop her. She tossed it on the counter behind him and ran her hands over his torso, pausing over his ribs.

She's worried. She'd only seen the tail end of the fight. She had no way of knowing the scumbag hadn't landed more than a couple blows. He might end up with a couple more bruises but nothing more serious than that. "I'm all right," he assured.

Sabella licked her lips and looked down at her hands. Her fingers flexed gently into his skin. Kane cupped her head, pulling it to his chest. Her arms circled his waist. He wrapped his free one around her and stroked her hair.

They stood like that for a drawn-out moment. Having her in his arms destroyed any of his leftover concerns.

When her lips pressed to his chest, Kane stilled. When her tongue flicked out, he loosened his hold. Her hands moved to his hips as her mouth traced a burning pattern on his skin. She kissed lightly up to his jaw. Kane dipped his head closer, taking in her scent. She brushed his hair back and rose up on tiptoes to lay a soft kiss over his swollen cheek. Kane swallowed.

Sabella's attention then shifted to his right hand. She lifted it in both her smaller ones. He intertwined their fingers. Her free hand traced gently over his knuckles.

"I make a terrible nurse," she said before placing a soft kiss over the bruises.

Kane used his free hand to bring her closer. She'd already changed into a tank top and pajama bottoms, which shifted under his hand to reveal her skin. "Best one I ever had."

Sabella smiled and tilted her chin up for another kiss. Kane was only too happy to oblige. The kiss deepened, and his hand slipped lower. Sabella's body pressed along the length of his through the thin fabric of her clothes and the more annoying tightness of his jeans. He was more than ready to strip them both of everything they still wore but didn't want tonight to end with him taking her against the bathroom wall.

His hands slipped just under her top. Hers traced over his chest and shoulders, coming to rest on his biceps. They broke the kiss at the same time. Sabella stepped back, putting the smallest distance between their bodies.

"I should go make up the couch," she whispered.

Kane's hands flexed over her waist, before he forced himself to let go. "I already did." He'd put things together while Sabella had been taking care of Gina in the bedroom.

Sabella nodded, lips forming a silent "o." Her hands dropped to fidget with the forgotten first-aid kit. Kane reached behind himself to pick up his shirt. The awareness between them was too intense, like it'd been months since they'd last been together. Kane placed his hand on hers, stopping its nervous actions.

Her eyes flew to his and some of the tension eased. Kane straightened from the counter and opened the door. Sabella switched off the lights, and he followed her out into the darkened apartment.

She stopped at the foot of the folded-out couch. A small lamp he'd left on still shone in the corner. Without looking, Kane tossed his shirt toward the duffel bag he'd brought in earlier.

They stood facing each other. Kane's hands traced the waistband over her hips. He slid his thumbs under it and, when she didn't protest, let the bottoms drop to the floor. She stepped out of them without breaking eye contact. Her fingers moved delicately down over his abs until they hit his jeans. She unbuttoned them then stopped. Kane let go of her long enough to slide his remaining clothes over his hips, kicking everything aside. She looked from his eyes, down his body, and back again in appreciation.

The light in the corner shone enough that her hair gleamed over her shoulders. Her hands still rested on his hips. Kane swallowed through a clenched jaw. He inched her top up. She lifted her arms, and he peeled it off, revealing more of her skin to the glow of the lamp and to his eyes.

Sabella's tongue flicked over her lips, drawing his attention. He slid his hands down her arms, preventing her habit of covering up when there was light on. He leaned closer for a gentle kiss. Her fingers tightened in his. She stretched against him, breasts grazing his chest, deepening the kiss. With her hands still in his, Kane hooked his thumbs in the straps of her panties. He slid their hands down the curve of her hips until that last scrap of fabric fell.

Breathing deeply, Sabella broke their kiss. Kane lifted her hands, relishing the rise and fall of her chest in the light, and hooked them behind his neck. He traced the lines of her arms and down over her sides until his hands covered her ribs. His thumbs rested just under her breasts, and she shivered.

Kane lifted her to lay her down on the temporary bed. Her knee bent instinctively to make room as his body covered hers.

His skin burned everywhere it touched hers. The tender emotion in her eyes heightened his desire even more.

They took their time with a gentle passion that was exactly what both of them needed.

Twenty-Five

Kane was the epitome of patience as Gina and Sabella selected colors in the paint store. They'd settled on base colors over breakfast—pale blue and green for the living and dining areas, light yellow and pink for her bedroom—and had been discussing contrast colors ever since. Granted, since Gina had walked in to see Sabella and Kane curled around each other, still naked though thankfully under the blankets, color choices made for a significantly better topic than the alternative.

Their exquisitely tender night seemed to have brought them to a new level of intimacy, but Sabella doubted Kane would welcome knowing Gina had caught them. Then again, he was considerably more comfortable with nudity than Sabella was, so perhaps he wouldn't care. He'd probably also not obsess about what last night meant for them.

When they had finally purchased sufficient tarps, brushes, trays, stencils, and paint—and loaded everything into Kane's truck—they headed over to Gina's apartment. Roger had gleefully agreed to join them, not that there had been any doubt. Gina had officially given him permission to take a half-day. She was growing progressively more tense as they neared her apartment. Her fingernails tapped erratically against the armrest of her seat. She didn't appear fearful but rather determined to reclaim her life, which was encouraging.

Kane parked beside the private entrance to facilitate unloading the supplies. Gina hesitated briefly when opening her new locks but pushed through whatever memory had caught her. Unlike Sabella, she had seen most of the men's fight. Both of them considered it unlikely that Alistair would return after the beating. The box containing his things still waited inside the door, but Kane brought it down to Sabella's car between trips with the paint supplies. With everything that had happened, they hadn't measured Gina's walls the night before, so they had purchased an excessive amount of paint, but the store clerk had assured them they could return any unopened cans.

By the time everything was upstairs and they had covered most of the living and dining furniture with protective plastic, Roger arrived, in a hilarious take on painting clothes. He wore jeans Sabella was pretty certain hadn't started out the morning as ripped, and a tight, black tee shirt that wouldn't last an hour with all the paint, but Roger cared more about "the look."

"Ladies," he announced walking in the door. "I have arrived to make sure you don't blow this…" He trailed off when he caught a glimpse of Kane, who also wore jeans and a tee shirt that hugged his biceps, though his was a subdued blue. Roger's eyebrows shot up, which Sabella interpreted as a sign of approval. "Is this the cowboy?" he inquired in a mock whisper.

At his distinctive voice, Gina came out from the bedroom, where they had placed all of the supplies. Sabella and Kane rose from taping down the last of the tarp. "Kane," Sabella introduced, "this is Roger, Gina's assistant. Roger, this is Kane."

"Gina's assistant? That's what I am now, is it?" Roger pouted. Sabella was often jealous of his ability to look cute while pouting, primarily because he frequently reminded her of this skill.

"Her associate editor, and our friend," she obediently amended. Beside her, Kane stiffened a bit as Roger looked him up and down in a manner that was blatantly sexual. "Behave!" Sabella chided.

"All right, all right! Nice to meet you," Roger said with a tilt of the head.

"Don't just stand there, Rodge. You're here to work," Gina teased. She had changed into an old, oversized, cut-up tee shirt that dipped off one shoulder and some leggings she wouldn't have any trouble replacing if they were ruined. Of everyone, she looked most ready to paint. Sabella had also brought an oversized tee to change into, but she wore some jean shorts and a pastel top for now.

"There you are!" Roger said, redirecting his attention. "It's a good thing you called me; it's about time we redid this drab place of yours." Gina cocked an eyebrow at the word *drab*. "*Tsk*. You know what I mean!" he added with a placating smile.

Gina had significant practice managing Roger, and he had learned essentially to read her mind, so when she turned back to the bedroom, he followed, no doubt to "consult" on their selected colors and stencils. Their voices carried back out to the living room, and Sabella smiled fondly. For whatever reason, the pairing worked ingeniously, and, over the years, Roger had become one of their closest friends. It was surprisingly nice, introducing Kane into her world, though she may feel otherwise when her friends chose to comment unabashedly. The word *scrumdiddlyumptious* would almost certainly be appearing in her near future—not that Sabella disagreed with such an assessment of Kane.

The aforementioned singer dropped his roll of tape onto the covered dining table and drew her closer for a half-hug and a kiss. With their arms wrapped around each other's waists, he asked, "Think I could steal you away for a bit?"

"Is everything okay?" she asked, noting his serious expression.

"You know I have to get going soon."

Sabella was tempted to imitate Roger's pout, but she couldn't pull it off, and it wasn't really news. Kane had taken his duffel bag and guitar from her place before they left that morning. They both needed to return to their real lives. That didn't mean she was ready to say goodbye.

"Ooh, lazy lovers alert," Roger joked from the bedroom doorway, claiming their attention. Sabella and Kane shifted to a decorous distance and faced the other pair.

"Do you mind if we duck out for a little while?" Sabella asked.

"Well, I do," Roger cut in, twirling the brush he held.

"Good thing I was asking Gina," Sabella retorted. "Kane has to leave soon."

Gina shot her a knowing look that was so ultimately her, Sabella had to smile, though she assumed Kane's request had in fact been relatively innocent. "Don't feel like painting?" Gina asked him.

"Y'know me," he responded, deadpan and with a falsely thick drawl. "Hate liftin' a finger."

Gina smiled and instructed, "Bring her back in one piece."

"Yes, ma'am."

Kane set aside his guitar and held his hand out for Sabella. She laced her fingers through his and shifted a bit closer. They sat under the same tree they'd visited on his first trip to see her. It was a much-needed break from the intensity of the past few days. Unfortunately, it didn't change the fact that Kane had to get back to his tour. Like it or not, their circumstances were about to change, again.

"So," Sabella ventured, nervously twisting her lips, "where's your next stop?"

"Reno." Kane looked down at their loosely intertwined fingers. It was going to be tough, but this conversation needed to happen. "So, listen. Bella, you're so unlike any woman I've ever—"

"I know," she cut him off, letting go of his hand. "You don't have to…" She licked her lips. Kane wasn't sure where she was going, so he didn't interrupt. "I know. I've always been pretty certain I'm nothing like your type—I'm not tall enough, or leggy enough, or just Southern enough." She forced a smile. "And with everything that has happened… It's okay, you don't have to explain."

"Okay…I mean, yeah, you're not really any—" Kane stopped himself. She thought he was ending things. "You're unlike the women I've known, and you're nothing at all like what I thought I wanted." He took her hand back in his. "But you're so much better, it's hard to believe. *Not* in the sense that I don't trust you," he added quickly.

Sabella watched him, eyes narrowed. Speaking clearly wasn't his big talent. Maybe he should have written another song. Kane took a deep breath and went on. "What I mean is, you're incredible." She looked down. "You don't behave like Southern women do, you're right, but it's so much easier with you. You're not all defensive, but you have this, you have a quiet, soft strength that runs deep. It's probably why, uh, why you're still putting up with me." She didn't quite smile, but she didn't stop him either. "Maybe you're not—what'd you call it? leggy?—but you're so damn beautiful. Unbelievably sexy, in case I haven't, you know, if I haven't made that clear. And I like how you just, you fit so perfectly under my arm.

"You're classy, but not in a snotty way. Or, worse, high-maintenance, or you'd have never been willing to deal with those guys, and, you know, everything with our shows. I know, I was an idiot to think you were at all, that you'd act at all like those other women. You're just, well, you're too honest and sweet, and a bit too unaware of your own charms, to use people. What I'm trying to say is…" She was back to looking at him, with slightly wide eyes. Kane's thumb played over her palm, trying to reassure her, or maybe himself. "You're *not* anything like I thought I'd want, even some months ago. But you're exactly what I've been missing."

Sabella opened her mouth, then closed it and licked her lips again. "You're going to make me blush," she joked, looking away again.

Kane crooked a finger under her chin, tilting it up gently until her eyes followed the motion. "I love you."

After a shocked moment, Sabella lips curved uncertainly. When she didn't say anything, Kane pushed down the fear that he'd been mistaken and kissed her. She kissed him back, and Kane thought back to the completely open look in her eyes the night before.

Still, when she pulled back, he couldn't shake an unsettled feeling. He dropped his hand. "What is it?" he asked, with forced calm.

Sabella's lips pressed together as if trying to keep the words in, but she finally said, "Alistair told Gina he loved her." Kane froze, jaw clenching. "And Riley, he said that to me, too, and I thought, naïvely, that I loved him. That ended so incredibly badly. For me, I mean, he seemed pretty okay with it."

"He broke your heart," Kane stated. A part of him hated the guy for hurting her, and for getting her love, for knowing her first.

"Well, at the time, it felt like it. It doesn't matter."

Kane wanted to comfort her, to reach out and stroke the hair she'd left down. But he didn't move, trying to figure out her point.

"Those things you said," she whispered, closing her eyes for a moment before continuing, "I feel like such a fraud. I'm not strong, or sweet, or any of that, and—"

Kane stopped the flow of words with a finger on her lips. "You're everything I said and even more." Her breath puffed against his fingers. He thought over her protests, piecing them together. "It's not about the words, about saying it. I know how you feel about me. You've shown me so many times, it just took me a while, took way too long, really, for me to figure it out."

Sabella's hand cupped the uninjured side of his face. "You're so wonderful," she murmured.

Kane shifted, pulling Sabella's hand around so she moved, too, settling against him. He pressed a kiss against her head. "You know I have to go, and I know you can't come with me." He squeezed her hands in his. "But we can figure it out. We'll change the circumstances how we want."

He felt her chuckle against his chest. They stayed there like that a while. Sabella's head rested on his shoulder. His arms held her. The wind tangled their hair together. Kane had no idea how they would continue from there. His mind should have been racing, but it was strangely calm.

"You're right, you know," Sabella said eventually. "It's not about the words, especially since in some sense or another, both of us spend our careers manipulating them."

Kane waited, feeling her take a deep breath.

"I'm not certain when I started feeling this way about you—maybe it was even simply you coming up, being here through all this, or maybe it was back in California—but I know that, at the very least, I've been standing on the edge of that particular cliff for weeks." She twisted to look up at him then paused for an endless moment before finally saying, "I love you, too."

Kane smiled, memorizing the emotions on her face, and kissed her.

They hadn't discussed any concrete plans before Kane left for Reno, but somehow Sabella wasn't concerned. The last several days had been filled with incredibly draining, intense emotions. In a way, their conversation in the park was no less intense, but the time she had spent in his arms had been soothing and reassuring. That same sensation of being sheltered that she had experienced on a bridge in Nashville what felt like so long ago had returned, heightened by her new knowledge of Kane's fervent protectiveness. She hadn't quite yet processed what he had told her, or her own response, particularly in conjunction with their current, de facto long-distance situation. She did know he had supported her without hesitation and that she wasn't prepared for their relationship to end.

"Plus, fantastic sex," Gina pointed out as they painted, unabashedly weighing in on the current state of Sabella's love life. They weren't aiming for a professional effect, so the living and dining areas were nearly finished, other than the stenciling.

"That's so not fair," Roger commented, finishing the wall beside the bedroom door. "That good-looking *and* great in bed? Maybe I should take a trip to Nashville."

"Yeah, I'm sure guys like Kane are just lying around, waiting for tourists," Gina told him.

"How nice would that be?" Sabella chimed in.

"Oh is one not enough for you? Guess the sex isn't *that* good," Roger tossed over his shoulder.

Sabella searched for something to throw at him. So far, he had managed to keep his tee shirt pristine, though his jeans were in fact covered in paint drips. "I am definitely more than satisfied with the one I have," she protested instead.

"Well, look at you," Gina commented, pointing out the pleased smile that accompanied Sabella's words. "You really do love him."

Sabella sobered, unsure how to share her happiness given the reason they were painting.

"Hey," Gina said, tossing down her paintbrush. "He's one of the good ones."

Sabella followed suit, laying her brush down on one of the trays. "He said he loved me, when we were out," she admitted. Gina's features resettled into a genuine smile. "I reciprocated the sentiment."

"Of course you did," Gina stated sagely. Her smile slipped, but she continued resolutely, "This is great."

"Super," Roger added, disgruntled. "Miss Savvy's fallen head over heels for a cowboy, and I'm here painting with a couple of ladies who've forgotten the point of their brushes. Next thing you know, Gina will go off with some cute delivery boy as I finish up her bedroom."

The girls rolled their eyes. "What delivery boy?" Gina asked.

Sabella elbowed her, conscientiously aiming for the arm. Roger was intentionally overly dramatic, but he wasn't above a hissy fit, either. As long as he was happy, he would keep painting, which was promising for the results.

"You know I'd choose hanging out with the two of you over any delivery boy," Gina dutifully corrected. A purely sad look crossed her face, which Roger didn't see, but Sabella squeezed Gina's hand in hers.

"Speaking of delivery boys, are we ordering out or should we get him to cook?" Sabella teased, changing the topic.

"Ugh, we can't eat here," Roger asserted.

"Hey, now!" Gina objected.

"Paint fumes," he clarified, wrinkling his nose. "You may have all the windows flung as open as they'll go, but we should take a break from this lovely scent, regardless. I, for one, still have need of my brain cells."

"You're being so snarky," Sabella noted.

"That's because I'm the only one working!"

"Aw…" the girls intoned, laughing, and moved over to give him a hug.

Roger swatted their hands away, pouting again.

"All right!" Gina scolded playfully. "Okay, how's this: we finish up out here and do the first coat in the bedroom, and then we can go out while it dries, and you can buy lunch for us two pretty ladies."

Sabella giggled. Roger's jaw dropped almost comically. "*I'll* buy lunch," Sabella interjected to prevent him from spluttering.

"Always the peacemaker," Gina said, wrapping her in a one-armed hug.

Roger regarded both of them with a long-suffering expression, before suggesting impishly, "We could always expense it."

Twenty-Six

By Friday, Gina's apartment had been successfully revitalized, and she returned to work with a somewhat subdued but significantly less severe approach to fashion, which was favorable for her career. Roger was placed under strict orders to meet her in the lobby every morning and walk her to her car in the evenings, though Sabella wasn't certain how much of a deterrent he would actually be, and more importantly, how long Gina would allow him to trail her. So, Sabella had come up with a better plan.

"Hey Benny," she greeted, striding up to the security guards in the lobby of the building where Gina, and Alistair, worked. She was meeting Gina for lunch but had arrived early with the box filled with Alistair's things. Personally, Sabella would have found it acceptable to cover the entirety with an accelerant and enjoy the flames, but she didn't want Gina to owe him anything or for him to have any excuse to contact her.

"Elle," Benny responded with a nod. He had met their friend, Melody, when she had come to seek Gina's advice, which had led to him growing relatively close with the girls. Benny actually knew Sabella's real name, but he respected her chosen pseudonym in this building. He was generally quite courteous and sweet overall, reminding Sabella of a muscled teddy bear with a buzz cut.

She slid the box onto the counter in front of him. It was labeled, so he accepted it without comment, moving it out of the way. The simple gesture somehow lifted all of the metaphorical weight off her shoulders. "How are the wedding plans coming along?" she asked him.

"Melody's going a little crazy," he answered with a fond smile.

Sabella laughed, wholly unsurprised. Melody was a petite, warm-hearted fireball. Benny wasn't one for chatting, particularly at work, so Sabella skipped to the point. "So, Benny, listen, there's this guy upstairs—"

He cut her off with a reproving yet apologetic look. "You know I can't give Gina anyone's number."

Sabella almost laughed again. She had forgotten that Gina had joked on more than one occasion about getting a cute guy's information through Benny. "No, listen," she explained, choosing her words carefully, "this is the situation: there is a guy who works upstairs who's bad news for Gina, to put it mildly. She has broken things off, but I'm concerned that he may corner her if an opportunity presents itself." Benny's grim expression reassured her that this was the right plan. "Roger's meeting her in the mornings, but, regardless…"

"You got it." Benny's eyes flicked back to the box, silently noting the name. "But, you know Gina," he warned.

"You're right, she won't willingly go for it. I was thinking you could tell her there have been reports of some nefarious activity targeting women in the area? Say you're looking out for her until it's safe?" she suggested winsomely.

"I don't know about saying all that, but I'll take care of it," he assured.

Sabella covered one of his hands with hers and smiled. "Thanks, Benny." The mistaken belief that Gina was seeing Kane may keep Alistair away for a while, but it definitely wouldn't hurt to have an additional pair of eyes in their building, especially when those eyes were as trustworthy as Benny's.

After returning from the working lunch that had actually included some work, Sabella settled on one of her easy chairs with her laptop. Usually, she would have chosen the couch, but the invisible, lingering remnants of the quietly smoldering passion of her night with Kane deterred her. She had intended not to contact him, at least for a few days, but that resolution hadn't lasted, primarily because he had sent her a text message when he reached Reno and called her briefly the following day.

When she logged into her email account, a message from Kane drew her attention. The entire text was a link to a video, with so many exclamation points in the title, it had to have been created by a fan. Applause from a preceding song introduced a clip from Kane's show the previous night that was so shaky, Sabella considered listening rather than watching. When Kane's voice sounded, she couldn't prevent herself from smiling and refocusing on the video.

"I know, well, I've heard, a lot of y'all been asking what happened to me," he said on the clip, gesturing to the bruises still coloring his cheek with his scraped right hand. Sabella sobered as he continued. "And, well, I'll tell ya. This girl I know, she was seeing, she was with this guy, someone who wasn't, you know, well he wasn't very nice to her. And I'd seen the marks, the bruises on her face, and stuff like that, I'd seem 'em, but I didn't know who this guy was. Not until a couple days ago, when I saw him, saw him raise his hand to her. Well, I figured he was lookin' for a fight, so I uh, so I gave 'im one."

Laughter and cheers followed his explanation. The rest of the video overlaid photos of Kane on a track of him singing. Many pictures included little hearts or concise adulations of Kane's looks. The last one had a heart encompassing a shot of Kane on stage, with the word *love* scrawled diagonally.

Sabella paused the clip right before it would end, leaving the image on the screen as an uplifting reminder, and resumed drafting an article she had begun that morning, about the warning signs of having a friend in an abusive relationship and the difference between men, whose strength destroys, and those, whose strength defends.

An hour or so later, a computerized chime drew her away from the research. Sabella scrubbed her hands over her face, massaging her frown away before clicking over to Skype to check the notification. The lingering tension in her shoulders released as she saw a request to connect from Kane.

She accepted the invitation and leaned back in her chair, tucking her toes on the footstool to balance the computer higher on her knees. A moment later, Kane called her, popping up on her screen with the paneling of the tour bus behind him.

"Hey, Bella," he said with an easy smile.

"Hi." Her lips stretched into a returning curve. "Since when do you use Skype?"

"I was convinced by the promise of seeing you."

Her chuckle faded quickly, and she glanced away from the screen.

"What is it?" Kane asked instantly, seeing through her.

Her gaze circled back to the flat image of him, his eyebrows now drawn together. "It's wonderful to see you, at least like this. But, it's also another reminder that this is the only way we can, for who knows how long. We haven't even discussed…" She trailed off, shaking her head slightly.

"How we're doing this," he finished for her. Silence spanned between them, only sounds from outside his bus confirming that the connection hadn't frozen. "I don't have all that much time," he said eventually. "I only called to say hi, see you. But we can, do you want to talk about it now?"

"No." Long-distance relationships were hard under the best of circumstances, and they both had entire, separate lives thousands of miles apart. "But we have to, don't we?" Without some kind of a plan, their future would be nothing more than phone lines and computer screens. And eventually, likely, not even that.

"Maybe." He paused for a beat before adding, "I've definitely got to head back to Nashville, after the tour."

Sabella nodded. "I know. And I need to be here right now, for Gina." Where did that leave them?

Kane's lips tugged to one side, his gaze lingering on the parts of her the little camera showed him. "Long distance's going to be a mess, isn't it?"

"Probably." Maybe he'd been so focused on that moment in the park, he hadn't thought it through. She hadn't either until after he'd left, but the logistics did matter. "I don't want to complicate your life, Kane," she said quietly. Swallowing roughly, she looked over the computer screen at her living room, at the couch where everything between them had felt so *right* just a few days ago.

"Hey." His voice snapped her attention back to him. "We can make it work," he assured without a hint of doubt. "Haven't figured out how, but if we both want to…" He trailed off, eyebrows arching a bit.

Sabella nodded quickly. Desire to be with him wasn't the question. Hopefully he was right, and they simply hadn't yet had the time and focus to find a solution.

Kane's cheeks rounded a touch, softening his expression. "Then we'll find a way."

Twenty-Seven

"So what shall we do first?" Gina asked a week later, plopping down across the queen-sized bed in their hotel room at Seattle's Belltown Inn.

Sabella lowered onto the multicolored, abstractly patterned armchair that would have outdone even Gina's usually colorful style. Over the last ten days, Gina had mostly returned to her vivacious, confident self, though she did remain somewhat subdued. The cliché about a thrown stone changing a lake forever rang true now—the experience had altered some core piece, invisibly yet, most likely, permanently. Though the rings had stilled—Gina's physical wounds had healed, and she had reassembled the surface—flesh, even metaphorical flesh, tore differently than water. Hopefully, Gina's invisible wounds would heal in time.

With any luck, their weekend away would help that process. It wasn't exactly coincidental that Kane's last tour performance was in Seattle the following day, but that wasn't the primary reason for their trip. Neither Sabella nor Gina had been to Seattle before, and it was a short enough drive to be reasonable for a spontaneous weekend away. Gina had even spent the entire morning at work.

"Space Needle?" Sabella suggested.

Gina rolled over to her back, looking at Sabella upside down. "Too touristy. Besides, don't you want to call Kane? I won't hold it against you."

"I told you, this weekend isn't about Kane. You agreed that we would see his show tomorrow night, and otherwise I want to spend time with you." Sabella couldn't wait to see him in person, but her best friend was the priority. Gina had even requested, and easily received, a promise not to check Kane's website in the meanwhile.

"You booked a room at the same hotel," Gina pointed out.

"It was last minute, they had an opening, and this way I didn't have to spend hours researching," Sabella defended. "Which doesn't mean I want to spend our entire weekend in this room, so what do you want to do?"

Gina rolled back over and sat up, flashing her impish smile. "We should go out."

"Out?" Sabella winced at the predictable suggestion. Gina's idea of a night out usually included drinks at a rowdy bar with lots of inappropriate flirting, which frequently resulted in more drinks. "Are you sure you don't want to explore the city?"

"Nightlife is a part of the city. We'll be touristy tomorrow. This is why you brought heels!" Gina climbed off the bed to pull Sabella up from the chair and over to the overnight bags they had dropped by the room's desk.

"I brought heels because you made me," Sabella reminded her, laughing. Despite her somewhat dramatized objections, it was nice, having a carefree weekend with her best friend.

"Well this is why I made you. Come on, there's supposedly this fantastic bar that's not too far from here, with live music or maybe a DJ. We could go early and grab some food, while scoping it out to see if we want to stay."

"Stay, or...?" Sabella asked suspiciously, though she was fairly certain of the answer.

"Or go somewhere else," Gina stated blithely, unzipping her bag.

"How did you even hear about this place?" Sabella inquired, following suit.

"Research," Gina answered mysteriously, with a taunting smile and a quick raise of her eyebrows. "Now show me what you're going to wear!"

The Crocodile, which truly was situated quite close to their hotel, offered a friendly and bustling atmosphere in their bar area. Sabella and Gina managed to reach it at the perfect moment, so they were able to slip into one of the few booths.

Despite their extensive primping, they arrived during happy hour, which wasn't an unwelcome surprise. Gina now wore a slinky, sleeveless dress, which bloused over a band that hugged her hips. A combination of browns and tans played with gold highlights throughout the fabric, complemented by a pair of bronze earrings. An edgy, cropped jacket and some high heels completed the stunning ensemble.

By comparison, Sabella felt underdressed, but she was happy to watch Gina confidently claim the spotlight. Gina, on the other hand, hadn't been content to leave Sabella in her jeans, so a flouncy black skirt, with thin streaks of lime and blue, swirled around her thighs. Under Gina's direction, she had combined the skirt with a matching blue blouse, which had a ruched torso, surplice neckline, and short, loose sleeves, and the pair of strappy heels she had dutifully brought. She had foregone a jacket since it was a pleasantly warm evening, and all she had packed was a fleece zip-up which didn't exactly complement the outfit. A simple glass-drop necklace and silver earrings brought some sparkle to the look. Gina had also insisted on a scrupulous application of evening makeup before pronouncing them fit to venture outside the hotel.

At the Crocodile, they ordered with complete disregard for any nutritional concerns, indulging in a couple margaritas along with some cheesy bread and pizzas, which had been prepared in an exposed, old-fashioned oven that dominated one corner. The food was sufficiently, but not overly, greasy, fresh, and hot, and the booth provided some seclusion, which allowed them to enjoy both dinner and people watching.

When the dining part of the bar began filling, and the area with the stage opened to the public, Gina, who somehow always looked amazingly put together even after eating a full meal, went to stake out a good—meaning subtly noticeable—spot, and Sabella veered off to touch up her makeup. Before leaving the restroom, she moistened her palms, twisted the loose part of her hair into waves, and resettled the delicate jade clip she wore. She verified she was alone, then twirled in front of the mirrors, using the swirling motion of the skirt and a deep breath to bolster her confidence.

When Sabella emerged, Gina was talking to a man slightly taller than her, who wore jeans and layered tee shirts. Sabella paused, but when Gina shook her head with an uncomfortable smile and subtly shifted away from the man, she briskly crossed the room to Gina's side. It was only after she interrupted the exchange with a brief greeting that she recognized the man.

"Hey there," he said with a small double take. His brows drew together over narrowed eyes, and his jaw shifted to the side pensively.

"You know each other?" Gina asked glancing between them.

"Wait, you ladies know each other?" Steve echoed.

"Gina, this is Steve. He's Kane's drummer," Sabella explained. "Steve, this is my best friend, Gina."

"Pleased to meet you," Steve murmured, gazing now unwaveringly at Gina.

She gifted him with a smile. "You too."

They fell silent. Sabella's eyes flicked between them before she asked, "I'm sorry, did I interrupt something?"

Gina glanced at Steve then directed her gaze to the floor. The knowledge that Sabella knew the man who had singled her out seemed to comfort her a little, but she still stood with her shoulders hunched and her hands clasped in front of her body.

"Nah," Steve said, registering the reaction, then settled comfortably into one hip. "It's good to see you," he told Sabella.

Sabella exhaled, relaxing somewhat. She hadn't been certain how Kane's friends would react to seeing her again, but the statement sounded sincere.

"Maybe now you'll help me convince Gina here to let me buy you lovely ladies a couple drinks," he added with a casual, flirty smile.

"What do you say, Gi?" Gina brought her gaze up, evidently still hesitant. "Or are we declining free alcohol tonight?" Sabella asked with mock horror.

"Perish the thought," Gina responded with a trace of her usual humor.

"Well all right, then." Steve nodded and moved toward the bar.

"Are you okay?" Sabella checked when he was out of earshot.

"Yeah. Yes, I'm fine," Gina answered, a bit shakily, then shrugged it off. "Guess I'm out of practice," she joked.

"He's a nice guy," Sabella offered, casually yet intentionally. "Although, come to think of it, I'm not sure I've ever seen him hit on someone."

"That's 'cause I've got good taste," Steve interjected from behind her, holding out Gina's drink.

"That was fast," Gina remarked.

"Everyone's gotta be good at something," he said then handed Sabella a beer.

"You forgot your own," Sabella pointed out.

Steve shrugged. "Bobby'll get it."

"Oh, you and Bobby came out together?"

Steve shot her a confused look. "Yeah, we're all here. For Kane."

Sabella turned to Gina, confused and prepared to say so, but Gina spoke first. "I looked at the website," she confessed over the growing hum of people around them. "Surprise," she added with a satisfied smile.

"Kane doesn't know you're here?" Steve asked, catching on. Bobby joined them then, carrying a couple more beers. He nodded instead of a verbal greeting. Apparently Steve had warned him away from Gina, because Bobby didn't try any of his typical flirtatious tricks.

"Well, I didn't know any of you guys would be here," Sabella explained. "Your show is tomorrow, right?"

"Sure is," Bobby confirmed.

"I'm so confused," Sabella admitted, looking to Gina. "You knew they would be here?"

"Well, I didn't know *they* would be here. I only knew he would be here," Gina clarified, gesturing toward the stage.

Sabella turned to see Kane, with his guitar, walking alongside another man onto the stage, which was set up with equipment for a disc jockey but also, as she now noticed, with a standalone microphone. Kane wore his jeans with a checkered shirt in an assortment of grays, with the sleeves rolled up and unbuttoned enough to display a blue tee shirt underneath. As the other man, dressed in corduroy pants and a polo shirt, strode to the microphone, Kane brushed his hair back automatically. The stage lights highlighted the movement, glinting off his hair, and Sabella's focus narrowed on the man she had missed significantly more than she had been willing to admit. Gravity could have stopped working in the rest of the room, and she wouldn't have noticed.

Kane surveyed the room absently as the other man introduced him. His gaze skimmed over the gathering audience, and he smiled briefly at the group of women who screamed for his attention when his name was announced. When his eyes reached Sabella, he stilled and blinked a few times. Sabella waited, motionless, until his lips curved faintly, and then she softly returned the smile.

Kane barely believed it when he saw Sabella from the Crocodile's stage. Mitch had arranged for him to play a few songs there, for the publicity. Plus, the place was a musical institution in Seattle. Kane really had to admit, to himself, that the man snapped up or created every possible opportunity to showcase Kane's music.

Still, it was a good thing he'd been scheduled as a special—*short*—addition tonight. All he wanted once he saw Sabella was to get off the stage and scoop her into his arms. He managed to play through a couple upbeat songs and plug his show. He also smiled and thanked the audience for their cheers, but his eyes always went back to Sabella.

On his way off the stage, he shook hands with the DJ who'd given up some of his stage time. By the time he'd put his guitar away in the green room and come back out, the DJ had most everyone dancing. That made it easier for Kane to round the crowd and find Sabella.

She stood near Steve and Gina, who seemed like they were getting along. Sabella let them talk, watching the room. She was turned away from him, so Kane took a moment to appreciate how stunning she looked. Her top hugged her torso, like the skirt hugged her hips, but everything flowed at the same time. She somehow shone, even in the dark room. Everything about her was purely tempting.

Sabella sipped her drink, and he walked up to their small group. When she saw him, she smiled, lighting up even more. "Hi," she said simply.

"Hey." He placed his hands on her waist, stepping closer.

"You look beautiful." His eyes dipped to her lips, then lower, to the necklace that sparkled in the dim light.

"D'you reckon they know they're not alone?" Steve asked beside them.

Sabella looked away, and he knew she blushed. Kane let go of her waist and moved one arm to her shoulders. He ignored his drummer but greeted the woman next to him. "Gina. You look good."

"You didn't sound half-bad, for a country singer," she answered wryly. He couldn't tell if any bruises remained, but that one comment already showed she acted more like the first time they'd met. "And I look fantastic."

"That you do," Steve agreed. Kane saw the look he gave her but decided not to comment. Gina didn't need another man telling her what to do. If she needed help, Sabella would know. He was pretty sure she'd tell him if someone needed to step in.

"It's great to see you both," Kane told the women. "I didn't know you'd be here."

"I actually didn't know you would be here," Sabella said. "Or that we would be precisely here, for that matter."

"This way you're both surprised," Gina commented with a pleased smile.

Kane would have asked what she meant, but he noticed a couple women with photos winding toward them through the crowd. "I have to go be social a bit," he told Sabella apologetically. "I'll find you as soon as I can, okay?"

"Of course." She nodded, understanding as always. Kane squeezed her closer for a moment then let go. He nodded at Gina and walked a ways toward the other women.

He spent some time chatting, signing autographs, and taking photos. He used the chance to tell people about their show at the Tractor Tavern the next night. It was their last stop this year, which meant it had to be great, memorable. A solid audience always helped.

When he looked up from one group of fans, Mitch was talking to Sabella. Kane almost interfered, but two more women slipped in his way. He glanced over a few times in between taking pictures. Mitch held his hands out away from his hips. Sabella stood firmly, listening to him, without shying away.

By the next time Kane looked up from signing photos or menus, she was dancing and laughing with Gina. Sabella's skirt and hair flew when she spun, completely distracting him. Their visit was definitely a good surprise.

They left the Crocodile pretty early, but everyone seemed okay with it. Steve asked Bobby to check in with Mitch before catching up. Kane went to grab his guitar and jacket, and then they both met the ladies outside.

"Our hotel has a rooftop deck. Pretty good view of the city," Steve said casually, out on the street.

"You don't say," Gina said, lips twisting with amusement. Sabella also suppressed a smile.

"What are we missing?" Kane asked.

"Same hotel," Sabella explained. "We were planning on seeing you play tomorrow night."

"And Sab didn't feel like choosing between hotels," Gina added.

Sabella nudged her with an elbow, pressing her lips together.

"Well, then," Kane said, turning the way they'd need to go. He sure wasn't going to complain about this turn of events.

"Shall we?" Steve offered his arm to Gina.

"Why not?" she answered, laughing, and placed her arm in his.

Kane slipped his arm around Sabella, and they started after the other couple.

"Oh wow," Sabella breathed when they'd reached the rooftop. The city shone around them, and the four of them had the deck to themselves.

Gina walked over to some lounge chairs with Steve. Sabella walked away from them and toward the railing. Kane followed her lead. The night had grown chilly, especially up on the roof, and Sabella shivered. Kane slipped off his jacket, holding it out for her.

"Thank you," she mouthed through curved lips. She held the railing loosely, looking out over the city, toward the Space Needle.

"Saw you talking to Mitch," Kane mentioned. "You all right?"

"Oh, yes, I'm fine," she answered, shifting to face him. "He apologized, actually—said he misunderstood."

Kane nodded. It was good the man had stepped up. Then he promptly put it all out of his mind. He used the jacket to pull Sabella closer so he could finally kiss her. She brought her hands to the back of his neck, playing with his hair. He slipped his hands beneath the jacket, wrapping his arms at her waist. Sabella moved her hands to his shoulders for balance, rising up to him. The kiss deepened.

A bright flash broke them apart. Both their heads twisted in its direction, to see Bobby standing with a camera. "Smile!" he directed a bit late.

Kane considered hitting him upside the head, but Sabella laughed. "How could we pass up a view like this?" she asked, humoring him.

She moved away, turning Kane so he faced Bobby. Kane braced his hands on the railing behind him. Sabella smiled, also turning to Bobby. She would have moved to the side, but Kane grabbed her gently and pulled her in front of him.

The camera flashed again when she laughed. Apparently, Bobby was paying attention. He took a few more shots with Sabella wrapped in Kane's arms.

"All right, enough!" Sabella soon said, pulling away.

Bobby lowered the camera. All three of them joined Gina and Steve. Sabella moved to Gina, splitting up the couples.

"That was cute," Gina told her.

Sabella answered, but Kane didn't hear her, since Steve asked Bobby, "What'd Mitch say?"

Kane should have paid attention, but he watched Sabella instead. She shrugged in his jacket, pulling the edges closed, then slipped her hands in the pockets.

"So what's going on tomorrow?" Bobby asked, pulling Kane's attention.

He started to answer something but instead heard Gina ask, "What's wrong?"

He looked back to Sabella, who was suddenly tense. She shook her head, but her hands were now clenched on her lap.

Too late, Kane remembered what she'd felt in his jacket pocket. *Damn it.* This wasn't the right time.

He walked around the seats, closer to her. "Bella." She looked up at him, but everyone else was watching, too. Kane took her hand so she'd stand then reached into the jacket's left pocket, palming the box inside.

"This isn't…" Kane sighed, letting go of her hand to drag his through his hair. She deserved better than some unplanned stammering.

"What's going on?" Bobby asked.

Sabella's eyes flicked in his direction, then down. Kane didn't spare him a glance. He tried speaking again. "Bella, I think you're amazing." Sabella's gaze returned to his face. She looked frozen, almost scared. Maybe he should put this off? But it was too late for that. "I didn't expect I'd get a chance to do this, to see you, so soon. And I know we have some things to figure out, like distance, or living arrangements, long-term things. This isn't what I had planned, but I love you. Every part of my life you touch, you improve. Infinitely."

That earned him a small smile, and she seemed to relax. Kane swallowed roughly. "After this weekend, no matter what, our circumstances, they'll change." His gut twisted. He'd thought he'd have more time to get his nerve up. "I need your help, to change them how we want, changing them so that we can stay together, maybe not always, but forever."

Kane flipped open the tiny box and lowered to one knee. Sabella's lips parted, disbelieving. She glanced over at their rooftop companions. Kane's eyes followed, seeing everyone sitting alert but still. He quickly looked back to Sabella, who had also resumed watching him. "Everything else, we'll figure out," he assured her, in case she was considering the practical problems. "Say yes."

The moment seemed to drag out, Kane's mind frozen as he waited. Sabella's shoulders lifted self-consciously, and she nodded. A smile slowly spread across her face. "Yes."

Kane shot up, lifting her up and twisting with her in his arms. "Yes?" he asked once more after setting her down.

"Yes!" she repeated with a bright smile.

Kane pulled the ring from its box to slide it onto her finger, then kissed her, rejoicing in the soft slip of her lips against his.

Whoops from the other men kept the kiss short. Kane shook hands with his bandmates, and Sabella hugged Gina, as both women laughed.

Steve sent Bobby to get some champagne they had on the bus—a gift from the club they'd played in Spokane. Meanwhile, Gina directed them in some more photos, to mark the engagement. Kane and Sabella obliged, laughing. They drew the line at posed photos of them kissing.

When Bobby returned, it was with the bottle, glasses, and Mitch. The manager walked over to Kane, as Steve poured and Sabella huddled murmuring with Gina.

"Congratulations," he said, holding out his hand. Kane shook it, too happy to have their fight ruin it.

Mitch took the camera from Bobby, getting everyone to line up with the champagne. They shuffled around, settling in front of the skyline. Kane slipped his arm around Sabella's waist.

"You learned to jump," Gina murmured, beaming at her friend.

"Looks like," Sabella agreed, grinning back at her.

When Sabella twisted to meet his gaze, smiling with every emotion he'd once given up on finding, Kane knew they'd jumped together.

— Acknowledgements —

A heartfelt thank you first of all to my amazing parents, for supporting this crazy endeavor; to Jillian and Aleksey, for my wonderful cover photo; to Christa at Paper & Sage for transforming that photo into an absolutely gorgeous cover; to Laura, Iris, Lucia, Rachel, and Lighty, for their sharp eyes and reliable honesty; to the ladies of my writing group, for their encouragement despite my doubts; and to Brian Wales, the very first person who pushed me to pursue publication.

— About Aria —

Aria's writing story started when her seventh-grade English teacher encouraged her to submit a class assignment for publication. That piece was printed, and let's just say, she was hooked!

Since then, Aria has run a literary magazine, earned her degree in Creative Writing (as well as in French and Russian literatures), and been published here and there. Though her first kiss technically came from a bear cub, and no fairy-tale transformation followed, Aria still believes magic can happen when the right people come together—if they don't get in their own way, that is.

Other than all things literary, Aria loves spending time with her family, including her two unbearably adorable nieces. She also dabbles in painting, dancing, playing violin, and, given the opportunity, Epicureanism.

Learn more about Aria and her books at:
www.AriaGlazki.com